D0451302

Also by Earl Emerson:

THE RAINY CITY
POVERTY BAY
NERVOUS LAUGHTER
FAT TUESDAY*
BLACK HEARTS AND SLOW DANCING
DEVIANT BEHAVIOR*
HELP WANTED: ORPHANS PREFERRED

*Published by Ballantine Books

YELLOW
DOG
PARTY

Earl Emerson

BALLANTINE BOOKS • NEW YORK

Copyright © 1991 by Earl Emerson

All rights reserved under International and Pan-American Copyright Conventions. Published in the United States of America by Ballantine Books, a division of Random House, Inc., New York, and simultaneously in Canada by Random House of Canada Limited, Toronto.

No part of this book may be reproduced or utilized in any form or by any means, electronic or mechanical, including photocopying, recording, or by any information storage or retrieval system, without permission in writing from the Publisher. Inquiries should be addressed to Permissions Department, William Morrow and Company, Inc., 1350 Avenue of the Americas, New York, N.Y. 10019.

Library of Congress Catalog Card Number: 90-24437

ISBN 0-345-37716-8

This edition published by arrangement with William Morrow and Company, Inc.

Manufactured in the United States of America

First Ballantine Books Edition: May 1992

For my brother,
Stephen Paul Emerson,
1951–1968

"I guess somebody lost a dream."
RAYMOND CHANDLER, *The Little Sister*

1

IT WAS RAINING WHEN THEY ROLLED ME OUT OF the big Lincoln and into the ditch.

Not a heavy rain, just one of those Northwest mists that cling to the landscape. Tiny dots of precipitation barely discernible to the naked eye. Sheets of drizzle shrouding the madronas alongside the roadway, tarnishing greens into grays and wetting the white center line to a keen, deadly polish.

Five of us rode out in the Lincoln; three brawny men with pistols, the clown in whiteface, and yours truly in jeans, a sweatshirt, and dingy Nikes.

Fifteen minutes earlier, when they jumped us in the tiny U-shaped parking lot behind the Umpqua Valley Community Hospital, one of them waved a Smith & Wesson Model 27 in our faces and another a Llama 9mm automatic pistol. The third man had no gun, and perhaps because of this, he began sweating almost immediately.

You had to give Kathy points for not screaming.

The one holding the 9mm had stepped out of the shadows in the hospital lot, his voice low and euphonious, cracking on his first words. He said, ''Tell us where Auntie's is and we'll call it even.''

Their hair was slicked down in wet, wormy strands. Aside from the guns, what bugged me were the scowls behind the Miss Piggy disguises they each wore, masks measeled with

1

dew, and, without any signal from the others, the way the Sloppy Guy reached over and locked up Kathy's right wrist in his clammy mitts. Under her clown makeup Kathy shot me a beleaguered look as she tried to wrench her slim forearm free. It occurred to me that they thought she was a boy.

"What do you pigs want?" I said.

"Auntie's. Tell us where it is."

"Naw. You're supposed to be looking for Grandma's. Wait a minute. The pigs weren't looking for anything. They were building houses and waiting for the wolf."

"Asshole," he said. "I don't want to see you here again."

Romancing the electricity that drumrolled up and down my spine when somebody trained a gun on me, I stepped close enough to smell the Big Red on his breath. "I don't know what you're talking about."

"You were just inside. You're not going to see her again, get it?"

"Talking about the lady in 110?"

"From now on, she doesn't exist."

"No problem. You put the artillery away, we'll be on our way."

"Not quite. First tell us about Auntie's."

"Who?"

Saturday night in Myrtle Creek, Oregon. The Umpqua Valley Community Hospital, along with the rest of the town, was built just off Interstate 5 in the southern part of the state in the midst of those high rolling brown hills that you think of as endemic only to California. Maybe a thousand feet of elevation each. Above and behind the hospital, an occasional live oak stood vigil. Across Heard Street behind the hospital were a couple of older houses, but I hadn't seen any activity. No traffic. On Saturday night, Myrtle Creek was a deserted municipal core of vacant buildings.

"Listen, Bud," said the one with the automatic pistol. "You tell us where Auntie's is and we set you loose. It's that simple. We could be here all night. But it's that simple."

"Never heard of Auntie's."

"Wrong answer."

"I never have."

"Maybe we should break your arm . . ."

"Maybe you should try." I grinned and looked around sheepishly. "Hell, I thought you were looking for the security station. It's over there. Here come a couple of guards now."

I gave a heartfelt squint across the parking area, enough for the man who had done all the talking to turn, and, putting all of my weight behind it, I punched him as he swiveled his face back to me.

The blow sounded like a watermelon being cleaved in half with a saber.

Blood spewing, he dropped heavily to the tarmac. The Miss Piggy mask twisted off and flopped to the pavement. His Llama 9mm clattered on the cement. The look on his face reminded me of a dumbfounded kid on a skateboard taking his first spill. His nearest associate let go of Kathy and leaned over to help, tearing his mask off to see better. I was at the wrong angle, but Kathy was in a position to watch their faces.

"Get out of here," I said to the clown.

Out of loyalty or shock, I had no way of telling which, she hesitated.

Me, I was busy testing the barrel of a Smith & Wesson with the back of my skull. Somebody caught my falling form and, semiconscious, I felt myself being dragged. After getting wedged into the back of the car on the floor and feeling a size 13 shoe pin my neck, I listened as we screeched out of the tiny hospital lot. I listened, but I didn't hear anything except a car defroster and the chunk-chunk of windshield wipers.

The excursion took five minutes, slivers of light ricocheting behind my eyes. Bile choking my throat. I could feel Kathy's feet on the backs of my knees, nudging to see if I was all right. She kept nudging.

It took only a few seconds to cartwheel me into the ditch.

My hope was that they would dump us in the tules, talk tough, and exit. Then too, it could be they were about to empty their guns into our eyeballs. All three of them wore windbreakers, slacks, black loafers, in addition to the Miss

Piggy masks. I had already assigned them each a designation: the Mean One, the Sloppy Guy, and the Talker.

The Mean One had popped me with his pistol barrel and sat in the back with his foot on my neck. Hulking, aggressive, he seemed the most muscular, 240 maybe, almost my height, as well as the most ruthless. If it hadn't been for him, we would have gotten away in the parking lot. He was also the coolest of the three, the only one who'd thought to block our escape route at the hospital, as well as the only one who didn't continually glance around like a nervous kid.

The Sloppy Guy had put the wristlock on Kathy and was now driving. Perspiring and fidgety, he kept opening his mouth with a dry, smacking sound.

Twice, the Talker, riding in front, bitched about his own blood slopping onto the car's upholstery. Hearing him advise the driver which doodad operated the headlights, I decided he owned the Lincoln. It was going to be delicate the next time he escorted some lady to the opera, what with the blood on the seats, broken teeth from kidnap victims, and whatnot. So far he was the only one of our assailants who had uttered a word.

Eight-thirty, maybe 9:00 P.M. by now. A lonely country road. No cars. Cloud cover a mere two hundred feet above our heads, with a fine drizzle. A solitary robin chirruped good night to the hills. I figured we had traveled five minutes east up the canyon, which I knew ended some seventeen miles up in the foothills beyond Myrtle Creek.

I was six foot one and 180, yet the smallest of these bean pickers had thirty pounds on me. The two who weren't sweating looked, under their Miss Piggy gear, capable of anything. I had already violated two of my most cherished personal guidelines: Never slug a man who has a gun in his hand. Never stick around after you slug a man who has a gun in his hand.

We'd been in Myrtle Creek, Oregon, all day, Kathy in baggy black trousers, Keds, an old tuxedo vest, and a bow tie. White gloves. Whiteface with black and red accent marks. Her top hat concealed a mane of black-brunette hair. Myrtle Creek had sponsored a truck show and parade, and Kathy had taken advantage of the crowds. Over the years she'd cooked up a pretty fair street act, comedy and juggling, replete with hat pass at the conclusion and the admonition, "Kids! Remember, if your parents don't give you any money for the hat, it means they don't . . . *loooove* . . . you." Kathy, an attorney by day, promptly donated the money to charity, but she cherished the act.

After the Lincoln stopped, the Sloppy Guy walked Kathy around to the front fender. His windbreaker was stained at the armpits, the air in the car still gamy with his anxiety. I'd noticed he was the only one of the three with a wedding band visible.

Venturing onto my hands and knees in the ditch, I peered up at them. Balloons of exhaust strayed across the evening. I thought I saw a tadpole swimming in the shadowy water in front of my face, a dark harbinger of the damned.

The two packing guns stood at the lip of the culvert, waiting. Vermilion was clotting on the speaker's false snout, his chin, his tan shirt and windbreaker.

"Climb out of there," he said.

I stood slowly. "You should pack that schnozz with Kleenex."

"What I should do is bust yours."

When I spotted the cord in the Sloppy Guy's hands, my throat dried and I began to feel activity in the pit of my stomach. My legs began shivering. In another couple of minutes, if the adrenaline kept flooding my system, I'd be able to pick up a car and leap tall buildings. The worst part of the business was I had no idea what they wanted.

Or who they were.

We were on one of those two-lane roads that seemed to slither forever into the rolling hills, going nowhere, coming from nowhere, new-growth pines like foot soldiers on the steep bank at the opposite side of the highway. On our side was a wide dirt and gravel pullout, the ditch, a wind-bellied barbed-wire fence, a field of tall brown grass, and several hundred yards away some live oaks; beyond that, a steep foothill clad in brown grasses. Abandoned farmland, all.

The air was damp and funereal. In half an hour the sun

would set and it would be pitch-black. It was a swell spot for a pair of graves.

Kathy and the Sloppy Guy were at the front of the Lincoln, Kathy unmoving, submissive. I couldn't tell if he'd loosened his grip, but she was working him in that direction. It didn't matter what they did to me, but one way or another, I had to get her out of it. The Talker and the one who'd smacked me with the Smith & Wesson stood in front of the driver's and passenger's doors respectively.

"Look," I said, ankle-deep in muck, a cold bib of dirty water discoloring my front. "I don't know who you guys think we are, but we're not them."

"You from Seattle?"

"A lot of folks are from Seattle."

"You a private dick?"

"There's a lot of them, too."

"Get out of the ditch."

"I do and you'll hit me."

He fingered his nose under the rubber pig snout. "You were on Twenty-fifth, weren't you? You saw Morgana."

"Don't know anybody named Morgana."

"And Auntie's? You were there."

"Keep yakking. I'll tell you when it starts to make sense."

"Wise-ass." The Mean One casually pointed his Smith & Wesson and fired into the water adjacent to my legs. The gun bucked in his hand. The loud popcorn-popping sound echoed in the still hills, startling the clown. The projectile missed my kneecap by inches.

"Where's Auntie's?"

Kathy was about to say something, but I muted her with a look. He fired another cap past my knees, causing a burst of water behind me. He didn't seem to be aiming; didn't care if he crippled me. The gun bucked with each shot. "Auntie's. It's a nightclub in Lake City. They've got strippers."

He fired a third round so close I felt the airstream from the bullet. Looking down, I could see that a contrail of white cotton had streaked the denim of my jeans.

"Somebody's going to hear those shots," I said. "And they're going to call the Douglas County sheriff."

The two with guns didn't budge, though the guy holding Kathy began to look up and down the two-lane highway. My tormentors had all the time in the world. The last time a car had rolled up this road was probably around 1973.

"Your name is Thomas Black. You're a two-bit private eye who works in Seattle. You've seen Morgana, and you've probably been to Auntie's. Tell us where we can find Auntie and you won't have to crawl home."

"Screw off."

"Let's try this. Jo Schwantz?"

Kathy and I exchanged looks. "What about her?"

"Finally getting your memory back? Keep talking."

"Thirty minutes ago I visited Schwantz in the hospital in Myrtle Creek. You know that. You must have been following us. Or staking her out. It was the first time I met Jo. I don't know these other people you're talking about." They mulled it over without taking their eyes off me. I was getting into a dangerous mood, not scared, just angry.

"Who is your client?"

"I don't reveal clients' names. If you know Jo's in the hospital, you know she isn't in any condition to talk."

"You're messing in things that can get you in a whole lot of trouble."

"I've been in trouble before."

"How did you know where she was? Jo?"

"Yellow Pages."

The only sounds were the Lincoln's silky engine, a buzzing transformer on a mist-covered phone pole overhead, and my own wooden heartbeat.

"Get out of there. Get out of that ditch."

"You pack that right, it'll heal a lot better. Ever see Kirk Douglas in *Lonely Are the Brave*? Get some strips of cloth and . . ."

"Out!" They were pointing their weapons. Both of them.

I jiggled my eyebrows, shrugged, and began climbing out of the shallow ditch. "Look, I don't want any trouble. I'll pay the medical bills. Just send them to my office. Geez, what was the name of Kirk Douglas's horse? Whiskey? Brandy? What a great movie. Carroll O'Connor was in it.

Did you know that? Long before he made it on the hypno box. Yeah, he was driving a truck full of toilets.''

Scrambling up the wet, grassy slope of the ditch, I remained in a crouch, blathering nonsense, pretending the wet grass and rocks weren't giving me a purchase.

When I got close enough, I used my left fist to center-punch the Mean One in the testicles. He folded in half and expelled all his air. I pivoted on my left foot and kicked Kathy's tormentor in the kneecap. He twisted, clutched his leg, and rolled down the side of the culvert heavily, splashing in the ditch and muttering, "Oh, Christ. Oh, Christ. Oh . . .''

And Kathy was gone.

The Talker said, "Shit," pressed his torso up against the Lincoln, and laid the Llama over the roof so he could take aim at her fleeing figure. He cocked the pistol. Head lowered, I rammed into his doubled-over companion, and the three of us went down like bowling pins.

Before I could get out of the tangle, the Talker had the cold muzzle of the 9mm screwed into my ear. After a second I could feel blood trickling toward my eardrum. He cocked the piece, and it sounded like two bricks being slapped together inside a sewer pipe. Kathy had vanished, and they were through piddling around.

He said, "Move, bastard, and I'll open your brain up."

"Fair enough. Sure. Sounds fair enough. I can live with that. I like a guy who states his position clearly and fairly and doesn't—''

"Shut up.''

"Sure.''

2

THE MEAN ONE CLAMBERED TO HIS FEET AND booted me in the stomach. With a gun in my ear, there wasn't much I could do. He struck me repeatedly in the small of my back, searching for my kidneys, a gimmick I supposed he'd picked up from the movies. After an interval, the Sloppy Guy hobbled out of the culvert and stepped on my fingers, dripping ditch water from his Weejuns. Then, in a haphazard rhythm, all three of them kicked me.

When they tired of that, they wrenched both my arms behind my back and tied them at the wrists with a cord that chiseled into my flesh. It surprised me that they didn't use handcuffs.

For a minute or two I was left on my face while they nursed their wounds, griped, cussed, regrouped, and gazed about halfheartedly for Kathy. The sky was growing dimmer, the air humid. The ringleader, the guy with the Llama automatic, wore half a liter or more of Calvin Klein Fragrance for Men. Kathy had bought me a bottle of the stuff once.

They hoisted me to my feet and began marching me across the open field toward the woods. The Talker nosed his pistol up to my head and cocked it. As we stepped over the sluggish creek at the bottom of the ditch and then into the field of tall, wet grasses, he wanted to be sure I didn't generate any more surprises. I found I could walk easily enough, though my stomach and back were cramping.

We had traveled 250 yards from the roadway when the Sloppy Guy limped over to a live oak and tossed thirty feet of hemp rope over a lower limb.

They might have gone all night without stumbling onto a setup this sweet. The road was out of sight. The oak was dripping with moss and dew, and in a fit of hopeless optimism I rapidly hypothesized that rot had decayed the limb they chose. The pine stump beneath it was three feet across, sawed unevenly two or three years before.

It was more of a slipknot than a noose. They rigged it up and dropped it over my head, tightened it at my throat like a mother knotting a Windsor tie for a schoolboy. Blue eyes. All three of them had blue eyes. I was trying to remember anything I could. Calvin Klein fragrance. Blue eyes. A Llama 9mm. The one I had slugged in the nuts had lumpy calluses on his knuckles. Karate.

"You're kidding," I said, when they dropped the rope over my head.

Odd how fast you run out of snappy patter with a noose draped around your neck. Jamming the gun in my mouth, they stood me on the wet stump and pulled the slack out of the rope. My eyeballs were beginning to build up pressure behind them. I thought I might have the cord at my wrists off in another minute. The Sloppy Guy, laboring at the knots with the fumbling diligence of a man who does not use his hands often, tethered the free end of the noose around the base of the oak. He was a mess, windbreaker pitted out, pain deforming his mouth, trousers sopping from the ditch water. As he tightened the rope, I tried to get a footing on the rain-slicked stump.

I was being lynched by three overweight pig impressionists in the middle of the woods somewhere in southern Oregon, and nobody was telling my why.

"One last chance, Bud," said the one who'd done all the talking. "Auntie's."

"Don't you think I'd tell you if I knew?" Constricting my larynx, the rope was also beginning to alter my voice.

"He knows," said the man who'd fired at me, still partially doubled over. He'd limped badly during our walk across the field. "Why would he work for her? Can't he see what she is?"

"There's guys'll do anything for a fee."

"I know who you are," I said, cursing my cupidity. The announcement brought a dead silence. "You guys were hired by Smitty to get even for that blind date I fixed him up with. Right? Nobody ever warned me about her politics. And I didn't know she carried Mace."

"Look, we don't want to hurt you," he said. "Tell us where Auntie's is. You think we want to hurt you?"

"You're giving a fair imitation."

"The only thing hurting you here is your mouth."

"I hope your car's all right," I said. "You didn't leave the keys in it? Pity to get stranded this far out."

"Wait!" said the one who'd fired at my legs. "Listen." They were silent. "Listen. You hear the car?"

"Oh, Jesus," said the Sloppy Guy, crashing off through the brush.

"Earle, get back here!" said the Talker, but there was no abridging Earle's frenzy.

"That clown ain't comin' back," said the Mean One. "He's all the way to the California border by now."

I shuffled once and nearly lost my balance, using my weight against the tight noose to maintain equilibrium. My face was beginning to swell. My cheeks were itchy. The arteries under my jaw were pounding. From behind now, because I had spun halfway around, one of them jabbed at my sore back.

One of my feet slipped off, and suddenly I was at an angle, more of my weight being supported by my neck.

My face was bloated, pounding with pooled blood. For three or four seconds I scuffled on the slick stump, teeth gritted.

And then off I went, swinging by my neck.

And it hurt so much I wanted to bellow, but of course the rope choked that out of me. The branch above creaked and sagged, but not low enough that my feet touched the earth.

As I spun, I could see two men, myrtle trees, billions of stars, two men, trees, and a blood-red sky. The pain was more intense and unyielding than anything I had ever endured. My scalp felt as if it were about to explode. My eyes were tiny balloons filled to bursting.

Somebody was fumbling with the rope. They spoke quickly. Magpies on amphetamines, I thought.

"Get him down! Cut it, quick!" "Fuck that!" "No, we gotta get him down." "Tough guy! Let him swing!" "You can't do this, Randy!" More fumbling. "I just did!" "We gotta get him down!" "Too late. Look at him. He's dead." "No, he's not . . ." "Take a good look, pal. His neck is broken." I was beginning to untwirl, to spin in the opposite direction.

"Let's get out of here."

And then silence.

And me the pendulum. Tick-tock. Expecting the pain to go away now that the blackness was here and the pain not going away, not even a little. Tick. Tock. Growing worse. And then the stars behind my eyes turning colors. And slipping into another kind of delirium, the hurt of knowing it was over, that my body was no longer fighting for air. The last jamboree. Tick. Finally over. Tock. So this was what it was like. To die.

Tick.

Somewhere off in the mist a robin chirped one last stanza for the dead man.

Tock.

3

I WAS EITHER WAKING UP OR ROLLING OVER IN my coffin.

The back of my skull was as big as a house. I gulped air, wriggled, and felt shudders throughout my body. Something unholy pricked my right cheek. An excruciating series of jolts shot through my spinal cord and ran down both legs, hacking at the backs of my knees. If I was lying in a pine coffin with a velvet liner, the excursion was definitely tourist class.

It took a while to unravel the scenario. The branch they'd looped the rope over had snapped, and I had plunged to the sod. But I was suffocating, squirming, dying, still choking.

Glissading in and out of consciousness, I lay flat on my face. I twisted, wrenched, and finally jerked my hands free.

Rolling onto my back, I dug at the rope around my throat. My neck was cool and swollen, and the rope was so deep I couldn't feel it.

I was beginning to drift off again in a haze of slow strangulation. Using fingers that might have been frozen for all their dexterity, I gradually loosened the slipknot. A hundred and eighty pounds of swinging private investigator had cinched it tight. My cheeks and brow were tingling.

Rolling onto my stomach, I pushed off to my hands and knees. Gradually my eyesight was restored, though it would remain blurry for almost an hour. My breathing remained troubled, and more than once I checked to make certain I had removed the rope.

When Kathy found me, I was standing in an attempt to get my bearings. I had fainted twice. "Oh, God, Thomas. What did they do? What happened to your face?"

"Am I starting to lose my looks?"

"You've lost your voice, too. Oh, dear Thomas. Oh . . . my . . . Lord." She finally glimpsed the setup, picked up the ropes, and stepped over the broken branch. "Are you all right?" I patted the top of her head by way of a reply, but it did little to assuage the tears streaming down her white clown cheeks.

She was shattered, quivering with it. I held up three fingers. "The pigs are gone, big guy. And the way they burned rubber taking off, I knew something lousy happened."

She snuggled her head against my chest so that I could smell the fragrance of her hair, now thick and black and drifting about her shoulders loosely.

When she spoke, I could feel her lower lip quiver. "Thomas, you saved my life. You know that, don't you?"

"Bull."

"It's true. They hanged you. They would have shot me. Thomas . . . I was so afraid I'd never see you again."

When I tipped forward to kiss her brow, the movement sent an excruciating pain through my spinal cord and knees. My lips were thick and soon tasted of greasepaint.

We headed for the road, all the little veins and vessels in my head straining and pounding and wanting to burst. I couldn't hear out of my left ear, had almost no balance, kept stumbling against Kathy. It impressed me that she was overwhelmed. That she thought I had saved her life. That she was weeping. I don't know why it impressed me, but it did.

As we hobbled along together, I realized I'd wet myself. I wondered if I was going to have memory lapses. If I was going to need somebody to drive me to Safeway for groceries. If I was doomed to spend the remainder of my days perched in front of soap operas and wondering whether the neighbor's cat was a communist.

When we reached the road, it was dark, no cars in sight. If

I'd had a gun, I would have shot out a transformer and waited for the power company. As it was, we walked, Kathy propping herself under one arm. Oddly my legs worked fairly well. But the prickly, scalding, exploding sensations in my face and neck and skull became more painful once the blood started to flow.

It was my swollen throat that worried me. The airway seemed to be growing smaller despite the movement that I hoped would oxygenate my blood enough to do some good.

"Thomas, I'm so sorry."

"It wasn't your fault," I said, the words coming like acid.

"You saved my life. They were going to kill us."

"Maybe."

"One of them was trying to shoot at me when I ran. You stopped him."

"Catch their plate?"

"I was too scared to get close. I saw them take you into the trees, but I didn't know how far you went. I was afraid they'd shoot me if they saw me sneaking back to the car. I just hid up there. I'm such a coward. Oh, Thomas, can you ever forgive me? You were so brave, and I just ran."

"Don't be an idiot. I would have run if I could have. You did the only sane thing."

"I should have at least written down the license. I never should have got you mixed up in this, Thomas. We're going to look like a pair of half-wits. It's just that the office has been so dead lately and I'm sick of personal injury cases and you know I won't take any more drug defendants who are all guilty as hell. Where are all the innocent accused?"

I croaked, "Getting hanged in the woods." It netted me a kiss on the cheek. "Getting hanged in the woods," I repeated, grinning foolishly. It earned a second kiss.

Fifteen minutes into our odyssey a lone car passed from the opposite direction. We would have rolled into the ditch to hide, but I could see from a distance the headlights were too close together for a Lincoln. An old geezer in a defeated fedora slowed his '54 Ford, looked us over, then gunned it.

Twelve minutes later a Myrtle Creek police car pulled abreast, his brilliant blue bubble-gum rack playing smatterings of light up against the oaks and madronas and roadway. He looked about as tough as a boy scout trying to sell tickets to the jamboree.

He was young and wore his hat inside the car, same as the old man in the Ford. Maybe it was the custom in Oregon. Wear your hat in the car and hang strangers. "Can I help you folks?"

4

AFTER DESCRIBING OUR ASSAILANTS AND THEIR vehicle, Kathy rushed off to round up fresh duds for us at the Rose Motel. They were X-raying me when Kathy returned, her face scrubbed as pink as a Yakima peach. The Myrtle Creek officer, a young man named Aldredge, turned sappy as soon as he saw Kathy without the clown getup.

It was predictable. Once in downtown Seattle I saw a stockbroker following her, trailed them eight blocks, and scared the bejesus out of him, pretending to be a vice cop, taking down his name, his employer's name, his mother's, and then his wife's phone number. "Been a lot of retards running around the city with hard-ons," I said, grimly. He was so sick at being caught I thought he was going to vomit. "Holy Christ," he said. "Do you know her? She a ballet dancer, or an actress, what?"

"Karate master," I said. "She'd as soon chop your nuts off and make a tobacco pouch out of 'em as spit."

Maybe it was her unusual violet eyes. Or the way she moved. She had a saucy, confident air about her, walked with a flashy strut, and dressed with panache. Shorter than average, she had a dancer's body, a sultry telephone operator's voice, and a way of roping you in with her big blue-violet eyes that you swore would raise the dead. Friendly and matter-of-fact with everybody.

An intern who looked to me as if she were still in high school poked, probed, palpated, twisted, sucked blood into a syringe, listened, groped, and finally announced that she could not detect any brain damage, but that I needed to come back for tests in the morning.

"What are you going to do if my brain's been pulped?"

"I've never been hanged before, so I can't guess how you feel. If it were me, I'd stay here two or three days at the very minimum." I had, she informed me, a ruptured eardrum, a sprained neck, a hematoma on the back of my head, severe bruising on my back and ribs, a pair of chipped teeth, and several nasty abrasions, including one ribbon of raw flesh snaking around my neck that was going to produce an ugly scar.

Kathy Birchfield was able to give the admiring Officer Aldredge a carefully considered statement. I added, "The one without a gun is named Earle and should be walking with a limp. The one with the chrome-plated Llama nine millimeter was named Randy."

"How do you know it was a nine millimeter?"

"It was inscribed on the slide. The other carried a Smith and Wesson Model 27. He did the shooting. But he was using .38s, not the .357s the gun is chambered for."

"You know weapons."

"Used to spend time at the range. I worked for the SPD for ten years."

Aldredge was twenty-four or -five and looked as if he hadn't seen his life flash before him too many times. He kept glancing sideways at Kathy as if he were gathering up his nerve to ask her to the sophomore hop.

"That's Seattle?"

"Yeah."

"If you don't mind my asking, why'd you leave the department?"

"Bum knee." Actually I'd shot someone in the eye, but I

frequently used the knee as an alibi. It was the official version, it was simpler, and it didn't make me sound like a wimp. In America it was getting so not liking to shoot people gave you a bad reputation.

He sat facing me, legs crossed, one black service shoe glistening like a chunk of ebony candy, studying the raw welt across the front of my neck. The look of compassion in his light blue eyes struck me.

Sometimes I wondered if hate didn't get in your bloodstream like a freak chemical enzyme. I was going to have to watch myself, or I'd end up polishing a bar of soap in prison. Revenge. What it was, if you cared to admit it to yourself, was a wretched and very childish embarrassment. They had overpowered me in front of a woman I thought highly of. They had nearly killed me. I simply couldn't bear the humiliation.

"We got your description of the car and the suspects out on the air," Aldredge said. The thumb of his left hand kept spinning a wedding band on his ring finger. "About this woman you came to see? We know about her. Dragged herself in here about four days ago, said she'd been in a car accident. She's drifted in and out of a coma since. The doctors say she's been badly beaten. The chief here took a personal interest. So far, we haven't been able to trace her."

"It was no car accident," said the nurse.

Aldredge said, "How did you track her from Seattle?"

Bridget Simes, the operative who'd located Jo Schwantz for us, stepped forward from the back of the room, her reddish ponytail swinging across her shoulders. I was so groggy and shaken I hadn't even realized she was in the room. She was tall, her face lean, the lines clean and classic. I liked working with Bridget, but she always seemed to have something holding her back. I never knew what.

Bridget said, "I found her. Ms. Schwantz had remarried not too many years ago after her first husband's death. That's really all I know about her except that she was down here."

"Lives in Seattle?" Aldredge asked.

"At least until recently. Never did find the house. I only worked on it half a day. In fact, tracking her here was a fluke." Bridget had been staring at me, presumably irritated over the fact that I'd promised her a simple case, no violent characters.

The officer looked at me. "You think maybe this Jo Schwantz got herself tangled up with some bad dudes and they zeroed in on you . . . trying to protect her, maybe?"

"That's one theory."

"You're not going to talk about it?"

"Hurts to talk."

"Yeah. Sure. I shouldn't have kept you this long." Aldredge stood up, gangly but not tall. The minute he reached his full height, he put his hat back on, as if something important had been missing. "You're going after these guys, aren't you?"

"Me?"

"Do us all a favor and don't do anything illegal, Mr. Black."

"If I even catch up to them."

"Oh, you'll catch up to them. Just remember the law of the land when you do."

"Aldredge?"

"Yeah."

"Ever been hanged?"

"Just don't do anything you'll regret."

"You didn't answer me."

"Yeah. Well, you know I haven't."

Kathy was giving me one of her looks, a mixture of affection and censure. She wanted me to forget the whole thing. Entomb my hate and get on with life. Officer Aldredge gee-whizzed about the lynching, then suggested we drive out there in the dark. I passed, but he lit up like a Las Vegas signboard when Kathy volunteered.

Before they left, Kathy said, "Sure you're okay, Thomas?"

I nodded, trying hard not to swallow the rock that was in my throat.

"I'll check on you before I turn in." At the doorway she pitched my motel room key at me. It sailed past my outstretched palm and struck the wall.

Room 110 was only fifty feet down the hallway. No guard. The door half open, Jo Schwantz's chart in a rack. I scanned her paperwork, but it didn't reveal much except that she was going by the name of Brown.

When she spotted me at the door, a scrawny nurse in her late forties bustled officiously down the corridor. She knew who I was. In a hospital this tiny everyone on the staff had dropped in to see the guy who'd gotten himself hanged.

"May I help you?"

I tried to clear my throat, but it telegraphed agony from my nasal passages all the way down into my chest. The nurse looked past me down the hallway at an orderly who sat at a small desk reading a fishing magazine, his presence an obvious comfort to her. He was too short and too paunchy to have been one of our assailants, I thought, realizing I was already looking at the world differently.

"I saw her earlier," I said, hoarsely.

"Visiting hours are posted at the main desk."

"I know." The nurse thought I was loony, but she stood back and waited in the doorway, arms crossed over her flat chest. "One more thing. She have any visitors?"

"You two and that woman detective seem to be the only people who care whether she lives or dies."

"I bet there's somebody else."

5

IT WAS A HIGH-CEILINGED ROOM PEOPLE DIED in, with a nightstand and a narrow bed jammed up against the wall. A dim lamp burned in the corner. Beyond the frosted window a rhododendron shed teardrops of moisture. Even for a hospital it was austere; no carnations wrapped in red cellophane, no Mylar balloons, no witty get-well cards. She might have been a transfer patient from Pleiades.

Her skull cocooned in white bandages, Jo Schwantz lay on her back. Her face was an eggplant, cheeks bluish-black, mouth misshapen. Even awake, it was doubtful she'd be able to see out of her swollen eyes. Her eyebrows were gone. It had been a long while since I'd seen anyone beaten that brutally. Her left arm was in a fresh white cast, elbow to knuckles.

In Schwantz's driver's license photo she resembled Candice Bergen, shoulder-length wavy brown hair, blue eyes, and a broad, smiling face. The videotape I'd seen of her last week revealed a self-assured woman with perfect posture. Her stats were five foot ten and 135 pounds. Born: 12-13-51. Her chart said she was subject to epileptic seizures, which made me wonder if at least some of her injuries hadn't been incurred in a car wreck. Usually epileptics couldn't get a license without special dispensations, and sometimes didn't want to risk it when they could.

I watched the slow rising and lowering of her chest. The room smelled of bandages, antiseptic, and vaguely of bleach. A particularly repulsive laceration on her chin had been stitched. She breathed through her mouth.

On the wall above the bed somebody had taped a child's crayoned drawing, a crude piece of art, done by a five- or six-year-old, of two women and a girl. One of the women was black. One white. Only the round heads were colored in, the rest of the figures mere sticks. At the top was written in a child's awkward printing: *Amber. Mrs. Swan's class, Room 1.*

I turned to the doorway and the nurse. "The picture . . . ?"

"We found it in her purse when we were trying to ascertain who she was. Kim taped it up. We thought it was kind of nice."

"How long was she here before she stopped talking?"

"Just a few minutes. Poor dear."

"She came in alone?"

"Tuesday about twelve-thirty in the morning. Maybe hitchhiked. Maybe got dropped off. Nobody's seen her car."

"Any evidence of rape?"

"Doctor said no. She was spared that anyway."

"So whatever happened, happened on Tuesday or maybe Monday?"

"Doctor thinks Monday."

"Is she in a coma?"

"Yes. A light one, we suspect. She could come out of it at any time."

"Or maybe never, huh?"

"Right."

"Brain injury?" I croaked. My voice was fading quickly.

"If you mean does she have permanent brain injury, we won't know that for quite some time."

According to Bridget, the address on Jo Schwantz's driver's license was long out of date, an apartment on Seattle's Capitol Hill. For years Schwantz had been renewing her driver's license and misstating her address. Probably had it forwarded by a friend. Curious. It was the first avenue of investigation the hospital staff had tried, too. The Myrtle Creek Police had put her name out on the computer in case somebody somewhere was mounting an organized search.

The motel was only five blocks away. I showered carefully and crawled into a tight envelope of clean, cool sheets where, in order to feel as if I wasn't suffocating, I was forced to lie on my back, the position Jo Schwantz had been in. For half an hour I reviewed the evening's events, replaying the scenario at the roadside. At one time physical action had been my forte, but I had queered this deal.

But then, with a transaction like this, probably the single most unconventional assignment I'd ever undertaken, who had been expecting to get jumped by pigs?

The case had originated in Kathy Birchfield's law practice, the way many of my jobs did. Four highly successful Seattle-area businessmen, all friends since high school, each closing in on forty, had hired me. After years of listening to stories of missing husbands, wives, sisters, brothers—hearing tales of thievery, extortion, incest, child-stealing, and every other perversion under the sun, I listened to their request and nearly broke into laughter.

Three of them were divorced, and one had never married: Floyd Boyd, Jimmy Canfield, Denny McCallum, and Rex Ronquist. The job they requested of me had been hatched a year ago at a private observance held annually since their second year of college when Canfield's yellow dog had been bumped off by a Ritz Cracker truck.

Yellow Dog Party, they called it, an annual beer bash and lie-telling extravaganza where between fifteen and fifty pals from their high school and college days gathered for most of a day and all of a night to catch up on each other's business activities, stock options, marriages, adulteries, sports accomplishments, and recent automotive purchases. They held it the last week of August, at first in Tacoma, where they'd all graduated from Woodrow Wilson High School in '69. The last few years they'd been hiring a suite at the Four Seasons Olympic in Seattle.

The four had approached me in Kathy Birchfield's Pioneer Square office in Seattle, Kathy their ally, Floyd Boyd, their spokesperson—Canfield, McCallum, and Ronquist sitting thigh to thigh on the sofa in their Hong Kong–tailored suits like three dry-mouthed high school boys waiting for the madam to trot out her string of harlots.

Floyd Boyd worked as a public-relations specialist for a law firm in town where the strength of his personality had enabled him to overcome the burden of his unfortunate name. In the autumn he was a shoo-in for a term in a state-representative slot in Washington, D.C. Republican. The Democrat running against him had just been accused of bid-rigging, and his defense was unraveling daily in the newspapers. Boyd would be the next representative from the Thirty-fourth District.

Boyd laid out the program while Kathy, in a gray suit, sat at the back of the room not saying anything. Her presence made the group on the davenport jittery, though Boyd handled the whole thing with aplomb.

"It's not frivolous, Mr. Black," said Boyd. "The problem here is that when a man reaches a certain age, he reviews the past and begins to feel he's missed opportunities. He grows older and more experienced and begins to realize he's let a few get away. What we're asking you to find here is our dreamgirls. We've each got a woman selected, and we'd like you to locate her and get us a date with her. Do you understand what I'm trying to say?"

"Have you tried an escort service?"

"Thomas," said Kathy, giving me a stern look. "You don't even know what they're asking. Hear them out."

"Sure. Okay, sister." She hated it when I called her "sister" in front of clients, but then, she would get even in her own sweet time. She crossed her legs demurely and looked out the window, eyebrows arched. After a long while, the three on the sofa wearied of looking at her smoky stockings and slim ankles and turned back to Floyd.

Boyd continued, "Not women, Mr. Black. We're not talking about numbers here. We're talking about a certain, special woman. Everybody has a dreamgirl, do they not?" Like a poor puttering salesman overrehearsed in the company line, he awaited an answer. I glanced around the room at the boobs on the couch.

"If you say so."

Humoring me with a cockeyed grin, Floyd Boyd continued, "A dreamgirl is somebody who moves you in a particular way. Someone you've spent a lot of time thinking about. Perhaps that feeling was reciprocated, perhaps not. Perhaps she was a high school cheerleader you were too nervous or timid to ask out. Perhaps a co-worker who had other commitments at the time you knew each other. We get older and change. We begin to come into our own, and we wonder what might happen as well as what might have happened."

"Let's hear about the women," I said.

"Sure. Well, Jimmy, Mr. Canfield here, would like you to track down Rhonda Lastusky. Rhonda was a cheerleader at our high school in Tacoma."

"Wouldn't your twenty-year reunion be this summer?"

"Three weeks ago at the Sheraton in Tacoma. As those things go, it was mildly amusing. Rhonda didn't show. Nobody seemed to know anything about her. The invitation committee was unable to track her."

"So I locate her and then what?"

This element of the enterprise embarrassed them, even Floyd Boyd, who seemed to be taking the whole balmy deal in stride. "Well," said Jimmy Canfield from the sofa, dangling his hands out over his knees and flicking his fingers around with each statement. Canfield was the biggest of these four, and, I thought, perhaps the handsomest in a way that was a cross between Tyrone Power and a minor-league ball player. Eye contact was Canfield's knack. "I'd like to see her again. Go out with her, if she's not married or living with someone."

"Date her in high school, did you?"

"Not really."

"Talk to her in high school?"

Kathy had told me Canfield was an insurance-company executive, had skyrocketed through the ranks until he was making close to half a million a year, yet his air of confidence was dwindling rapidly under my onslaught. "Not really."

"I see. Who else?" I looked at McCallum, sitting in the center of the trio on the sofa.

Boyd replied for him. "Denny's dreamgirl is a little closer to home. She has season tickets to the Mariners. He's never met her, but he's admired her from his own seat in the Kingdome for quite some time."

Denny McCallum had very thin hair through which a tanned pate shone, despite which he was one of those men who were destined always to look childlike. Not young, it was just that you knew precisely what he had looked like at ten. He was thickening around the middle and had alert, but often fearful, blue eyes. He knew what could go wrong in life and kept a careful watch out for it. He seemed the least committed to this scheme.

I said, "Why not just approach her at a game and talk to her?"

"It gets a little complicated," stuttered McCallum, his face flushing. He had a squeaky voice that readily betrayed emotion. "She's usually with a guy, see? I don't think there's anything much going on there, but she's usually with this guy. It might even be her brother, cousin, something. How do I know it's not her brother? It's just a little strange going up and asking her with him there. Maybe he's her husband. Maybe he's the jealous type. I mean, I could go to a Mariners game in a polo shirt and come home in a cardboard box, know what I mean? You're trained to handle that sort of thing, aren't you? I mean, you could find out who he was. You could probably do it without pissing anybody off."

"Sure."

Rex Ronquist volunteered his story, leaning forward and pulling an expensive kangaroo-skin wallet from his hip pocket, withdrawing a tattered magazine clipping and offering it to me between two manicured fingers. I took it, glancing at Kathy, who still hadn't taken her eyes off the street below. The clipping was old, half a page that had been folded and carried around that way for years. In this venerable setting it somehow managed to shock me. It was a nude from a girlie magazine. A young dark-haired girl on her knees before a fireplace, one arm resting on the back of a Samoyed. The caption said, "We all pant for Abby."

"Carried her picture around with me in Nam," Ronquist explained. "I had a lot of pictures over there, but she stuck with me. Clipped her out of this magazine before I left. *Babes with Bosoms,* it was called. I was only eighteen. I can't even remember where I picked up the mag. I could'a found it alongside the road for all I know."

"This doesn't look like it's been to Vietnam," I said.

"The one I carried in Nam didn't have nuthin' left of it by the time I shipped home. This is one of the other pictures from the article."

"You have the body of the magazine?"

"Out in the car."

"How about you, Mr. Boyd? Want to sleep with your third-grade teacher? Or have you selected some bespectacled valedictorian out of *Nifty Knockers?* Or a flight attendant who damp-mopped a highball out of your lap in 1979?"

Boyd didn't say a word, just gazed over at Kathy, as did

the three startled and somewhat shamed men on the davenport. Kathy turned from the window and gave me a searing look. "Okay," I said. "I apologize. I've got a big mouth, and I've been having a tough week. Continue."

"I don't see the point," said Boyd. "You don't sound as if you want the job."

"Let me worry about that," said Kathy, in a tone that clearly brooked no dissension. It startled Boyd and all three on the couch. She spoke as if she were my supervisor. She wasn't, but I let it fly.

Floyd Boyd was the smallest and tidiest of the four, reminded me of a dapper little gay opera critic Kathy had introduced me to once, though I had no reason to think Boyd was gay. He was just a bit prim in his impeccably tailored suit and immaculate coiffure, brushed high on top and cut short at the sides, the latest *GQ* look. He moved precisely, as if he were afraid of tipping over, with an old man's fastidious hand gestures. He had a tiny face, plump, and without lines despite the fact that he had to be close to forty. He'd been a local television newscaster for many years, and I was vaguely surprised at how short he was. He had ridden his local celebrity into a job as a public-relations consultant, and now he was flogging the animal into Washington, D.C.

Though they had in essence fired her, Kathy obtained a good number of referrals through Leech, Bemis & Ott, one of whom was Boyd, and she was reluctant to refuse this proposition, no matter how fatuous. Having ties to a state representative couldn't hurt her any.

"Mine," said Boyd, "is a little sticky. I never actually met the lady, but I admired her for many years on the local PBS station. I don't know what she did there, but she used to come in and help run their pledge drives. PBS is about the only station I ever watch. In fact, I don't know why I have a channel changer, even."

"Yeah, me, too."

"She was on for several years, and the way I recall it . . ."

"Got her name?"

"Not really. But I have several hours of videotape featuring her. I'm sure someone at the local station . . ."

"Sure. So what happens when I find these women and they're married?"

"No problem," said Canfield, whose yellow dog had started the annual shindig. "We've already discussed all the possible complications. Happily married? We don't want to interfere with anything. We bow out."

"Okay. But I didn't say *happily* married. I said married. I'm not going to help you cuckold any unsuspecting husbands."

Boyd stepped in, unflappable and cheery. "Married is fine. They're out. But three of us are divorced. We're thinking why couldn't these women be divorced as well? All we want is a nice dinner with them. One date. That's all. One date. If we can't prove ourselves in one evening, then we deserve the brush-off."

"Was that the bet?"

"We didn't bet anything. We just thought . . . What we'd like is for you to find them and convince them to come to Seattle and have dinner with us. All expenses paid, of course."

"This could run into some dough."

"We know that."

"And when they refuse?"

"In that eventuality we're prepared to sweeten the transaction. Five thousand dollars just to show," said Boyd. "We are not hooligans. We have undertaken this rather silly-sounding project because we are now men of means, men of the world. It is our belief that if the four of us each have dinner with these women, in at least one of the cases, possibly more, something of note will develop."

"You're betting which one can score first, right?"

Boyd gave a gentle, politician's laugh and looked across the room at his buddies. I had the feeling nothing could deflate this man. "I assure you, Mr. Black, it's nothing like that. We are serious men. We consider this something in the character of an experiment in human nature."

"The way I see it, you're asking me to pimp for you."

Boyd touched his hair. "I just don't know how I can convince you."

Kathy Birchfield stood, straightened her skirt, walked around the conference table past Boyd and over to me. "One minute, gentlemen," she said, towing me out of the room by my cuff. She hadn't looked anyone in the eye, least of all me.

When she'd closed us in her small office with the planter and the stained-glass windows, she pushed up close to me, dabbed her finger to my eyebrow to rid me of an imaginary speck of lint, and said, "You know I need this. You know Boyd can be helpful in the future. For that matter, so can the other three. They're just a bunch of overgrown schoolboys chasing a fantasy."

"This could take some time."

"So hire it out. It'll be easy money."

The weather was finally turning nice after a rainy spring. "I was hoping for some time off."

"Please don't make me look bad. They can go hire some hack anywhere, but they wanted you."

"Geez, Kathy."

"Look, you've been working on the Sullivan thing since January. This should be a lark compared to a rape-murder. These guys aren't guilty of anything except a little wish fulfillment. Use Bridget. Whoever." She cradled my face between her hot palms and pursed her lips as if speaking to a baby. "Do it for me, Thomas."

"I set the guidelines."

"Don't you always, big guy?"

When we got back into the conference room, Kathy sat by the window. "A few ground rules, gentlemen. You each put ten grand in a trust fund Kathy will set up. If I have to, I will use the money to draw in your little honeybees." Two of them on the sofa smirked at that crack. We were all men now, conspiring the way only men talking about women could conspire.

McCallum said, "I thought we agreed to five grand."

"That was your idea. Ten sounds better. If the money is not necessary, you'll get it back. You pay all expenses on a weekly basis. I find your woman. I explain the situation. She doesn't like it, that's her decision. You do not find out where she is. She wants to tell you where she lives and what she's doing, that's up to her. I will choose the location for the date and escort the woman home. Understood?''

They nodded.

Because of another client who came into Kathy's office that afternoon, the dreamgirl project didn't get off the ground for another two weeks when Bridget Simes, in my employ, located the PBS-drive lady, Floyd Boyd's fantasy. Bridget located her on Friday, late, and early Saturday morning we set off on our six-hour drive to southern Oregon.

By that evening I had been pushed around by pigs, knocked cold, kidnapped, shot at, and lynched.

 "WOW. PLUM-COLORED BRIEFS. I LIKE 'EM. They match my eyes.''

"Forget it, little sister. Your eyes ain't gonna get that close.''

It was eight o'clock Sunday morning when Kathy overran my motel room. She viewed it as a sorry sign that I didn't like being caught half-clothed. "Your back looks like hell, Thomas. I didn't think you ever bruised. Why didn't you tell me?''

I pulled on one leg of my jeans dizzily. When I spoke, my throat ached. "I wish you'd wait until I was decent.''

"You're the most decent man I know. Except Philip.''

"I'm half-naked," I whispered. "I get tired of this.''

"Don't be silly. It didn't even scare me. Mother said I would be scared. I wasn't.''

"I'll bet your mother wouldn't be here."

"With bells on, she would. Mom has a thing for handsome private eyes."

A few minutes later we spoke to a sleepy-eyed Bridget Simes through a half-closed door. To my surprise, her companion lounging in the background was a heavyset dishwater blonde ten years older than Bridget. I had assumed she was here with a boyfriend, not a girlfriend. Bridget wore a long T-shirt, her small breasts poking at the raspberry-colored cotton, her scarlet toenails spread across the threshold.

"I'll be in Seattle in eight hours," I said.

"We'll give you a buzz later."

"Watch yourself, Bridget."

"You know it."

Before heading north to Seattle, we stopped at the hospital and looked in on Jo Schwantz. She hadn't moved a millimeter since I'd seen her last. Before we left, I reached over to the nightstand and dropped my card, the one without the machine gun engraved on it.

Only one vehicle in a two-block radius bore Washington plates, a shabby Dodge Dart. It was parked on N.E. Division; registered to Josephine Beatrice Brown. Her name must have been Brown before it had been Schwantz. Or perhaps it was Jo Brown now. The locks didn't work, so we climbed right in, noting the car had not been in an accident.

Thirty-nine thousand miles on the odometer told me the engine had at least a hundred grand on top of that. The retreads were slick. No spare. In the glove box I found maps of Oregon and Washington, three dog-eared paperback thrillers by John D. MacDonald priced at $1.25, and a pair of women's sunglasses with scratched lenses. In the back I spied a stray crayon, an empty box of Lemon Heads, and one of those plastic eggs that hold cheap toys and drop out of what used to be bubble-gum machines.

On the front passenger seat lay a woman's slip, dappled with dried blood. I found the ignition and trunk key under the driver's seat, and forty-two dollars in wrinkled ones and fives jammed into the ashtray. I left the money and the keys where they were, realizing a tow-truck driver or the neighborhood kids would likely appropriate this booty before Jo.

"They're taking it very seriously," said Kathy. "Unlawful imprisonment, assault, attempted murder. They don't get that sort of thing around here. The Myrtle Creek police want to hand it over to the Douglas County sheriff. I don't see why not. They figure since we were abducted from their hospital, it makes it their case."

"Besides, Officer Aldredge thinks you're swell."

"Here, look at this." She rooted a pair of photocopies out of her purse. Identi-kit drawings of two burly-looking men, neither of whom I recognized.

"When did you do this?"

"Last night."

On the drive home I squeezed and contorted my big frame into several awkward positions before Kathy indicated her thigh. One foot propped on the seat, I lay down and inclined the back of my head against her denim-clad leg. It wasn't a position that made me especially comfortable, but I was drowsy, and feeling Kathy's thigh against the back of my neck wasn't altogether unpleasant.

"Can you still drive?" I asked, as the weight of my head settled against her.

"No problem, big guy."

"Hey, Pancho?"

"Sí, señor."

"This has been bothering me ever since it happened. When I popped that guy at the hospital, why didn't you take off?"

"It was my fault. Stupid. The guy you hit went down. The other guy let go of me and stooped over to help, with his mask off. I looked at his face and I knew him. I guess it surprised me. I should have run, but it surprised me so much I just stood there. I knew the guy."

"So who was it? Somebody you used to date?"

"Don't be ridiculous. I haven't dated a kidnapper in months."

"Who?"

"Beats me. It was just weird. You were telling me to run,

and I was staring at this guy. I've been racking my brain trying to figure out where I know him from.''

"You didn't tell Aldredge?"

"Aldredge told me to phone if I remembered. Any time. Day or night."

"I'll bet."

"All the boys like me."

"It's because they think you're easy."

"I *am* easy." She dropped a hand lightly to my stomach and massaged, as if about to reach for more critical regions. I picked up her hand and returned it to the steering wheel.

"Do me a favor. When you recall where you saw this clodbuster . . ."

"Tell you first? Natch. Thomas? Who were those guys?"

"You used to date one. You tell me."

"Do you think those three had anything to do with Jo Schwantz getting beat up?"

"Maybe. Maybe they thought they were protecting her. What'd you find last night with the cop?"

"I found Big Lick Lane and Cedar Grove Sunday School—a one-room schoolhouse, but I couldn't find where they took us. There are three forks out there, and now I'm not sure which we were on."

"It's a unique situation, Kathy. You know what *they* look like, and they know what *I* look like. But *they* don't know what *you* look like. So *you* can identify *them,* and they can identify *me.*"

"You're going after them, aren't you?"

"What made you think I wouldn't?"

"I'd let the Oregon police handle it."

"No, you wouldn't."

"If you get close, one of them's apt to assassinate you before you realize who he is. Forget this happened. Go back to work. Ride your bike. Get a tan if the weather ever clears up. I don't want you hurt."

There it was. The disagreeable implication that no American male wanted to hear, that he couldn't take care of himself. Not that I was so tough. But it annoyed me. And what was worse, it bothered me that I was annoyed.

Attorney Katherine Birchfield practiced law in Pioneer Square in a lineup of remodeled offices she shared with three other attorneys. I sublet a back room with a window off First Avenue. Kathy was my attorney. I was her private investigator.

Most people, for some reason, found it hard to swallow that my best friend was of the opposite sex, and even harder that we hadn't gotten romantic at some point during our relationship. In some circles a private eye with a middling income, a house, nice pickup truck, and all of his digits might be considered a catch. To my chagrin, Kathy's current boyfriend, Philip, believed us from the first. Not an iota of mistrust in the man. Lately, Kathy had been trying to pretend it didn't piss her off when I called him Dudley Dooright.

Being loosely affiliated with one of the hottest young criminal attorneys in town didn't weigh me down any. There were a lot of iffy situations where a client wasn't sure if he wanted a lawyer or an investigator, even more where he was in need of both. When I took a case, the attorney was there in the same office to dole out advice. When she took a case, vice versa.

Kathy was making a valiant effort to specialize in criminal law, her only problem being her initial vision of battling only for the innocent. She had come to find that of those yanked into court by the criminal-justice system, the innocent popped up about as often as buffalo nickels.

That spring we'd spent two months putting together a defense for a tattooed high school algebra teacher named Jake Sullivan who'd been accused of raping his estranged wife, then strangling her. Somewhere in my six weeks of interviews I determined Sullivan was a compulsive liar who cheated on his taxes, moved property lines to his advantage, sold a horse he knew had cancer to his wife's sister, and, in all probability, had slain his wife and who knows how many other people before her.

On the last day of Sullivan's trial a new client named Boarman came to Kathy. Another loser, Boarman had been arrested outside a tavern with a bloodstained knife in his pocket and thirteen witnesses inside the tavern who pegged him as the one who'd put an assortment of puncture wounds into Leroy Carter's chest, back, thighs, and neck during a dispute involving whiskey, a pool game, a ten-dollar bill, and Leroy's flirtatious girl friend, Lula May.

Criminal law wasn't all it was cracked up to be.

Yellow Dog Party, as we were calling it, had been a prospect for Kathy and me to do something on a lark. Something that didn't involve the unrepentant.

"By the way, little sister. I never did ask you. Where is Philip this weekend? Trying to fill up his autograph book at a convention of nude mud wrestlers?"

"At a fifteen-miler in Canada. He thinks it'll be easier on me if I'm not tagging along at every race."

"Gallant and manly to the end."

It was an eight-hour drive back to Seattle, and I wasn't up to spelling Kathy at the wheel. She stopped once an hour and demanded I get out and tramp around. Even as I bitched, I realized how much good it was doing. I was stiffer than a dead Eskimo.

In Chehalis she stopped at a roadside greasy spoon, and I fussed about what I might eat that could make it down my constricted throat. Ice cream, applesauce, chocolate milk, and Popsicles. Agony, all. Sucking hard candy had been like swallowing lye. Before we left, Kathy ducked into a convenience store attached to a Chevron station and came out with a brown paper sack.

"What's in the bag?"

"Whipped cream." She was jiggling it as she drove, the marble in the can pinging around. I heard the pressure letting off and looked up from her lap in time to see her discharging a jet into her mouth.

"What the hell are you doing?"

"When I'm sick, sometimes it's the only thing I can get down. Here. Try."

"Thanks anyway."

She rattled the marble and took another hit. "No. I'm serious. Here."

"I know you're serious, but I . . ." And then she was blasting whipped cream against my lips. Blurrrfffpt! She gave me a chance to swallow while I wrestled for the can, then blasted me again.

"Kathy . . . Hey, that's good."

"It doesn't hurt your throat?"

"Ummm. No."

For the next fifty miles we passed the can back and forth like a pair of pirates getting smashed on grog. Blurrrffffpt. Blurrrffffpt.

7

WE GOT BALLED UP IN THE SUNDAY EVENING I-5 corridor mess, mired near the Aroma-dome in downtown Tacoma for a wreck, and an hour later stuck in bumper-to-bumper indignation on 50th N.E. in Seattle. A fine drizzle beaded up on the windshield. Kathy didn't bother to lick it with the wipers.

"Would have been faster to take the Ravenna exit and double back on Roosevelt," I said.

"What I should have done, I should have gone north on Seventh, then taken Fifty-fifth over and across."

"Ravenna."

We inched past two of my favorite places, a tiny box of a movie theater called the Seven Gables and the white-walled University branch of the public library. Firehouse Number Seventeen was on the corner.

Home was a two-bedroom bungalow near Roosevelt Way N.E., actually one block over on Eleventh N.E. The neighborhood was strewn with college kids renting rooms, retired couples, widows, and here and there a family raising children.

Mine was a long, narrow green house shaded in the back by a forty-foot crab-apple tree that gave Kathy's teenage nephews ammo for our late-summer skirmishes upon which Kathy frowned when she wasn't participating, clad in a catcher's mask she'd picked up at a garage sale. My neighbor, Horace, automatically dialed the police when he saw us pitching apples.

The basement had long ago been converted into a bachelor apartment, which I had rented to Kathy. It could have fetched more than she paid, but then she wouldn't have had cheap digs, and I wouldn't have had her.

She evacuated her belongings from the truck, gave me a peck on the cheek, and disappeared through her doorway under my rear porch.

I wandered over to my roses in the gloomy backyard, feeling a tad dizzy from eating nothing but whipped cream, from the long drive, and from the inner-ear damage. And from the desire for revenge that barreled through my system like a runaway fever.

The yellows were my favorites in this subdued light. Sunsprite. Guadalajara. Gold Medal. I cut three budding Adolf Horstmanns and stuck them in a vase on my kitchen table.

After I unpacked my overnight bag, I managed to choke down a batch of scrambled eggs sans my usual ketchup. I checked the fridge, but there was no whipped cream. I had a deep bath thundering into the tub when the phone rang. A collect call from Bridget Simes, her voice dry and distraught. "Thomas?"

"How are you, Bridget?"

"I'm okay. I called the hospital, and they assured me there had been no change, so Jesse and I drove up to Crater Lake. When we got back, she was gone."

"Jo Schwantz passed away?"

"They say she came to late in the morning, and by mid-afternoon was walking around the corridors with a walker, trying to build up her strength. I guess she saw her opening and took off. She ran.''

"She say anything to anybody?"

"Not a whisper."

"There's no likelihood somebody spirited her away?"

"I had a long talk with the hospital staff. It was Sunday, and you know how dead that little hospital is. It's more like a first-aid kit with doors. They were keeping a close eye on her.''

"Not close enough."

"She took her clothes, her purse. And Thomas?"

"Yeah."

"You know the drawing somebody taped over her bed? If she was snatched, the drawing probably wouldn't have vanished. She took that.'' I had been banking on certain communications from Jo Schwantz, and this was a disappointment. Jo knew who beat me up. Jo knew who hanged me. Jo knew whom I was chasing. Jo had to know.

"Thomas, I found her once. I can find her again."

"Forget it, Bridget. I've got someone else for you to find. She's right here in the rainy city. By the way, how did you locate Schwantz in the first place?"

"I took a Polaroid off that videotape you gave me of the PBS pledge drive she'd been co-hosting. It turned out fairly decent, so I went to Channel Nine down by the Seattle Center and asked around. She'd worked there as a volunteer off and on for a couple of years, and most everybody knew her under the name of Jo Brown. The address they had listed on their records was the same one on file with the department of licensing. I'd already gone there and found it bogus. Nobody at the TV station had seen her for over seven years, but when I went through my standard spiel about did they know her mother, father, her car-repair shop, her dentist, that sort of thing, one of her old friends recalled Jo asking for the name of a doctor. The way she remembered it, Jo's physician had retired and she hadn't much liked the M.D. who was taking over the practice. This woman, Jamie Antonio, had referred Jo to her own doctor. A Dr. Mild.''

"You visited Dr. Mild?"

"I was prepared to bribe someone. If you show up after hours and promise not to steal anything, you can usually let loose of a hundred-dollar bill and get a cleaning woman to help you thumb through their files—nobody the wiser.

"But Dr. Mild came right out. You should have seen him. A regular milquetoast. Anyway, I played it straight because I usually find—when I'm not bribing the help—playing it straight works best; told him I was looking for this woman— but not why—and that she seemed to have disappeared. I'd already gone through my friend at TRW, but she didn't seem to have any credit under the name Jo Brown, wasn't listed in any of the routine directories. So Dr. Mild tells me he's worried about her. Jo Brown. It seems he received a phone call a day earlier from a Dr. Gillespie in Roseburg. Jo had checked herself into the hospital, barely able to walk, had seized once, and was all beat up, denying anything but a car accident.

"Gillespie found a Phenytoin prescription in her purse with Dr. Mild's name on it. They called Dr. Mild a few hours later and said she'd lapsed into a coma and did he know her next of kin. Mild tried to phone her home in Seattle, even sent his receptionist down there to check it out. The neighbors said nobody'd been home for a couple of days."

"You have that address?"

"Just a minute," said Bridget. I could hear her girlfriend talking to her in the background. Bridget came back to the phone and gave me a 900 number on Twenty-fifth Avenue South.

"Twenty-fifth? Those pigs were grilling me about Twenty-fifth last night."

"You're right. I should have picked up on that and told you about this earlier."

"Don't worry about it. Take care, Bridget. And drop by when you want to tackle the next dreamgirl."

I was in the living room scanning the Sunday *Times-PI*, my hair damp from a bath, when I heard Philip Bacon's car pull up the drive behind Kathy's eight-year-old Firebird. He walked to the rear of the house and rapped on her door. I expected to hear voices through the floor, but instead I heard footsteps around the side of the house as he tried to figure out whether she was home.

Philip was a tall, good-looking man with one brown eye and one blue and enough unruly hair to transplant onto a whole litter of bald cats. He'd been Kathy's guy for several months now, but I was expecting her to off-load him shortly.

I watched from the semidarkness of my living room but did not open the front door to offer that Kathy had been up all last night and was probably zonked. Looking confused, he drove off in his BMW.

I breezed through the paper but found nothing to take my thoughts off Jo Schwantz and her three guardians, or whatever they were. I was afraid to doze, fearful that I would suffocate in my sleep.

That night they came for me in the fog again. This time they brought their own lady clown. She was small and lithe and curvaceous, her eyes brighter than I thought possible, as if they had violet lasers behind them. It wasn't until they had me on a stump, a noose around my neck, that the clown doffed her raincoat to reveal a skintight Lycra outfit with holes cut out at the breasts, a Fellini nightmare of titillation. I tried to say something, but the rope strangled my words.

It was 7:00 A.M. when someone sank onto the edge of my bed. Half-asleep, I'd heard her clomping up the inside basement stairs, using her skeleton key on the old-fashioned lock at my inside kitchen door.

"Don't move, Cisco. I just came up to be sure you were well and to tell you I was off to work." I rolled over, knuckled my eyes, and inhaled her. "Hard night? I see you're better. Good." It took me a few moments to separate dream from reality. I was hot, perspiring. "You all right this morning, Thomas?"

"I was dreaming."

"I can see you were dreaming. Anybody I know?" She gave me a leer.

I stretched and yawned. "What?"

"Last night I was so wiped out I don't even remember the drive. I put my head on the pillow and was gone. Fourteen hours. And still I woke up frazzled. I don't know if I'll get through the day.''

"You look fabulous.''

"And you're a first-rate liar. Is your neck better?'' She reached out and cupped her cold palm against the stubble on my cheek.

"Sure. Fine.''

"I just wanted to be sure you knew I was grateful. The more I think about it, the more I realize if you hadn't taken a chance, we'd both be out in the bulrushes somewhere.''

She leaned down and kissed my brow. "Philip dropped by around seven-thirty.''

"I didn't hear a thing. Did you tell him I was asleep?''

"He had a couple of dolled up Bahamian hookers with him. They were all pretty smashed or I would have invited them in.''

"You're a real card.'' Kathy's perfume lingered in my bedroom long after she walked out of the room. She gave the horn a tap and headed the Firebird out onto Eleventh.

For two days I vegetated in front of the television. Fred Allen said television had been invented so people with nothing to do could watch people who couldn't do anything. I was smack in the middle somewhere. I napped, deadheaded my roses, sat in the sun, thumbed through mail-order cycling catalogs, watched forty-year-old grade B westerns, mostly Roy Rogers films I'd taped, and shot at slugs from the window with my Daisy Red Ryder BB gun. For me, old cowboy movies acted as a poultice.

When it occurred to me, I got on the computer in the spare bedroom and pecked out random notes on the Schwantz case.

A couple of old friends dropped around to pay their respects and to inspect my injuries. Tuesday morning Bridget Simes dropped by, and I gave her all the information on Denny McCallum's Kingdome dreamgirl. At noon I phoned the police in Myrtle Creek to see what progress they'd made. Everyone was out. I left a message. Aldredge called back at four. "Not a thing, Mr. Black. We thought we found the motel those three birds stayed at, but we didn't.''

It was brutal when people in their twenties called you Mister.

Tuesday evening I felt rusty and restless. It had sprinkled that afternoon, though patches of blue were charming the city now, and I was sitting on the back porch in a wooden chair sold to me out of a flatbed truck by Gypsies, had just blasted a slug near the concrete bird feeder, when Floyd Boyd, Denny McCallum, and a girl walked around the corner from my driveway.

I was gnawing on a carrot, had found myself with an insatiable craving for carrots since my throat began healing, maybe just to prove to myself that I could still eat them. I put the gun up quickly, BBs rattling inside the storage barrel.

"Black," said Floyd Boyd, as he stepped forcefully past the half-open gate. Behind him came a prepubescent girl in a gray sweatshirt, black sneakers, and blue jeans sawed off and hemmed above the knees. She resembled Boyd, the same horsey teeth and mouth, although the mouth didn't disturb the agreeable looks of either one. Behind them, Denny McCallum stepped into the yard hesitantly. McCallum and Boyd both wore suits, had no doubt come directly from work.

"Gentlemen," I said. "And lady. What can I do for you?"

A trace of hope threading his voice, Boyd said, "Kathy told us you found mine. And ran into some trouble."

"Kathy should have referred you to me."

"Did you, though? Did you find the lady from Channel Nine?"

"I'm still working on it."

"Are you all right? Kathy said you were under the weather. I phoned a couple of times. Nobody answered."

"Sometimes when I practice my trombone . . ."

"May I borrow your telephone? It's out of state, but I'll use my card. Got a beeper message on the way over here to call the committee in D.C."

I stabbed a thumb toward the open back door. "Can't stand in the way of the national interest."

"I need it, too," said Denny McCallum, bashfully.

"In the living room." He followed Boyd up the steps, leaving me with the girl.

After they were well inside the house, I turned and saw her sizing me up, very serious about the neck brace. "Ever do any big-game hunting?" I asked.

"No, but I've ridden pigs."

"So what's your name?"

"Echo."

"Floyd your dad?"

She nodded. "He's going to be a congressman. I met the mayor. Dad's going to introduce me to the vice president of the United States in a few weeks."

"That's something you won't soon forget." The BBs in my Daisy Red Ryder jostled when we shook hands. "My name is Thomas Black. See that gray thing in the grass over by the Jacob's ladder, that plant with the blue flowers? 'Bout five inches long?"

"A snake?"

"You're not from around here, are you?"

"Utah."

"Slugs, we call 'em. Let's see what kind of shot you are." She wedged her cheek up against the comb of the gun, her off eye closed, the long dark lashes settling against her cheek. The men took their time on the phone, long enough that Echo had not only mastered the blade and notch sights of my carbine but scored a bull's-eye near the compost heap.

"So where do you ride these pigs?" I asked. "Utah?"

"Uh-huh. My uncle's farm."

"You probably eat a ton of sausage. If we had any sense, we'd turn our slugs into wieners."

She chuckled. "On my uncle's farm. One day my friend Ginny said, 'Why don't we ride one of your pigs?' So we did. It was insane. My uncle had cows and horses and goats and four dogs. Thirteen cats. And pigs, of course. What happened to your neck?"

"Whiplash."

"Were you in a car wreck?"

"Seattle has the biggest slugs in the world. Last year they caught one, twenty-seven pounds. The only way they caught it—it was scooting out of the neighborhood with a barbecue pit half-eaten down its gullet—they threw a stick of dynamite down the barbecue's chimney." I made an explosion sound with the back of my throat, which was a mistake, because it ached horribly.

She chuckled. "My uncle's farm is in Utah. But we don't live there anymore."

"In Utah?"

"I live in Utah with my mom. But not on the farm. We lived on the farm after Dad left. Now we're in Salt Lake City. Mom works for a dentist. But she's going to school. She's going to be a lawyer."

"Good for her. And your dad moved back here?"

"Him and Mom got a divorce when I was little. Mom didn't want to come back to Seattle. She said it rained too much. She said Dad had a girlfriend, but he didn't. I don't know why moms and dads lie about each other."

"And you're visiting?"

"Until August twenty-eighth."

"Almost two months. Good for you."

"And Dad's going to be real busy getting ready for D.C. He's going to be a congressman, did you know? Mom's coming on the train to get me in August."

"Has your mom remarried?"

Echo tucked her chin in, gave me a clouded squint and some facts. "Of course not. She and Daddy are getting back together."

"Is that what she said?"

"No. But I know it." She stared off at my compost heap. She had programmed the future out of her own aching need. I hoped she wasn't going to be disappointed.

"Twist your neck?" It was Floyd Boyd on the porch behind us. "Those cervical strains can be serious."

"He's got whiplash," volunteered Echo.

"I forgot to introduce my daughter," said Boyd. "Echo, this is Thomas Black. Mr. Black is a private investigator."

"We've met," I said.

"Gosh. A private eye like on TV?"

"Exactly," I lied. Denny McCallum remained in the house, his distant voice whiny on the phone.

Boyd crinkled up his face, unbuttoned the dark suit jacket, and tramped down the steps. "I'm just curious, that's all. You found her? The lady from Channel Nine. Where was she? Is she married?"

"What do you know about her?"

Boyd stepped back as if I'd tossed him a burning coal. "Me?"

"Yeah."

"Dad? You don't have a girlfriend, do you?"

"No, honey. This is just a woman Thomas is finding. I don't have any girlfriends except you."

"And Mom."

"Right." Boyd was a glossy, sophisticated piece of business, but I had to respect the bumbling glow he emitted when he spoke to his daughter. He'd been divorced several years, had only the one child. She was pretty, intelligent, and obviously meant the world to him.

"What do I know about her? She was on the PBS drives for a good number of years. She wore glasses the first few years. After she got contacts and changed her hairstyle, she was a knockout."

"You never knew her name?"

"They didn't give it out on those videotapes."

"That's not what I'm asking."

"Black, you get more finicky each time we meet. No. I never knew it. If I had, I would have told you so that your search would have been that much easier. I'm not in the habit of costing myself money. Close by, is she?''

''I'm working on it.''

''I don't understand how you could find her and then lose touch.'' Boyd was unquestionably vexed at my orthodox interpretation of our contract. Clearly he thought a slackening of the guidelines was in order once the horses were lathered up.

''Look, Floyd. It wasn't my idea to keep you guys abreast of every little development. I rarely do that with clients. Kathy's doing it for you guys as a favor. I'll find her again, and when I do, she may or may not be interested in your offer.''

''Why do you say that? You didn't talk to her about it this weekend?''

''No.''

''Then I might not ever hear more than you're telling me?''

''Exactly.''

''You don't know if she's married?''

''I don't know that telling you is in the contract.''

''You can't give me a hint?''

''Nope.'' This badgering was unlike Boyd, who had heretofore seemed the most confident of hunters. Now that I was getting close, he'd turned to Jell-O.

He took a deep breath and gazed at his daughter, who was under the crab-apple tree bending down to sniff a Cathedral, one hand tucked between her bare knees. I took my clippers, walked over, cut a long bud off the plant, and presented it to her, thinking we must look like some sort of Norman Rockwell magazine cover. The exploded slug at our feet made it perfect. She grinned and looked up at me with eyes as blue as paint. Already, she had several mannerisms of her father's, one being a slow, cowlike blink of her eyes when talking. The manner in which she held her hands when she took the rose was her father's as well. On Echo the mannerisms were winsome; on Floyd, slightly effeminate.

''Well, sorry to bother you. We're just going out to dinner with some boosters. Thought we'd drop by and see how you were. I'll be in touch,'' Boyd said, as he and his daughter walked down the driveway past my pickup truck, Boyd moving with the cocky confidence of a man who'd never in his life been ambushed by a school bully, been slapped by an angry girlfriend, or had a check bounce. His daughter slipped one hand into his, the other nursing my pink Cathedral bud.

Inside, I found Denny McCallum staring dismally at the telephone in its cradle. "Trouble?"

Unnerved, McCallum looked up. "No. Nothing. Really. Business as usual. My ex-wife. I guess she's not an ex yet. Penny keeps getting emotional on me. Thinks we should be seeing a counselor. I told her it was way beyond that, but she keeps insisting. Now she's got my lawyer telling me I should go to the counselor. What the heck, he says. Go to a couple of sessions. But I don't need to see some shrink so he and my wife can gang up on me and tell me I left fish guts in the trunk of the car and embarrassed her in front of her tennis-club friends."

"Did you?"

"What?"

"Leave fish guts in the trunk?"

"Yeah, and I spilled turpentine on the dining-room floor. And sometimes I eat a whole spud right off the fork. She knew I was like that when we got married. She's just emotional."

"Women tend to get emotional when you divorce them."

"Yeah, well . . ."

Denny worked in a small company down on N.E. Boat Street above Portage Bay, designing and then overseeing the manufacture of machinery for paper mills. He made good money, but his employment afforded little opportunity for contact with people—consequently his social skills hadn't been exercised much. McCallum was one of those shy guys who carried a million grudges because he wouldn't open his mouth and complain at the right time. He'd been volunteering on Boyd's campaign all summer, aping Boyd's apparel, tailored suits, and handmade European shoes, though usually, on Denny, a shirttail poufed out or a shoelace tracked astray.

Denny had thinning blond hair over a pate tanned in a booth. He was thick across the middle, maybe forty-five pounds overweight. Despite a tan as even as a coat of enamel, he had one of those faces that blushed easily.

At our last caucus he'd gotten tipsy, and let out that he'd left his wife in anticipation of hooking up with the woman from the Kingdome. Sparks would fly. His divorce was riding on it. It had never occurred to him that the woman from the Kingdome might be spoken for, that she might not cotton to him, that he might not cotton to her. Or maybe it had occurred to him, since he was the most fidgety of the four.

"You, uh, you don't look so hot," said McCallum.

"Little trouble."

"Kathy Birchfield said something about getting into a fight."

"Is that what she said?"

McCallum did a lot of verbal backpedaling, ever fearful of being caught with the wrong words between his lips. "Well, not exactly. She said 'hassle.' I figure a guy has a hassle and ends up in a neck brace with his face all cut up . . . maybe that was a fight. What else would it be? But that's your concern. I was only wondering . . . it didn't have anything to do with that gal from the Kingdome?"

"I've got somebody going to tomorrow night's Mariners game. We should know who she is in two days."

"I wonder if I went to the game tomorrow night if I might muck things up? I mean, I've been watching this woman for a long time, and to get this close and then muck it up . . ."

"Makes no never mind."

"But if you're going to be there . . ."

"An operative will be doing this. You won't even know who it is. Guaranteed."

At twenty-four, he'd married the first woman he ever dated. They'd been together fourteen years. Nothing wrong with that—some of the greatest love stories of our time happened that way—except, from the outset, Denny thought he'd missed something.

"Must be tough being a private eye. Must get into a lot of scrapes," McCallum said.

"Not too many."

"But you've been beat up before?"

"Still have most of my teeth. There are guys on the Sonics who don't have *any* teeth." I plucked a pear out of a bowl on the dining-room table and chomped it.

"Yeah, but what's a few teeth when you're pulling down a million a year, eh? It's gotta be tougher on a guy like you. I'll bet that's why you keep in shape. And the guns. You carry one, don't you?"

"Rarely."

"Geez," said McCallum. "A private eye without a gun."

"Think I'm going to need one for your dreamgirl?"

"It's not that. It's just . . ."

"America's gone to hell in a hand basket, eh? Presidents without ethics. Judges without common sense. Laws without teeth. Private eyes without guns."

My snideness sparked a smile on McCallum's lips, a smile he reserved for mothers-in-law, caustic bosses, and pushy salesmen. I noticed it didn't spread to his eyes. McCallum tried hard not to judge others, which was funny, because he seemed to be doing it constantly. I could see by the way he was looking at me that he'd come to some negative conclusions where I was concerned.

On the way out my back door he stopped, turned on my kitchen faucet, hunched down, and drank directly from the pipe. While he ambled down the driveway, I cleaned the faucet and wondered how I'd gotten sucked into this Okefenokee of wish fulfillment.

9 WEDNESDAY I WOKE UP WANTING TO KICK down doors. I showered and let the hot spray address the soreness in my neck, toweled off, put on slacks, a dress shirt, and a sportcoat. I wrapped the soft brace around my neck even though I wasn't sure I needed it, and smoothed the Velcro seal. Braces were an everyday sight. Rope burns were for freaks.

I knelt in the back of the closet and pried open the hidden wall panel where I kept my pistols, brought out the pieces to a .45 automatic, and assembled it, wiping the parts down with an oiled rag as I handled them. I hadn't touched a gun in over two years. My hands, I noticed, were steady.

Rolling the cartridges in my palms to feel the heft and deadliness of them, I took out a clip and slowly fed the fat, round-headed bullets in, pushing slowly against the spring. My mind was numb; my eyes barely alive to what was going on in front of them. I heeled the clip into the handle of the pistol, then pulled back the slide, let it slap a bullet into the chamber. I flicked off the safety, squeezed the grip safety, and aimed at the doorknob, a perfect sight alignment, the knob sitting behind and atop the sights. The explosion and the flying doorknob came as no surprise, though I hadn't consciously thought about firing. The ringing in my ears seemed to have a cause outside of my own actions, but I couldn't quite comprehend what it might be.

Sluggishly, as if in defeat, I unloaded the gun, took each of the cartridges out of the clip, and stacked them neatly in the box they had come from. I wiped the pistol down with the oily rag, then placed it in the back of the closet. Walking outside to the garage, I found another doorknob, brought it in, and installed it. I discovered the hole in the plaster behind the door where the bullet had bedded itself into a stud, spackled the hole, and let it dry. Then I painted over it. Ten minutes later I had breakfast and tried to pretend the episode had never happened.

I would find these men and I would make them pay, but not at the expense of my own sanity. Not with a gun.

Overcooked Quaker Oats was all I could get down for breakfast, since my throat would tolerate nothing more exotic after yesterday's carrot festival. And my voice. I wasn't sure how long it would hold up. It was lower, gruffer.

Four men and four dreamgirls. It was quite a list.

A high school cheerleader. She was Canfield's.

The pretty woman who sat nearby at the Mariners games. McCallum's.

A nude pinup. Ronquist's.

And now it was time to find Floyd Boyd's. The TV lady. There were three Schwantzes in the Tacoma book, but they all spelled it without the *T*. No Seattle listings. I went through the Eastside book, found two, and phoned. Both ancient. Neither professed to know a Jo Schwantz or Jo Brown, though one of them claimed he could trace his ancestry back to Diogenes.

I already knew DMV had her address wrong. The City Directory didn't contain Jo's name. I called City Light pretending to be Jo, but they had no record. Ditto Washington Natural Gas. Another call produced three Joseph Browns, but no Jo. I had a friend who worked for Pacific Northwest Bell who promised to go through their records. I added combinations of middle and first names.

If Jo was subscribing to the *Times* or *PI*, it wasn't under her own name.

I phoned a Seattle policeman I'd known from the pistol team. Pfortmiller. "Herb? Thomas Black here. Hey, sorry to bother you so early but I've got a question. A Llama nine millimeter. Ever see one?"

"Saw a .45 once. You spot 'em in the catalogs, but nobody I know carries it. They had a poor reputation back in the seventies. Supposed to be making some nice firearms now, according to what I've read, but I still don't see any."

"Could you call some of your friends around the gun clubs and see if anybody has a nine millimeter? I'm looking for a guy around six feet tall. White. Husky. Maybe two thirty-five. Blue and brown. Somewhere between thirty and fifty years old. He's well-educated. He was carrying a Llama nine millimeter Saturday night in southern Oregon. Probably owns a white Lincoln, '88 or '89. I don't want him to know anybody's looking for him."

"Sure. I should get back to you by early afternoon."

"Thanks, Herb. I owe you."

"Like always."

As I was scanning the videotapes of Jo Brown/Schwantz,

my contact from the phone company called back and announced that they had no record of her. I sat back and watched the videos. Floyd Boyd had come off as the poised one in this concoction, yet Boyd had stockpiled the KCTS tapes for seven-and-a-half years. Was that poised or was that spooky?

I'd been reviewing Boyd's history, and couldn't conjure up any way to connect him to the high jinks Saturday night. He'd been divorced eight years, yet his eleven-year-old daughter thought he was going to get back with his ex. Boyd couldn't have been a bachelor more than about ten minutes before fixating on Jo.

Jo Brown had been a spokesperson for the public-television station pledge drives. Routine stuff. Stand in front of the camera and tout nature films, reruns of *Mr. Rogers' Neighborhood*, then urge viewers to phone in pledges. In early tapes Jo's face was cluttered with large, heavy spectacles, and she seemed awkward and ill-at-ease in front of the cameras. In later tapes she apparently wore contacts and looked entirely different. Smiling. Her hair was done up behind her head, giving her face definition, her mouth gleaming with perfect white teeth. She carried herself with confidence, spoke right up. It was as if she had been redone by some make-over master. There didn't seem to be any way on earth the wreck of a woman I'd visited in the hospital in Myrtle Creek might be related to this one.

I nursed my '68 Ford truck down to the Mobil station on 45th N.E., gassed it, checked the oil and water, then took N.E. Pacific to Montlake, crossed the Cut on the bridge, and fought traffic up Twenty-fourth Avenue until it angled into Twenty-third, until most of the faces on the street were black. I passed Garfield High School and then headed east on Dearborn.

It was a tall, dilapidated house, two stories, with peeling paint and a broken window in the attic. Its neighbors were squeezed in like the hopeful poor in line for lotto tickets. Down the street sat a ten-year-old Cadillac in immaculate condition. In front of the Caddy a junker Ford LTD canted with two flats. A rusty bicycle sans tires was chinked under the LTD. Some of the yards were immaculate. Others were eyesores.

I strode through the open gate of the cyclone fence, stepped up onto the porch, and found the innards of the doorbell hanging out of the siding. Gelatinous gauze curtains stretched across the top of the door's fan-shaped window. The wooden porch needed paint and creaked so that any minute my weight might have taken me through to the spiders. I knocked, hoping a pig didn't answer.

Nobody did.

Only a few of the neighbors were home.

Most were probably at work. One house was abandoned, an old doorless Gibson refrigerator in the yard. Nobody I called on knew anything about Jo Brown/Schwantz or the house I thought she lived in.

I took Norman Street back to Twenty-third, followed Jackson down the hill, beyond the Vietnamese shops mushrooming at Twelfth, under the freeway, through a sleepy Chinatown, and past the construction at the King Street Station. I crossed First and parked several blocks north under the Viaduct.

Along with two other lawyers, Kathy leased offices in a renovated three-story stone building in Pioneer Square. The city had made a noble effort to reclaim what had once been the heart of the town, but wine-bibbing derelicts, traffic congestion, and beggars with cardboard signs delineating their sorry life histories put a crimp in things.

After jogging up two flights, I bypassed Kathy's office and unlocked the frosted-glass door to my small cubicle. Still breathing heavily, I located a pair of binoculars in a cabinet against the wall, cloistered myself behind the curtains, and focused.

"I thought Blondie's bus route didn't start until later?"

"Kathy . . . look at this guy." She came over and placed her head alongside mine. "Heavyset guy across the park by the light standard? Recognize him?"

As if I were a child caught playing with a cigarette lighter, Kathy gently took the binoculars and moved in front of me. I could smell her hair, feel her body heat.

"Next to the light pole?"

"Big guy. Gray suit. Hands in his pockets. Looks like he's waiting to snatch a baby. Maybe slide a firecracker into a blind man's soup."

Kathy handed me the field glasses. "He's not one of the two I saw."

"Just wondering."

"I thought you weren't going to do anything for a week."

"Just a little walk to the Cobb Building to visit Jo Schwantz's doctor."

"I'll go with you. I'm ready for a break. I've been studying depositions for hours."

"Don't bother."

"I'll just get my jacket and change shoes."

We hiked up First Avenue to University and then up the hill three blocks to Fourth. A deep-water port catering to shipping from all over the world, Seattle was built on seven hills, all of which overlook Elliott Bay. A rusty Japanese freighter was moored offshore. A tooting ferry chugged toward the terminal several blocks below us, as if ready to sink from the burden of station wagons bogged down with drowsy tourists, empty Nikons, and loaded Pampers.

The sky was drab, a light breeze kicking up off the water, the smell of salt air mingling with the fumes from passing vehicles and with the smells oozing out of old brick buildings. Walking briskly, we soon regretted our jackets. We might have gone down Third Avenue, but the bus-tunnel project spanning the length of Third would have upset Kathy, who was disgusted with the relentless construction and railed against a city administration that contrived more each day.

Dr. Mild's office was on the tenth floor of the Cobb Building, directly opposite the elevators. A well-preserved woman of about sixty with shoulder-length hair, bangs, and a voice that sounded as fresh and soothing as the lady robot announcer in an elevator, took our names and told us Mild was with a patient.

Kathy was thumbing through a copy of *Mental Health*. "Looking for clues on how to straighten out Philip?" I whispered. Kathy gave me a look, and I tried to think up another crack.

"Gee," continued the receptionist. "You're not here about the woman who was beat up in Oregon?"

We went back to the desk together. "How did you know?"

"Well, I didn't," she said, matter-of-factly. "But we get patients, not private detectives. And after the police came in, I naturally assumed . . ."

"Police? When?"

"Friday, I guess. Yes, it was last Friday because it was raining, and he came in with drops all over his shirt."

"A Seattle policeman?" Kathy asked, as a man in a white smock escorted an elderly man with a cane out to the reception area. We watched as the doctor launched him on his way.

He turned to me, stuck his hand out limply, smiled, and said, "Purvis Mild. Heddy said on the intercom you wanted to see me. I don't usually take patients without an appointment, but if there's some rush . . ." He was looking at my brace.

I introduced myself and Kathy. "You saw my operative last week, Bridget Simes. We're looking for a woman named Jo Schwantz. Maybe Jo Brown."

"Doctor . . ." the receptionist interrupted. "What was the name of that policeman who came in here Friday?"

"Glenn," replied Dr. Mild, fixing me with his pale gray eyes.

"Did he resemble either of these?" I asked, unfolding the two composites Kathy had done in Myrtle Creek. I'd had them reduced and fitted onto one sheet.

"Well," said the receptionist. "I think he could almost be the one on the right. If you stretched him out. But I don't really guess so."

"I would have said it was more the one on the left," said Dr. Mild. "But not really."

Two patients entered, and the automatic bell on the front door jangled. Neither was large enough to have been one of my attackers on Saturday night. It was only when I realized

they were women that I knew how all-consuming my rancor
had become.

Mild steered us down a hallway to his office, which sported
a pair of windows looking out on the Rainier Tower across
the street. He seated us in plastic-backed chairs, crossed his
ankles, and folded his arms on his chest. He was small and
freckled, a shock of curly rust-colored hair nudging his collar. His chin was long, and his eyes were warm and sympa-
thetic. Bridget had called him a milquetoast, but she was
often too harsh in her conclusions.

"Now what can I do for you?"

"We're looking for Jo Brown."

"Patient information is confidential."

"I understand that. The trouble here is you might end up
identifying some woman in the basement of Harborview
wearing nothing but a toe tag. I think she's in real trouble,
and I'd like to find her. I'm trying to help her. Nobody will
ever learn where we got our information."

Dr. Mild considered the situation. "If I wasn't already so
concerned, I wouldn't say a word."

"We realize that."

"I received a phone call last week from a Dr. Gillespie in
Oregon who said Josephine Beatrice Schwantz was there, and
they had found a bottle of Phenytoin in her purse which I had
prescribed. Told me she was lapsing in and out of a coma. I
forget the name of the town. Nobody had a clue how she'd
gotten there."

"Myrtle Creek. Drove herself," I said.

"Then you've found her?"

"Found and lost her. Late Sunday she started exercising,
and before nightfall she had disappeared."

"That's an awfully quick recovery."

"Doctor, what's Phenytoin prescribed for?"

"Seizures, among other things. Could you tell me why you
are looking for her?"

Kathy, who noticed my voice eroding, said, "You have
to trust us that we mean her no harm. We're working on a
rather convoluted legal project, and Jo was just a small
part of it. Now she's become a larger part, but only because

we're frightened for her. We're working with the Myrtle Creek Police.'' Kathy looked at me, reluctant to mention men in pig masks with pistols. "Anything you can tell us will help.''

"Gillespie said she'd been battered. Bones in her face broken. Teeth knocked out. Arm fractured.''

"Yes. She's frightened, Doctor. That's why she left the hospital,'' Kathy said. "Somebody is after her. Any ideas?''

"Our relationship was not that close.''

"What about her children?''

"I delivered her second child.''

"Amber?'' I ventured.

"Yes.'' Dr. Mild walked around his desk, opened a drawer, and pulled out a file.

"How old would she be now?''

"Amber? About six. Jo is, let's see. Thirty-eight.''

"Did you ever treat Jo for a beating, Dr. Mild? Hematoma. Broken fingers. Anything like that?''

"Never.''

"You met her husband?''

"Her first husband.'' He hesitated, as if wondering how much to add. "But that was years ago.''

"How many marriages has she had?''

"Two, as far as I know.''

"What about an address?'' He gave me the house number on Twenty-fifth South. "I was there this morning,'' I said. Kathy gave me a stern look. "Nobody was around. You were going to say something about her first husband.''

"I suppose maybe I was. He was thirty-five. Had a heart attack and that was that. He was not my patient.''

"You have her second husband's name?''

Mild leafed through the file on his desk. "Randolph H. Schwantz. For employment we have 'insurance executive.' No company. I don't know, maybe he was between employers when she filled it out.''

"Got a separate address for Schwantz?''

"All I have is Twenty-fifth.''

Hardly the type of area an insurance executive would choose. "What was the previous address you had for her?''

The number he gave me was a place Bridget had checked with negative results. "And before that?"

"Nothing."

"This other guy who came asking about her? What did he want?"

"The officer? Just where to find her. I told him about Oregon."

"How did she pay? Jo Schwantz?"

"Are you sure you need to know this?"

"Everything helps."

"Cash. I know that without looking it up because generally I try to give my cash patients a break."

"Doesn't it seem strange to you that she pays cash when her husband works for an insurance company?"

"Now that you mention it, I suppose it does."

"You said seizures?" Kathy asked.

"Jo has a mild form of epilepsy. With medication it's controllable. I can't even remember when she had her last episode."

"Does she work?"

"Her first husband, I believe, was a musician. He had a small insurance policy. She mentioned it once. I guess if I ever thought about it, I assumed she had invested the proceeds from the policy and was living off that."

"Anything else you can think of?"

Dr. Mild ran a hand through his curly locks. "She was a pleasant enough woman. Witty. Gracious. College-educated. One of those fairly shy people who grew more attractive as they got older and got more confident. I had the feeling she'd come from a wealthy family, but that's just conjecture. She was real insecure about the possibility of having seizures in public. It had happened to her a number of times as a teenager, and naturally it left her feeling vulnerable."

"Who do you have listed as next of kin?"

He glanced at the paperwork. "A mother in northern California."

"Not the husband?" Kathy asked. Mild shook his head. "She was still married?"

"As far as I know."

"Mind if we have the mother's address and name?"

"I suppose not. I've given you everything else."

In the elevator a young man with both arms in casts from the shoulders down, steel rods holding the casts off from his body, gave me a knowing look that anointed me into the tribe of provisional American cripples. Without realizing it, I'd joined a subgroup with special parking privileges and the right to be stared at by kids.

Kathy smiled at him and said, "Kind of tough to play badminton in that getup, uh?"

"Fell off a horse," he said. "Broke both collarbones."

"Must be tough," I said.

"Yeah. What about you?" The doors slid open, and Kathy and I stepped into the marble foyer.

"I forgot her birthday, and she whacked me with a tennis racket. You wouldn't think a woman this cute could have such a nasty temper." Kathy spun around to tell him I was kidding, but the doors closed.

"Thomas!"

"Huh?"

"You are feeling better, aren't you?"

"Some."

 MATCHING MY GAIT KEPT KATHY breathless.

"That was a stupid thing, Thomas."

"Telling him you smacked me?"

"Going to Schwantz's house by yourself. They're from this state. Those three."

"We know the Lincoln had Washington plates. That's all we know."

"What do you think those goons are going to do when you show up?"

"Help me color-coordinate my wardrobe?"

"They're going to take that neck brace and spin it like a duck's butt on a frozen pond."

"Not bad. I'll give you a nine-point-one for that."

"Don't be so blasé, Thomas. This could be your life we're talking about. You are at least carrying a gun?"

"Ooops."

"And why not?"

"Because I spot one of them, I'll use it."

"Are you serious?"

"Yeah, I think I am."

"Thomas, I want you to back off. Let Aldredge manage it."

"He was a nice guy, but I think a rustled goat out behind the Umpqua Hotel is more his style." Kathy rolled her eyes.

Upstairs in the office I phoned Smithers at home. We'd mustered into the Seattle Police Department together, and he was still working the second shift unless they'd reassigned him in the past month. "Smitty? I didn't wake you?"

"Time to get up anyway."

"Know a guy in the department named Glenn?"

"Gary Glenn. Sure, I know him. So do you. Came in a year or two before we did. He's working the South Precinct. Same shift as me. He was the guy who accidentally walked in on that armed robbery at Salty's on Alki. Off duty. Wearing civvies. These two punks told him to lay on his face with the other customers. Frisking everyone. He knew when they got to him, they'd find his gun and badge. So, the punk is standing over Gary holding a pistol to his head, and Gary rips his piece out and fires past his ear. Without even rolling over. Drops the guy. Caps the other one as he's scrambling out the door. These guys had sheets on 'em you wouldn't believe. Glenn couldn't hear out of one ear for about a year from shooting that close." Smithers clearly wanted Glenn to marry his sister. And take his second sister as a mistress.

"He have blue eyes?"

"Glenn?"

"Yeah."

"Couldn't say. I mean, the last time we was smoochin', I forgot to look."

"He working out of a car?"

"Natch."

"What's he like?"

"You don't remember?"

"I remember a guy who wouldn't talk to most folks."

"That's Glenn. Keeps to himself. He's married to a real nice gal, but he plays around. Married but still dating, if you know what I mean."

"Have his home number handy?"

"Hang on." A few moments later he gave it to me.

"Thanks, Smitty."

"Thomas?"

"Yeah?"

"I don't know what you want with him, but be careful around Gary. He's gotten into a whole lot of trouble the past few years. There's nobody around who thinks he isn't going to get fired real soon. In fact, they're running an investigation right now. Somebody claims he pressured a couple of teen-aged hookers into having sex with him. It's going to be messy when it hits the papers. Plus he's on record as saying most of the crime in the city is caused by blacks. Big trouble. Glenn's one of those guys you can trust as long as your back is safely against a wall."

"I'll keep that in mind."

On the phone Glenn's voice was slow and authoritative. I was beginning to remember him. A lot of cops started off like Glenn, but for most the cure was thousands of hours of boredom on the job and all those cutting little injuries to the ego humans are susceptible to. Nobody had ever been able to whittle Glenn's ego down.

"Gary?"

"Who's speaking?" His voice was cold as a mortician's hands.

"I don't know if you remember me. Thomas Black. Retired a few years back. Used to work the Mount Baker District and Rainier Valley.''

There was a long silence. ''You the one capped that kid downtown?''

''A while back. Yeah, I guess I am.''

His lack of further comment on the shooting came across as the kind of reproach I'd felt from certain quarters when I left the department. ''What can I do for you?''

''I spoke to Dr. Mild. He said you were in Friday asking about a patient.''

''Not that I can recall, I wasn't.''

''You were asking about a woman who lives here in town.''

For a few moments I thought he'd hung up. ''What's it to *you*?''

''I'm a private investigator now, working mostly with a lawyer. We're looking for Jo Brown or Schwantz.''

''What do you want with her?''

''She's missing, and I'd like help finding her.''

''People are only missing when you don't know where they are.''

''You trying to tell me you know where she is?''

''I'm not telling you anything.''

''Do you know where Jo is?'' This silence was even longer. ''Gary?''

''What the hell are you into?''

''It's real simple. I'm looking for a woman.''

''You call me up out of the blue. You say you're a private detective. I don't need to hear this. I don't need a failed cop playing private dick running around backtracking my work. Who the fuck are you?''

My memory of Glenn was indistinct, filtered by the years. I thought about telling him the reason I was so keen on finding Jo, but I wanted to take a good look at him before I mentioned kidnappers and lynchings. Besides, the likelihood of receiving sympathy from Glenn was nil.

All the recent events in my life had been rendered down to Saturday night. Funny thing. If you're going to get hanged out in the woods, you'd expect it to be by a bunch of beer-swizzling louts with raggedy baseball caps, not three dapper, overweight dandies dressed from the Arnold Palmer collection.

"Look," I said. "Jo has been beaten. All we're trying to do is help."

"Stay out of this." He hung up.

Glenn maintained a territoriality about him that brooked no meddlers. The irony was that with people like that, there could have been any number of hidden agendas. It could be as absurd as playing on a volleyball team that had whipped his at the Police Guild picnic ten years ago. Or his inquiries about Jo could have been incidental to another case, entirely unrelated to Oregon.

Beulah Hancock, our receptionist and typist, was at the open reception island, teed-off about something. Beulah weighed more than two normal women, came almost up to my chin, and had a dozen boyfriends. She was a pistol. Beulah looked up at me and said, "Have you ever felt like slapping someone? Just anyone?"

"Just the last few days," I said. "Tell you what. We can slap each other. Trade off until we've got it out of our systems."

Beulah gave me a coy look, rolled her chair back from the low counter, and said, "Don't you think you'd better save that kinky stuff for someone special?"

I smiled.

The baby-stealer I'd seen lurking outside our offices earlier was gone. I took First South to Holgate, Holgate up the bridge over the industrial area, up to Beacon Avenue South on top of the hill. Beacon is a boulevard with an island of grass and trees for most of its length, one-way thoroughfares on either side.

The South Precinct was a low, modern building at the intersection of Beacon and Myrtle, across from a park. I left the truck in back and meandered inside. The longer I was away from the job, the fewer people remembered me. Coming back like this was almost a slow death. The sergeant was a woman I'd never met. I didn't know the guy at the desk either. After a few moments of chitchat I went back out and sat in the truck, listening to Jim Althoff on KING radio as he razzed a proponent of directed reincarnation.

One of the few things I remembered about Gary Glenn was that he always showed up early to pick up scuttlebutt from the other shifts. Nobody else had ever been so jealous of being first.

It was just before eleven when Gary Glenn showed up in a shiny black four-wheel-drive Chevrolet Blazer. He parked at the far end of the lot and, carrying a gym bag, walked slowly toward the back door. He wore new jeans and a close-fitting plaid shirt with the sleeves rolled up on his biceps, shirt unbuttoned to mid-chest. Aviator sunglasses. His black hair was molded down around his brow like a helmet. He was a big man, much larger, though not taller, than I am, and walked with the look and feel of someone who had just gotten off a very large horse. Inside, I'd asked as casually as possible if Glenn carried a Smith & Wesson Model 27. He didn't.

When he got the door to the building open, he gave a casual flick of his head and noticed me sitting in my red Ford pickup, a window rolled down against the muggy midday heat. After fixing on me a moment, he realized who I was. His look grew hard, and I held it for twenty seconds before he went into the building.

He was the right size to have been the third man Saturday night, but then so was the cop inside at the desk. For that matter, so was the lady sergeant.

11

I AMBLED DOWN THE SIDEWALK AND UP to Jo Brown's house. A two-story job built in the early 1900s. The brown trim had faded around the windows and doors. The pinkish outer walls were peeling.

I knocked, twisted the knob on the front door, and knocked again. It was locked. On the sidewalk halfway up the block two girls holding hands watched me. The older one was tall and gangly, probably baby-sitting the smaller. The little one was keen to see what I was about, but her caretaker towed her out of sight.

The back door had been kicked off its hinges, but somebody had remedied the broken jamb by screwing on a hasp and padlocking the door shut from the outside—a Sesamee lock with a four-digit combination at the bottom of the cylinder.

Back here the yard was better-tended, the unmowed grass not so tall. A child's swing had been tied to the lower branch of a cherry tree. An unpainted swaybacked wooden fence screened me from curious neighbors. I had bolt cutters in the truck, but I wrote down the numbers on the lock. Two, seven, four, four. I had had a lock like this once, but I had never flubbed all the numbers. Usually only one or two. I popped it open a few minutes later by changing the four, four at the end of the combination to five, five. After checking to be sure nobody was watching, I went inside. The first thing I did was open a side window on the first floor to provide a second means of egress.

It was a neatly kept though shabby house, two dinky bedrooms upstairs, a kitchen, utility room, living room, and dining room downstairs. The stained tub in the bathroom was the old-fashioned claw-leg type, the rim lined up with tub toys. Penciled slashes and dates on the bathroom doorjamb were labeled "Morgana" for the tall one, "Amber" for the shorter. Morgana came up to my eyebrows. They had been asking about Morgana Saturday night.

Spices had been spilled onto the bubbly kitchen linoleum: cinnamon, black pepper, and sugar. There was an overturned chair and a knife sticking into the kitchen door.

The living room was a shambles.

It looked more like a murder scene than an assault.

Near the front door an easy chair was capsized. A shattered wooden chair lay on the floor like a road kill. Bits of colored glass from a broken lamp jeweled the carpet. Most of the action had transpired against the wall next to the stairs.

That's where the wallboard was caved in and where the blood spattering was the heaviest. Dark brown flecks. Blood had flown off in all directions, sullying the wall, the floor, and spotting the newspapers strewn across the room. It was a Sunday paper from two weeks ago.

I couldn't find an address book or list of phone numbers, but in the jumble in the master bedroom upstairs I discovered several family portraits. Jo, a man, a young black girl, and a younger white girl. I didn't recognize the man, although Kathy might. But the two girls . . .

Rushing to the front bedroom window, I chinked open the pastel Raggedy Ann and Andy curtains. Not five minutes ago I'd been staring at Jo's girls. What threw me was that nobody had mentioned that one of them was black. Dr. Mild had neglected to tell me, as if the observation might somehow betray him as a closet bigot.

Saturday night the hangmen had been looking for the girls. "Where's Auntie's?" they had demanded. "You've seen Morgana."

Their names were Amber and Morgana, and now I had a photo of them, along with their mother and an unknown male. It had been Amber's artwork taped to the wall in the Umpqua Community Hospital. I'd been depressed for three days now, and for some reason hooking up the child's drawing in the Umpqua Hospital with the photo of the little girl in pigtails did something to me that wasn't entirely good. The anger I felt toward my three Mr. Piggys was becoming less than rational. I swiped one of the studio portraits.

From what I could see of their room, Amber leaned toward stuffed animals, Morgana toward *Mad* magazine. She kept several of them beside her bed, as well as a shelf full of paperback books printed by the Alfred E. Neuman folks. A backlog of library books that had been due yesterday were stacked on a dresser. The only signs of intrusion were two smashed dolls. Both dolls were black.

A ragged sepia splatter dominated the center of the bed in Jo's room. Near as I could tell, the intruder had peeled back the blanket and urinated onto the sheets. Burglars did that sometimes. So did madmen.

There were no men's clothes in the closet. Not a token anywhere in the house to indicate that a man lived here.

The woman had left little of a personal nature. She'd been paying the bills under an alias. Jackie Brown. Her canceled checks were all drawn on a Jackie Brown account at Rainier Bank. Her personal effects had already been looted.

Downstairs, Scotch-taped to the refrigerator, I found a variety of child's artwork mostly drawn on typing paper; a couple of fashion-designer attempts by the older girl, black and white Barbie-doll figures in evening gowns—some of it not bad; houses and animals drafted in pencil by the younger. I studied the sketches for a while. One of the drawings by the little one was titled in fading pencil and charmingly crooked letters: *Antis*.

Whoever gave Jo the beating and sacked the house had overlooked this nugget, an elaborate pencil sketch of a two-story dwelling with a tilting chimney. The house number was 805. Hell, it could be right down the block. I was in the 900 block now. But then, there were a lot of 800 and 900 blocks in Seattle.

Locking the back door, I walked to the street and stacked the overdue library books on the front seat of my truck, then hiked north. Eight-oh-one didn't exist on Twenty-fifth South. Nor on Twenty-fourth or Twenty-sixth.

On the sidewalk up the street a crack dealer was doing a herky-jerky dance to a ghetto blaster that polluted the otherwise-quiet street with its cacophony. From time to time a car would idle in front of him and a transaction would take place.

"Hey, guy," I said to a boy of about eleven wheeling past on a Schwinn too large for him. The chain was so rusty it made me wince. "You know somebody named Morgana?"

Dragging one foot to stop himself, he stood in the roadway and looked me over. He was wearing a torn T-shirt and jeans. Neither of his sneakers had laces. His left elbow was scabbed over with what looked like road rash from dumping the bike. "Morgana? Sure, I knows her."

"Where is she staying?"

"She stay right there." He pointed to the Schwantz house.

"Got any idea where else she might be?"

"She stay there."

"Not anymore."

He shrugged and jump-started the bicycle. "I seen her at the park today."

"Which one?"

He was thirty feet away now and rolling. "Judkins," he shouted.

"Thanks, guy." He nodded without taking his eyes off the street.

Trying all the neighboring houses, I found an elderly black woman living on the opposite side of Twenty-fifth two addresses north of Jo's residence willing, if not eager, to talk to me. Her house had virtually the same floor plan as Jo's, although reversed. Through a triangular tear in her screen door, I handed her one of my business cards with a machine gun on it. She gave me a little smile.

Her name was Ada Crabb, and she was in that peaceful world people hit somewhere beyond eighty.

"My. Are you a private cop?"

"I'm trying to find the people who live in the house across the street. With the brown trim?" I pointed.

"Oh, Lord," Ada Crabb said. "You might as well come on in. I've got a lot of things to tell you. No, I don't know where they went, but I have some things to get off my chest."

She sat me in a doily-infested chair by the window, in a sweltering house with the heat cranked up. One wall was devoted to photos of relatives, all younger than Ada, along with black-and-whites of ancestors who'd already gone to their reward. Her furniture, a walnut set, was polished and slick. She had been snacking from a plate of Oreos, crumbs pocking her housedress. Falling into her favorite chair in front of the TV, she killed the sound with a remote changer she operated like a gun, and peered at me over crooked bifocals. She wore big black witch shoes, a worn housedress sporting around seven hundred colors, and a strand of fake pearls. Her wedding and engagement rings had cost a bundle back when she'd gotten them.

Ada Crabb had never been a pretty woman, and time hadn't rectified the insult. But she had a spark in her eyes, always looking out at others instead of in at herself, hungry to glean what she could of the person in front of her. Still intrigued by the world despite her proximity to leaving it.

"Those people," she said. "I've been sitting here for days telling myself I should have done something. But I'm just an old woman. What could I do?"

"About what?"

"He was a big guy. That's all I know. It was dark out, so I didn't get that much of a look. And my eyes aren't being kind to me these days. But he was big. And he had an ugly voice. He went around the back, and a little later you could hear hollering from inside. And those two little children in there. I thought I was a brave person until that night, Mr. Black. And what's more, I thought I was too old to learn anything new about myself. But I guess you're never too old to figure out you're a poop. I surely wish I had it to do over again. I'd give anything for another whack at it. But then, when you do call the police, they don't want anything to do with you. So I wonder if it would have done any good."

"Are you saying the police weren't called?"

"They never showed. Nobody called them. We just watched. Later on I took the streetcar downtown and tried to fill out a missing-persons report, but they wouldn't let me. They have some silly rule that you have to be next of kin."

"Unfortunately, in this city, you do have to be related. It saves the SPD a lot of wear and tear."

"How many missing people does it save?"

"Good point. They've only got one detective assigned to missing persons anyway. When did all this happen?"

"I don't know. Last week sometime. Monday. She shouldn't have let him in."

"If it makes you feel any better, I don't think she did. It looks like he kicked down the back door." Ada Crabb chewed on a cookie, feeling miserable about the whole thing.

It was sorry work ratting on yourself. "Can you tell me what happened, Mrs. Crabb?"

"The lights were all on inside, so you could see everything. He was slapping her. I kept thinking somebody else was going to telephone the police, but I guess nobody did. Maybe they were frightened like I was. It was the size of the man. And the way he moved. You just knew you didn't want to cross him.

"I knew he'd even the score with anybody who interfered. After a while, the two youngsters came out from around back. Each of them had her own little suitcase. Morgana used to come sit right where you are and talk to me. She'd bring Amber with her. They watched their mother taking a licking from the sidewalk, then they hurried on up the street. I haven't seen 'em since. And I'm just sick about it."

"What about the woman?"

"Jackie? Oh, he was there with her for a long time. After a while he pulled all the drapes, and I couldn't tell what was going on. I was shaking and sick to my stomach. After a while he drove away."

"A white Lincoln, was it?"

"I couldn't say. I don't pay much attention to cars since I sold the Nash. A high school boy bought it in 1970. Thought he was getting a swell deal." She chuckled.

"You think one of the other neighbors might have seen?"

"Maybe. Maybe not. I sat in the window longer than most anybody."

"Did he take the woman with him?"

"Jackie went away later, a little after midnight." Ada Crabb thought it over. "Where are the girls?"

"Probably hiding."

"If I was a man, I'd find that stinker and bust him."

"You knew the family?"

"Mostly the girls. We talked about what's on the TV or what was happening to the neighborhood. Real fine children, Mr. Black."

"How long have they lived here?"

"Two years, about. Yes, it was, because it was the summer two years ago when the Morrisons moved out of there. Ann

Morrison had been carrying on with that Mitchell fella up the street.''

"Ever talk to their mother?"

"Once in a while they'd stay too long and she'd fetch them. She worked waitressing. Different places. She would come home dragging. Morgana would do the baby-sitting." Ada Crabb smiled and worked over an Oreo with her dentures.

"Do you know where she worked?"

"Couldn't say."

"The girls call you Auntie?"

"Ever since my Reginald died, kids have been calling me Grams. Reginald worked in a service station for over twenty years right down there on Yesler. Abrahamson, the owner, was a fair man. When he sold the place, Reginald worked for the Johnsons. He died right up the street there, walking home from the station. Had a sack of groceries he just fell on. Melba Harper came running down the street here to tell me. I remember it like it was five minutes ago. I was watching kids for folks in those days. Melba took over the youngsters and I trotted up there. Nobody had any common sense. Nobody thought to pick up his store teeth or eyeglasses off the sidewalk. Lord knows, dying is undignified enough without a bunch of idiots standing around watching like they bought tickets.''

"I'm sorry. Does the family have any regular friends come around?"

"On Christmas, Marnie would come and pick me up, but they would stay right at home. Same on Thanksgiving. But they were nice. You don't see families like that these days. Even if they were mixed."

"The mother ever have gentleman callers?"

"Never had much of anybody stop in, that I could see."

The Douglas-Truth branch of the Seattle Public Library was on Yesler. The woman assistant smiled at the titles as I waited to pay the fines on the books. Four horse stories, a romance novel, eight picture books.

"If life were just so simple," she said, when I shoved six quarters across the counter.

"Yeah," I said. "Nothing's simple anymore, is it?"

12

CHANCING ON A PAY PHONE OUTSIDE the Thriftway at Twenty-third and Jackson, I called Beulah at the office and was told Denny McCallum had phoned four times. Also, a gentleman named Bumpus had been pressing for an appointment. We set one up for four-thirty. I punched another quarter in and dialed Denny McCallum.

"Black?"

"What do you need?"

"Look, Black. I know there's something funny going on. You got into some trouble, and it had something to do with *my* dreamgirl, didn't it?"

"I haven't made contact, Denny."

"It was her boyfriend who busted you up, huh?"

"Haven't met her boyfriend, Denny. Tonight my operative is going to the Mariners game. If this woman shows, Bridget will ask her to call. You're not going to get beat up."

"Beat up? You think I'm worried about getting beat up? I mean, that guy's big, but he doesn't worry me. I take care of myself. I've handled situations before. Call me? She's gonna call *me*?"

He had flip-flopped from boldness to cold dread so quickly I had to clear my throat to keep from laughing. "You won't be mentioned until I see her in person."

"But he was the one, wasn't he? The one who busted you."

"I said no."

"Then who?"

"This is not a topic we're going to discuss."

"Christ . . . I don't need this. So how do I get out of it? You just refund my money? Yeah, why don't you do that? Gimme a refund."

"It shouldn't be more than a day before I speak to the woman."

"Couldn't you do it tonight?"

"You said you wanted out."

"Geez, I mean, I hate to get this close and then lose her, but geez, don't you think I should bail out? Except the others might get POed. Think they'd get POed?"

"Do what you have to, Denny."

"So if you were in my boots, would you bail out?"

"Let me think. Uuuuuh. No."

"Jesus. You just want your fee."

"Right. I just want my fee."

"Is there any danger, though? That's what I want to know. That boyfriend looks big."

"In or out, Denny? I've got to meet a man in ten minutes about a baggage car full of Brazilian parakeets. And then I have a Cactus Society meeting. Think it over for a couple of hours. I'll call back."

"No. No. I'm in. Definitely. I just need to know one thing. Are the other guys still going through with it?"

"Nobody but you has offered to call it off."

"You think I'm a piker, don't you?"

"I gotta get those parakeets out by three."

"Okay. Okay. Except what if she's married?"

I broke the connection.

Hunting for the two girls soaked up most of the afternoon.

I migrated through the surrounding neighborhoods with the drawing in my hand and unfolded a wrinkled city map that was so old Martin Luther King Junior Way South was still dubbed Empire. Dearborn was the 800-number street for the south designators, so it could be anywhere off of Dearborn, but then, there was 800 east, Columbia. There was also the possibility that the house was on a street, not an avenue, which would place it somewhere along one of the streets stemming off Eighth Avenue. When I thought about it, I reasoned that two little girls lugging suitcases were not going to march over to Eighth Avenue. Or farther than that to the north.

That left Dearborn, up and down. Possibly Columbia, sixteen blocks to the north.

Guesswork was all I had. Saturday night the three pigs had been asking for Auntie's and for the girls. Now I had two interconnected missions. One should lead to the other.

One item. Upstairs in the girls' room there had been knickknacks from the Leschi Café, napkins, menus, and sugar packets, objects that made sense now in light of Ada Crabb's remark that Jo was a waitress.

When I drove down the hill to Lake Washington and Lakeside, diehards were sailing on the lake from the three moorages within walking distance of the Leschi Café. I knew this road by heart, every pothole, biked it six times a week when I wasn't in traction. The placid cyclists spinning along inspired me to twist my neck experimentally. A barrage of agony cracked along my spine.

The manager of the Leschi Café was a young curly-haired man in a white shirt and tie and trendy balloon pants with glittery threads running through the fabric. He informed me "Jackie Brown" had worked there five weeks before failing to show up last Tuesday. She was, he said, a pleasant-enough person, although she hadn't made many friends, had worked hard and never been tardy until the day she simply didn't show. He waylaid a chunky redheaded waitress who'd been working Sunday and asked her if she recalled a disturbance involving "Jackie." She didn't.

I interviewed two other waitresses who knew Jo. Eager to gossip with a private eye, neither had much to say. Ordering fish and chips, I sulked at one of the white sidewalk tables, watching the traffic, the fluid women in black dresses driving down for lunch in their Volvos and Subarus, the resolute joggers, the cyclists.

Flattening the child's drawing out on the seat, I drove every fragment of Dearborn I could find, scouting for 805, for any dwelling even remotely similar to her sketch. In the artwork an elderly woman sat in a rocking chair in a window—two girls in another window, and in the upper dormer a woman with bright red lips and outlandishly curly locks; Jo, I assumed. You had to treasure the way little girls sketched their mothers.

Two hours later I had traced all of Dearborn South as well as East Columbia from Seattle University almost down to the lake. I had cruised the various play areas at Judkins Park. Negative.

It was 4:28 when I got back to the office. My neck was throbbing, and I was drowsy enough to climb into bed and take a good long nap.

"Gawd, Thomas," said Beulah, looking up from one of my standard client contracts. "You look like hell. Having a bad day?"

"I haven't inherited any money yet."

"Mr. Bumpus is over there," she whispered when I got closer. "He's steamed. Wanted to see you earlier." There were three people in the anteroom, two women perusing magazines and waiting for one of the attorneys, slim legs crossed, and Bumpus, a disheveled package plunked on the edge of the sofa as if he'd just fallen through the roof. He was in his late sixties, wore dirty green work pants, dusty cowboy boots, and a V-neck undershirt that hadn't seen the inside of a washing machine for a while. A grungy cowboy hat lay on the sofa beside him. He had a shock of salt-and-pepper hair with longish addenda out his ears. His craggy face was directed mournfully at the carpet.

"Send him in when I buzz."

I slurped a drink from the cooler in the hallway, glanced down the corridor at Kathy's office—the door was closed—and riffled through the mail at my desk while I dialed California. The phone rang twelve times before I gave up.

Half a minute after I buzzed, Bumpus bulled into my office, pumped my hand with a crushing grip, and sat in the red chair across from me. "You the detective?" I started to nod. "Got this here problem, and I need your help. I'm sure you can do something with it. How much is it worth to get rid of a coffin?''

''Say again.''

''Coffin. You know. Burial box.'' He made gestures with his arms, sizing the thing, the fleshy muscles in his arms wobbling. He was still hearty and working, to judge from his peppy movements and callused palms. ''Somebody sent the goldarned thing to me in the mail. I ain't got no use for it. The wife don't like it one bit. She's hot enough to fuck.'' He wiped his brow with a paisley handkerchief.

''Where is it?''

''Got two ball players I hired over at the high school hauling it up here. Just get rid of it for me. That's all you gotta do. Sink it in Green Lake for all I care. Throw it out in the blackberries.''

''Anything special inside?''

''Hell, it's heavy enough. But I ain't looked. I got a note with it said some blockhead from Iowa wanted me to resurrect her husband. Look, I was sellin' autographed photos, not miracle cures. I sold out my interest in the time-share campgrounds and got into something more lucrative. Oughta see my account books. They're sellin' like hotcakes.''

''Who are you selling autographed photos of?''

''Jesus Christ, Himself. People will buy anything. Nineteen ninety-five. Interested? The mother-in-law will always go for it.''

''Maybe later. Why haven't you opened the box?''

''I just want it out of my way.''

He pushed a letter across the desk. It was from a Rolanda Horton in Waterloo, Iowa, and she wrote that since Bumpus seemed to be on such good terms with the Savior, she would take three autographed photos and could he please ask the Son of God to raise up her Alvin, who'd only been gone a few days from the date UPS took him in hand.

''What's it worth to you?'' said Bumpus.

''Couldn't touch it for less than five grand,'' I said, certain the figure would rout him. When you didn't want a job, you asked too much. Bumpus dug out a sheaf of hundreds, meticulously counted fifty onto my desk, and absconded. Damn. A few minutes later a wooden crate of white pine was waiting for me in the now-cramped anteroom.

It was just past five. I tapped on Kathy's door and entered. She had changed into some sort of period costume. An early eighteenth-century outfit complete with décolletage. It was a dress I hadn't seen before but wouldn't have minded seeing again. Kathy was an eccentric when it came to clothing. It was daily torture for her to have to don one of her conservative business suits for the office.

"Thomas. You look depressed."

"Going for a ride in a time machine, or what?"

"We're just doing this. Why?"

"There's a new movie in town everyone's talking about. At the Guild Forty-fifth. I thought we might take it in to-night."

"Thomas. I'd love to. But Philip has already arranged something. I know. Why don't you come with us?"

"Forget it."

"You wouldn't be any bother. Just the three of us. It would be fun."

I walked to the window. Speak of the devil. Philip was in front of the building with a horse and carriage, two attendants in black livery. He wore a white wig, a sword, knee-high stockings, and a costume he must have rented. A voluptuous bouquet of roses sprouted from his white-gloved hand. From here they looked like Sonyas, a variety popular with florists.

"By the way," I said. "Dudley Dooright phoned and said he had to stop by the cemetery to pick up some flowers."

Kathy came around her desk, leaned toward me, and pushed her breasts up under her dress. Her black hair was pinned up elaborately, her violet-blue eyes wide and innocent.

"What do you think?" she asked. She leaned over and gave me the normal view, then boosted the whole affair again. "Maybe I should pack some Kleenex in there? What do you think?"

"I think you've got plenty packed in there."

"You're just being diplomatic. I want the truth." She went

to the glass door and looked at her reflection, yawing this way and that. "Sometimes I wish I had big knockers like all your girlfriends."

"I don't know what you're talking about."

"You know you like humongous boobs."

"Look. So how about two days at the ocean on the weekend? The Sandpiper, same as last year? I need some space. Some time to walk on the beach. What about you?"

"Oh, Thomas. I'm sorry. We're going up to Snoqualmie Falls for breakfast Saturday. Philip's had the reservations for months."

"No problem. Did I show you this?" I displayed the artwork I'd taken from Jo Schwantz's house.

"From the hospital? In Oregon?"

"Same artist. Different drawing."

"Auntie's?"

"I think so." I told her about my day, about the dried blood in the Schwantz house, about the girls. About Denny McCallum wanting to back out.

Beulah buzzed. "Philip's here."

"Look, Thomas. You're more than welcome to come tonight. It would be great fun. Philip won't mind."

"No? What does he think of me?"

"Nothing, really."

"Never said anything?"

"Not that I recall." Kathy took a step backward and regarded me. "You don't like him, do you?"

"I like him just fine. It's just that a guy who wears black socks with his Birkenstocks is not the kind of guy you should be swapping spit with."

She smiled coyly. "I'm going to cure him of that. Besides, a man with only one flaw is rare."

"I didn't say that was his only flaw."

Kathy was smiling now. She moved close and put her hands on my chest. "What else?"

"Well, what does he do for a living? He seems to be hanging around a lot. Does he even have a job?"

"Thomas, you're whining."

"Private eyes don't whine."

"For your information, Philip is a teacher. Fifth grade at Sanislo Elementary in West Seattle. Teachers get the summer off."

"I knew it. Teachers get paid in Monopoly money. The second flaw. No assets."

"That might be true, except Philip inherited a tidy little estate from his grandfather. He's independently wealthy. He teaches because he loves kids." Kathy kissed my cheek, and went to the door. "If I didn't know you better, I'd say you were jealous, Thomas Black."

"Private eyes don't get . . ."

"Yeah, I know."

When I came out of Kathy's office, the lawyers who shared the premises had vacated for the day. Beulah was tidying up. Only Kathy and Philip were in the anteroom, surveying the crate.

"New furniture?" Philip asked. His hair was perfect. He had dimples. A trim little mustache. He looked like a model in *GQ* except that he was smaller. Five eight, maybe. The only blemish I could detect was that he had one brown eye and one blue. Unfortunately, to women, this genetic defect was apparently entrancing.

"A job," I replied. "I'll have a janitor help me move it to the back room."

"I can help," said Philip.

"I'll do it later." I didn't want him looking too useful.

"But what is it?" Kathy persisted.

"Um. A box. From Iowa."

"I can see that. What's in it?"

"Brazilian parakeets. I'm going to keep them in the empty room in back."

On their way out, Kathy's bustle twitching to and fro, Philip presented her with the Sonyas. "Oh, how nice," she said. "You stopped off at the cemetery." They both laughed. Beulah laughed. I didn't see the humor.

When we were alone, Beulah trundling around on the rolling chair, sorting papers and taping notes to the edge of the counter for tomorrow morning, she glanced up at me and said, "What's really in the crate?"

"A client."

Convinced it was jest, she dismissed the remark and smiled. "They look awful good together."

"Who?"

"You know who."

"Kathy and the F-person?"

"Philip is spelled with a P. You know they do, Thomas. I'm glad we're alone. I've been meaning to talk to you about this. You know, when a man and a woman have the sort of relationship you and Kathy have been trying to pull off, it can only go one of two ways."

I leaned my forearms on the counter. "Continue."

"Don't patronize me. I'm serious. I see something happening here, and I have to comment before it's too late."

"Fair enough."

"Have you two ever . . . made love?"

"I've done it. I think she's done it."

"Don't clown around, Thomas. With each other."

"The truth?"

"The truth."

"We've come close."

"I thought not. Well, I've had similar relationships, and after a while you get forced to decide what sort of buddy you're going to be. The going-to-bed-with kind, or the going-to-lunch-with kind. You, my friend, and Kathy, too, seem to me to be the right-in-between kind, but you both act—for some godawful reason—like pals. I thought maybe you'd tried it and it hadn't worked. You see, it's like this, Thomas. Sooner or later one of you is going to find a partner. And there goes the friendship. Poof. I see no way around it. Either *you* become her partner, or you kiss her off when she finds one. You can't have it like this forever."

"I could."

"I've seen it crash too many times."

"Not with Kathy and me, you haven't."

"Yeah, I know," said Beulah. "Best friends. I think it's sweet. That's what makes it so heartbreaking."

13

I WORKED ON THE COMPUTER, TYPING up the day's discoveries into my DREAMGIRL file.

Manhandling the white pine crate into the spare room in back took a gang of janitors from the building, plus two de-horns from across the street at a fiver each. If Bumpus knew a pair of high school ball players who could truck it up three flights, I'd hate to be paying their food bills.

Dinner consisted of minestrone soup, rolls, and pasta with clam sauce at Trattoria Mitchelli around the corner on Yesler. I sat on a stool at the bar and scanned the paper. Nine different candidates had filed for mayor. Another DC-10 had crashed back East. After paying the bill, I straightened out my life by nibbling a dessert from the Cow Chip Cookies express window across the street. That evening I phoned California again. Jo's mother was either on vacation, in traction, or out on a hoot.

At eleven Bridget Simes called. "I'm sorry, Thomas. You were asleep, weren't you?"

During the hour I'd been in bed, my voice had gone rusty in a way that alarmed me. "What've you got?"

"Two things. One. I went to the game tonight. Found her in the one-hundred level. I was expecting something out of *Glamour*, but she's not that exceptional."

"Sure she's the one?"

"About positive. Went over and gave her my card, told her I thought she could help me out in a case I was working. She was very accessible. And a little high. I'll be generous and say it was a beer buzz. Name's Eartha Braintree. Tidy little mark with clipped blond hair and a lot of exposed nerve ends. I can see where somebody might be attracted to her. She's a baseball fanatic. Mercifully, I got out of there before the first inning. The only thing I find more boring than baseball is spectator chess." Bridget gave me two phone numbers for Braintree.

"Married?"

"I think she sleeps with a guy. My guess is it's one of those long-term relationships fast headed for a dead end. He was there, and he was already drunk. I'd bet my Maidenform bra they don't keep their clothes in the same closet. She works at Nordstrom at Northgate. Said she'd be there tomorrow.

"Something else. On the way back from Myrtle Creek I got this idea of stopping at all the little motels. Took me half a day but I found this place, Meyer Motels in Albany. A week ago Monday night Jo checked in around three in the morning. The guy said she was all beat to smithereens. She was driving around with a broken arm, for godsakes. But she paid for a room and left at ten in the morning. I told the guy at the motel to call if she came back. People have a tendency to use the same stopping-over points."

"Think he'll call?"

"Doesn't hurt to leave baited hooks around. He wants to be a private eye. We had quite a little bull session."

"Thanks, Bridget." I was asleep before my head slammed into the pillow.

The next morning I made phone calls. I spoke to a woman I'd done a few favors for at DSHS and asked her to check whether Amber and/or Morgana Schwantz had been placed in a receiving home recently. Or ever. I gave her the alternate name of Brown. She said she'd check the mircrofiche at the Department of Social and Health Services and call back. I talked to Missing Persons downtown and asked whether anybody had filed a report on the girls. Nobody had. I phoned Jo

Schwantz's mother again, in Yreka, California. Jo's maiden name had been Corelli.

Nanette Corelli sounded brittle, slow of limb, and slower of mind. "Yah?"

"Mrs. Corelli?"

"Yes."

"My name is Thomas Black. I'm a private investigator in Seattle. I've been trying to get hold of you."

"Been out winning at bingo. Got six cards last night. What can I do you for?"

"Do you have a daughter in Seattle?"

Her voice freighted with emotion, she said, "I have a daughter. Josephine."

"Can you say where she is?"

"I . . . why . . . who . . . ?"

"Jo's been injured. Badly. Until Sunday she was holed up in a small hospital in a one-horse town north of the California border. I have reason to believe people are hunting her."

"Oh, Lord. I knew it. Sweet Lord, I just knew it. Jo's got herself in trouble once more. That girl. I swear. My other daughter, Margaret, never . . . Ohhhhhhh . . ." She sounded close to a faint. I should have couched what I had to say in chitchat, crept up on the bad news.

"Look, Mrs. Corelli. Can you tell me where Jo is?"

"I ain't seen her."

"Maybe you could tell her I'm looking for her and that I want to help. Tell her I'm the private investigator who visited her in the hospital."

There was a long silence. "Mr. Black, I haven't seen Jo in sixteen years. Not since she run off and married that nigger."

She let that soak in: an announcement I sensed she had passed out a slew of times, like a handbill from a geek touting the end of the world. She sounded smug about all the pain and dishonor she felt.

"Anselmi disowned her after he found out. I kept in touch for a few years, but Anselmi saw the phone bill and raised the roof. He was sooooo . . . cross. Threw out all her things. Mr. Black? Do an old woman a favor. Tell me where my daughter is. My husband's gone to his reward, and I don't have no one left but Maggie and Josephine. I don't even care no more that she been with that colored.''

"When was the last time you spoke to her, Mrs. Corelli?"

"I reckon she called a few years ago, Christmas."

"Not since then?"

"No, sir. Not a peep."

"You don't get in touch, is that what you're saying?"

"I guess we don't."

"Mrs. Corelli, I believe she was headed your way a few days ago."

Her voice got quavery again. "A man come to the house here . . . I guess it was this Monday morning. After he left, I got skeptic. Said he was some inspector for the housing authority. Ever heard of 'em? He spread out some credentials, but I didn't pay no mind, and then like a nincompoop I let him traipse all through the place."

"What'd he look like?"

"He ain't never missed no meals. Polite. Had a big thing like a diaper taped to his nose. Said he hurt hisself hunting varmints. Glanced over ever' place. Garage. Even the attic. I thought he was doing me a favor till I had some time to think on it. You ever heard of the housing authority?"

"He was looking for Jo, Mrs. Corelli."

"Oh, my . . ."

"When I find her, I'll tell her you love her. Would that be acceptable?" The other end of the line went very quiet. It took a few moments for me to realize she was sobbing. She'd butchered relations with her daughter, and now the sadness in her life was beginning to mushroom.

"Let me tell you this," she said, through the tears. "Something very strange has been going on around here. Every night for the past week . . . round about seven, the house receives a person-to-person call for Jo."

"From where?"

She was blowing her nose, her voice tremulous. "No idea. Is that frightful or what say?"

"Next time accept the call. Find out who it is. I think I know, but try that. One more thing. What do you know about her second marriage?"

"Second?"

"Her first husband died. She has two daughters now, Mrs. Corelli. Did you know that?"

"I knew that." She spoke so fast the words ran together. "Iknewthat. SureIdid. So what's the . . . second girl must be about two?"

"More like six."

Nanette Corelli said she'd call if she heard from Jo. I wasn't sure she would, but I was reasonably certain the next time I spoke to her that I would be able to tell from her voice whether she was lying.

Pfortmiller called and said he hadn't found a thing on the Llama 9mm. "If somebody around here owns one, I don't know who it is."

"Thanks, Herb."

Phoning the King County Assessor's Office, I gave them Jo Schwantz's address on Twenty-fifth South and asked who'd been paying taxes on the property. They gave me an address on Mercer Island for an Anthony Hallinan. I looked him up in the Eastside phone book. A slow-talking woman with a washed-out Texas twang answered the phone and told me Tony had already left for work. He was an attorney in the Maynard Building, about a block from Kathy's office. When I reached him, Hallinan could tell me only that Jo Brown had been leasing the house for two years, that she'd never given him any grief, and was never late with the check. He claimed to know nothing of her personal life, but I got the feeling he wouldn't have shared it with me if he had.

"Did she have a husband when she moved in?"

"She's always lived there with just her daughters, as far as I know. Maybe she shacked up for a week or so, except she didn't strike me as that type."

After gassing up the truck, I took Aurora downtown to avoid the midmorning siege on I-5, worked the defroster and wipers against a fleeting July drizzle, parked near the office in Pioneer Square, checked in, was told Denny McCallum had already called twice, then hiked uptown to the King County Administration Building. I riffled through a ton of marriage records. Seven years earlier in December, Josephine Beatrice

Brown had married Randolph Harold Schwantz. They had been granted a divorce a little over two years ago. Randolph had been awarded custody of both children, which I thought was unusual, since one of them wasn't even his. Except for the bare bones of it, the judgment had been sealed, not unusual after an acrimonious court battle.

I walked over to the public library at Fourth and Spring. I went through every phone book and reverse directory in the state looking fruitlessly for Randolph Schwantz. He wasn't listed in any of the city directories either. My contact at the phone company couldn't find any unlisted or new listings for him.

It was still early when I drove back up Yesler Way to the Central District. Not quite ten o'clock. The mist had lifted, the streets were dry, and I thought I saw some dim blue between the quilts of gray to the southwest. I traced yesterday's route, looking for 805. There were three likely candidates along Dearborn.

At the first house a black woman in a robe answered, three wide-eyed toddlers behind her in various stages of deshabille. She had never heard of Morgana Brown, Jo Brown, Amber, or anybody named Schwantz. I showed her the family photo I'd snitched yesterday, but she drew a blank.

Nobody responded at the second 805, but for some reason the house looked too sedate to be snarled in this enterprise. Nobody answered at the third either. The other 805s were off E. Columbia.

Thirtieth plain had one. I parked on Thirty-first and walked a block on Columbia. Nobody came to the door. The backyard was untended, and there was no evidence of children. To me it seemed an old person's house, an old person's yard. A very old person who no longer hobbled around to weed or water and couldn't afford to hire things out. Every drape was drawn, several clipped together with faded plastic clothespins. The neighborhood was on the fringes of one of the prime combat zones for the drug trade. There was a shooting a week on Cherry a few blocks away. A crack deal every three minutes. You could park in front of the Harvey Apartments and watch the sweaty buyers and the cool sellers.

I found a pay phone at a convenience store at the corner of Twenty-third and Cherry and called the King County assessor. I gave him a list of addresses, and we went through them one by one. The one on Columbia was in the name of a Binstead. Martha Binstead. The second no-answer on Dearborn belonged to a guy named Stuart Green.

Parking on Columbia, I laid my binoculars in my lap and kept an eye on 805 Thirtieth. I might as well have been on Dearborn staking out Green's place. Six of one. Half a dozen . . . I waited an hour with no result, recorded the business in a journal I kept in the truck, then headed downtown on Cherry, derailed to James, and took the Freeway north. E. Columbia would keep. Denny McCallum was waiting for his dreamgirl.

Traffic on the freeway was thick and the Northgate Mall parking lot wasn't any better. A green-eyed young woman pushing a vacuum cleaner in the Nordstrom shoe department told me where I could find Eartha Braintree.

She wore her hair cropped very short, the white-blond ends contrasting sharply with the darker hair beneath. Eartha Braintree was working a cosmetics counter in a uniform dress. She looked high-strung, haughty, and off-putting. The first time I passed, she was ducking down behind the counter, surreptitiously slipping something into her purse. Looking around nervously. It was just a wild guess, but I had a feeling she was stealing from the store. Like a vulture's talons, her long fingernails forced her to handle things painstakingly. It would have been real sport to see her pick a dime off a glass table. I rambled through the department, out into the mall, and located a pay phone in front of the Bon. I dialed. "You still in, Denny?"

"Black? I've been trying to get you all morning. What's going on? Have you talked to her yet?"

"She's about a hundred yards away. Short hair. Bottle blonde. Enough fingernails for a whole junior high typing class?"

"Yeah, yeah, that's her. But I don't think she dyes her hair. She's too classy."

"Somebody dyed it. Just wanted to make sure you hadn't chickened out."

"Hey, buddy, I'm going for broke here. Just don't let it cost me an arm and a leg."

"Look at it this way. You swoon her and get married, the money'll be in the family."

"There is that. Anyways, call me right back, will ya?" Denny was the tightwad of the bunch. Though he drove a new Corvette each year, he kept a For Sale sign in it in case some cluck was dumb enough to offer more than he paid. Denny was the kind of guy who would fritter away ten dollars of gas driving around to save sixty-nine cents on a socket wrench.

After Eartha Braintree decided I had waited long enough, she sauntered over and asked if she could be of assistance. She wore the Nordstrom smile and a mask of sophistication and cold competence. I smiled back. Her skin was flawless and pale. And she was much prettier than Bridget led me to believe. She wasn't wearing a wedding ring. I handed her my card.

"That's funny," Braintree said, in a delicate, yodeling timber that sounded like the good witch in *The Wizard of Oz*. Since last Saturday and my continuing throat problems, I found myself paying attention to voices. Hers didn't match her glacial exterior. "Last night . . ."

"Bridget is a colleague of mine. We've got a proposition for you, Eartha, and while it might sound unusual, you'll be doing me a big favor by hearing me out. I represent an admirer of yours. He's got a college education and then some. He's married, but he's in the process of divorcing. Thirty-eight years old, well-established in his profession, and not all that bad-looking."

"What are you trying to pull?"

"He saw you somewhere and thought you were intriguing. He wants to take you to dinner." I pulled out a Polaroid of McCallum I'd snapped at one of our meetings. "If you say yes, we'll set up a dinner. I'll escort you to the restaurant, and I'll escort you home after. All he wants is a blind date. The worst you could be out is a few hours of your time and a nice meal. The Canlis, someplace like that.''

Eartha Braintree's skin turned almost orange as she blushed. Her nails played on the glass countertop like tiny horse hooves clattering across a frozen plane. ''The Canlis is for stuffy snobs.''

''You choose, then.''

''You. Right? You want to date me?'' Her voice was cold, her gray eyes caustic.

''Believe me, if I wanted a date, I'd ask. I'm not shy. My client is a good man. Should you care to bring your own chaperon, feel free. I can give you the name of a lieutenant in the Seattle Police Department who will vouch for me. My client has gone to a great deal of trouble.''

''Drop dead.''

She was halfway down the counter when I added, ''A thousand dollars for your trouble. Cashier's check.''

Now she was really hot. ''Just what do you think I am?''

''One dinner. I can give the check to an independent attorney to hold until afterward.''

Eartha Braintree rolled her eyes until the white showed. ''This is the craziest thing I've ever heard. I mean, I met a guy here in the store once who wanted to fly me to Acapulco, but this . . .''

''Isn't it nuts?''

''And he'll pay?''

''Yup.''

''So what's top offer?''

''Two grand.''

''Three?'' I started to walk away. ''Wait. Okay. How about two and a half?''

''How about two?''

As negotiations escalated, I had a feeling she thought I was going to sell her to a brothel in Japan, since she mentioned twice that she'd seen a movie about it. She asked for an advance, but only a fool would advance money to a suspected kleptomaniac. She finally agreed, and we made the rest of the arrangements.

*   *   *

I parked in the same spot half a block from the house on
Thirtieth. In Amber's sketch the chimney was tilting slightly
to the left, same as here. Most older chimneys in Seattle
leaned to the southwest, because that's where the predominate winds came from, the wet breezes devouring the mortar
on that side. Also, the windows in the sketch were identical
to the windows in this house, except the shades weren't
pulled.

I knocked, but nobody answered. I tramped around the
block, found three kids playing on Marion, and showed them
the family photo. They all shrugged.

It was not a bad neighborhood. The Central District, or CD
as it was known locally, had been the posh part of the city
sixty years ago, but now it was run down. It had been mostly
Jewish, and then after the war blacks gradually began to
predominate. Now it was almost exclusively black. Bit by
bit, these neighborhoods were reclaiming some of their
former ambience and prestige.

With no chow and no latrine, I slumped in the truck and
watched the house until shortly after one o'clock. I almost
missed them—two girls walking up the alley, heading for
Martin Luther King Way. Hand in hand. They might have
come from the house, but I couldn't be certain. A tall, gan-
gling black girl and a small white girl wearing pigtails and a
starched shirt. Threading my way through the neighborhoods,
I followed them in the truck, observing from a block away,
half a block, two blocks. I could easily have lost them, but
they were guileless. It took them twenty-five minutes to get
to the Thriftway supermarket at Twenty-third and Jackson. I
parked in the lot and wandered inside behind them.

It didn't take a wizard to spot the older girl stuffing mer-
chandise under her sweatshirt, a package of barrettes, a Sweet
Valley High book from the magazine rack. She eyeballed the
batteries, but shoplifting was so prevalent in this area they
kept the batteries behind the counter in the photo department.
Morgana paid cash for two Dr. Peppers and a bag of frosted
animal cookies. The checker eyed her sweatshirt, but wasn't
assertive enough to make a scene.

Outside in the lot I approached the girls as they broke into the animal cookies. I got ten feet away and veered off. The stark fear in their eyes warned me away. The little one began trembling. I had sudden visions of dried blood on the walls in her living room. Their mother being beaten. The two of them toting suitcases away in the dark.

Both were about to break into a blind run. I turned back, climbed into the truck, and drove to 805 Thirtieth. I would speak to their guardian. It would be easier.

But nobody answered. The house felt deader than the first time I had knocked.

The girls were gone from the streets, but I knew where they were staying now, and they were presumably safe. I would be back.

When I got to the office, I called the Myrtle Creek Police. Aldredge was there. He'd been working on it, but had nothing. He'd checked every motel in Roseburg and the two in Myrtle Creek. He'd looked around to see who stocked Miss Piggy masks, but hadn't been able to find an outlet nearby. I phoned my friend at DSHS to see whether she'd scored. The girls had not entered the system.

"Thomas," Kathy said, as I walked into her office. "How are you feeling?"

"I'm getting ready to climb Everest in a few days."

She made a face. "I've set up a meeting with Boyd and the others for later this afternoon. I forgot what time. Beulah knows."

"I'm not feeling *that* much better."

"Come on, Thomas. It's just a meeting."

"I bet these guys take a meeting before they crap."

"The more meetings, the higher your bill. How are you doing?" I told her about Morgana and Amber. "I don't understand. Why didn't you talk to them?"

"I played a couple of hunches. One, they're okay for now, which is what most concerns me. Two, they were so scared it made me want to bang my head against a post and cry. And I don't think, standing there in that parking lot, that I could have made them realize I was one of the good guys. It had all the earmarks of a disagreeable episode."

"Think their mother is hiding in that house with them?"

"I doubt she'd let her girls promenade around the neighborhood. Or shoplift. But maybe she would."

Kathy stood and moved to the window, glancing down at the street. I moved beside her, and we watched two scrawny street women screeching at each other on the corner. A pair of beat police jogged slowly toward the fracas, hoping it would be over before they arrived. "So you found Denny's dreamgirl. He'll be pleased."

"She's a kleptomaniac."

"Oh?"

"I'd bet my Campy gear cluster on it."

"What'd she think of the deal?"

"She thought two grand would do very nicely, thank you."

"You had to pay?"

"Trophy wives. I can't believe I'm helping yahoos search for trophy wives."

"Testosterone poisoning is what I think. The semen backs up to the brain, the eyes glaze over, and the synapses melt together like cheese on toast. Anyway, the Yellow Dog Party is toward the end of August, and they each want to have met their dreamgirls by then. At least Philip isn't like them."

"The F-person?"

"What? Did you just call Philip 'the F-person'?"

I smirked and she took a not-entirely-playful, looping swing at my shoulder: missed.

I walked to the bank to draw the cashier's check for Eartha Braintree, returned, and typed up notes. I kept thinking about the blood-spattered walls in Jo Schwantz's rental house. About the two girls in the parking lot. About their huge eyes. The little one's quivering lower lip and trembling limbs.

You rarely saw that sort of naked fear. Not anywhere outside a crime scene. Certainly not on two little girls. When I'd approached, Morgana had clumsily shielded Amber with her body. You had to admire a kid with more spunk than your average adult.

14

DENNY MCCALLUM SHOWED UP FIRST, danced a faltering jig with his reflection in the glass window in the main door, drew a comb out of his wallet, and dragged it through hair thinned, I conjectured, from too much combing. Cocksure, he winked at Beulah. Denny had a habit of being in command only when there was no payoff. I'd seen him shake down waiters, charm elevator operators, and curse one-legged panhandlers. Two things occurred to me. One, he walked like a duck. Two, I was losing my charity.

"Well?" he said.

The others materialized through the main door, and we all adjourned to my office. It was the first time since I'd been bushwhacked in Myrtle Creek that we'd all been together, and I was beginning to compare their cockeyed quest to the real world.

Floyd Boyd who lusted after the woman in the PBS videotapes.

Rex Ronquist who hankered for the woman in the nude photo.

Jimmy Canfield who'd asked me to track down a high school cheerleader.

And, of course, Denny McCallum, sweat beading his upper lip, eyes as dull and thoughtless as those of a man who'd just been gassed in a dentist's chair. "Well?" he asked.

"Dinner tonight. The Adriatica. Window seat overlooking Lake Union. You've got reservations."

"Christ. You don't give a guy much time. I wanted a haircut and things."

"Your hair's fine," said Floyd Boyd. "You're just nervous. I'll give you something you might need, though."

"What's that? Huh?"

"A French envelope."

Boyd, Ronquist, and Jimmy Canfield erupted into a chorus of Bronx cheers and catcalls. Rex Ronquist smiled until his eyes were slashes. "Look at him. He's already got so much blood going to his unit he can't think." Ronquist was a small man who walked solidly and tipped himself from side to side when moving, the way a weight lifter would. He had a mustache, soft brown hair swept back into a wave, and wore glasses that darkened in the sunlight. The skin on his face, which never tanned, was a myriad of smile wrinkles, and his general attitude toward life seemed to be, "Ain't it grand?" He was employed by an economic think tank on the Eastside.

Ronquist was funny and harmless. Since Vietnam he'd been married and divorced three times.

"Who's next?" asked Ronquist. "Come on. You can tell us. Who's the next dreamgirl you're going after?"

"Maybe I better be going home so I can get ready," said Denny.

"There goes that unit again," said Ronquist. "Maybe we better tie a bell on it."

After the laughter died down, I said, "The reservation is for eight."

"What's she like?" Denny asked. The sincerity in his voice deadened the room. Eartha Braintree might be a harbinger of all their dreamgirls.

"Quite pretty."

"She built?" Rex Ronquist asked, grinning.

"Now, you might be talking about Denny's future wife," said Floyd Boyd. "Let's be discreet."

"I'm not going to marry the girl," said Denny, clearly chagrined. "I'm just going out on a date. I mean, how could

I say we'll get married? How do I even know I'll like her?"

"How do you know she'll like *you*?" bellowed Floyd Boyd, coughing out more laughter.

Jimmy Canfield took advantage of a break in the conversation to dip into a tray of hors d'oeuvres Beulah had ordered up, snapped on the tiny portable Sony in the corner while he was up, and tuned it to *People's Court*.

Watching him move, it occurred to me that Canfield was the right size, and perhaps the right disposition, to have been one of our attackers Saturday. At just under six feet, he was about two hundred pounds. In a jacket he might look heavier.

Canfield was a good-looking man, with brushy salt-and-pepper hair combed straight back, dark eyebrows, the kind of rugged features one might see in a male model wearing hip waders and flicking a fly rod. He had a way of fixing you with his steady brown eyes that made you feel Jimmy Canfield didn't have a thing in the world to hide. Jimmy was the largest of the group and the one who kept himself in the best shape.

"Who's next?" he asked. His teeth were big and even. He had big-boned hands and enormous forearms; played slow-pitch softball in summer, flag football in autumn, city league basketball in winter. "Come on," he said. "You can tell us."

I smiled. "Depends on who's the most difficult to run down. I've got a man working on Ronquist's—St. Louis, the last I heard. And the agent who found Denny's will be taking on yours."

"All right!"

During the next lull Jimmy Canfield questioned me about the neck brace. He'd enjoyed a year of medical school before dropping out to tackle the business world, had become an executive with a large company based in Seattle, Simpco Insurance. He once mentioned a traffic dispute in which he'd been harassed by two drunken teenage boys in a Roadrunner. He'd bloodied both their faces and tossed their ignition key into the lake. "Wish somebody would have slapped me around like that when I was younger. Maybe it would have saved me some headaches." He laughed in his peculiar high-pitched giggle, which sounded like one squeaky note on a clarinet.

Jimmy Canfield broke out his second Heidelberg and passed a can to Ronquist.

Canfield said, "Really. What happened to your neck?"

"Somebody tried to hang me."

"You shitting me?"

Everyone stopped talking.

Watching Canfield's face, I supplied the details. The others in the room were built too small to have been directly involved Saturday night, but I watched them, too.

15

TWENTY-FIVE MINUTES LATE, EARTHA Braintree showed up in the passenger seat of a black Nissan 300 ZX, hastily kissed the hulking, unshaven driver good-bye and met me on the sidewalk in front of Pioneer Square Park in a tight indigo dress and a fur wrap, although the evening was warm, muggy, and gray. The clerks at the cosmetics counter at Nordstrom must have helped with the paint job. She looked like a model in *Vanity Fair*, except their models look you in the eye. I told her she looked nice, and we walked around the block. She gave my Ford pickup a jaundiced look.

"It's okay," I said. "The last person to ride in it was a lawyer, but I had it fumigated."

"Parker should have taken me to the restaurant," she said, scooting in.

"Kind of awkward having your boyfriend tag along on a blind date, wouldn't you say?"

"Is that what this is? A date?" She fidgeted, crossed her legs, uncrossed them, then felt under her to see if my seat cushions had snagged her dress. "Say, listen, Black. When do you hand over the check? Now, or after?"

"What's the difference? You can't cash it until tomorrow."

"Why not just let me see it?" I displayed the cashier's check but didn't release it when she tugged.

An intimate place where they dazed you with genteel politeness, the Adriatica sat at the base of Queen Anne Hill on an embankment overlooking Lake Union. The restaurant had been converted from one of those grand old Seattle houses. Upstairs it was all muted colors, muted music, low arches, and modern paintings. I was the only guy in the joint without a tie.

Denny McCallum sat at a table for two overlooking the boats and float planes on Lake Union, and beyond that, Capitol Hill, which was mostly huge old houses in the trees and apartments where they'd leveled the trees.

McCallum's beaming presence unnerved Eartha Braintree, and it took me a moment to realize she had assumed all along the date was actually with me. I took a table upstairs in the bar, ordered an appetizer, some dish called calamari fritli skorthallia, which turned out to be pretty good, and a soda. Nothing else. I was hungry, but I had no idea when they'd conclude, and I wanted to be available to drive Eartha home.

Denny had seemed uncharacteristically debonair, so much so that I had a hard time believing he didn't have a stomach full of painkillers. Eartha Braintree squirmed and peered out the window, and then at the other patrons, before she stomped upstairs to the ladies' room, five expeditions in the first forty minutes. From my table in the bar I could see the door to the ladies' room.

Finally Eartha skittered up the staircase with her wrap, rushed into the rest room, and then attempted to flee the premises minutes later. I caught her at the main door next to the leaded-glass windows.

I said, "Try the chocolate soufflé?"

"I want to go home."

"What's the matter? Gas?"

Palm up, she shoved her hand at me. I presented the check in its envelope, and she leaned so close I could feel the heat of her cheek. She hissed, "I felt like a goddamned escort service."

"Look," I said. "I don't think it was . . ." But she was out the front door and down the stairs. I smiled at the young hostess who was discreetly eavesdropping, then pulled the door closed behind Braintree. The black Nissan was in the street, a prearranged rendezvous.

I found McCallum at the table beyond the first arch. "Well," he said, baffled. "I thought that went rather well, didn't you?"

"Hard to say, Denny."

"Not for me." He was grinning. "I got another date with her. I was even thinking . . . Did you, uh?"

"I paid her."

"Oh, gee. I thought maybe . . ."

"Two thousand."

"Yeah, well, uh, what'd you think of her?"

"Nice teeth."

He grinned. "Yeah, I thought so."

Most of life's nuances seemed to give McCallum the slip, so he didn't have a clue what had transpired. When the waiter brought two chocolate soufflés in their hot, round dishes, having had only an appetizer, I couldn't resist, sat, and horsed down Eartha's while we gazed at the lights on the lake, the freeway in the distance, a sailboat chugging across the water under power. Neither of us spoke.

It was a foolish notion that took me back to Jo Schwantz's neighborhood that night. First I went to Stuart Green's place. Green lived at the only nearby 805 address that I hadn't checked. He was watching pastel reruns of *Miami Vice* on cable. He said he didn't recognize the photographs of Jo and the children, and I believed him. We chatted for a few minutes. He worked for City Light. His lumbar region had been giving him trouble.

I parked a distance up the street and walked to Jo Schwantz's. I walked along the dark side of the structure and, holding a miniflashlight in my teeth, diddled the lock on the back door. Twenty-seven fifty-five. I located a light switch at the back door, but the power had been disconnected. On the floor rice and other foodstuffs snapped underfoot, the thin echoes coming off the walls as if I were in a sepulcher. A cuckoo clock in the other room ticked. I wondered if somebody was winding it or if it just ran forever.

This late at night it was a heartbreaking place, in the dark, with the tenants scattered all over the compass. The house was lifeless, hollow, had the same aftershock feeling of a deserted crime scene.

There were discoveries to be made in this house. Had to be. If I searched long enough, I'd glean hints of who and what had driven the family out. Of where Jo was. Of who had assaulted me and why. I decided to go upstairs and rifle Jo's belongings a second time.

He must have heard me unlock the damaged back door and waited in the living room near the front door. When I came around the corner from the kitchen, I heard him cock a pistol.

My face flushed.

I ducked backward, and a fraction of an instant later a gun went off. The doorframe above my head blew apart. A splinter hit me in the face. He hadn't been aiming at anything except my skull.

Backpedaling, I slipped on the rubbish on the kitchen floor and lurched sideways into a counter, cracking my shoulder. Then my head. It was hard to move fast in a neck brace. On hands and feet I crab-walked for the exit but heard the front door slam before I could escape, footsteps on the wooden porch shuddering the structure.

I listened as a car in the street fired up and peeled out.

I had been scanning the streets for white Lincolns all week, and I would have noticed if one had been parked in front.

It had been too dark and too sudden for a glimpse of his face or even his silhouette, and I was reasonably sure he hadn't seen me either. Judging by those quick, heavy footsteps, my assailant had been a rather brawny man.

I slapped out the rice that was indented in my palms, walked to the front, and looked out on the street, but all was still. I went back to exploring the rooms. Everything looked as it had yesterday. The variations were a cracked-open front door and the faintly nostalgic odor of gunpowder. Downstairs hadn't been touched, but Jo Schwantz's bedroom on the second story had been looted. I spent half an hour pawing through the wreckage, then took a look-see at the girls' room. The stuffed animals hadn't been bothered.

After locking up, I was cautious coming around the house, but there wasn't anybody in the neighborhood who didn't belong. Getting shot at kept you deliberating for a good while. I knew a guy on the police force who digested the adventure for two years, then resigned. A civilian acquaintance had his windshield shattered by a freeway sniper, and although he'd suffered no physical wounds, had frittered away the next twenty-four hours in bed, unable to get up even to take a pee.

I traipsed across the street to Ada Crabb's, the weakness in my thigh muscles underscoring how much tension I had been under. Ada answered the door in a worn nightgown with yellow bears stenciled onto the fabric. "That you, Mr. Black?"

"How are you doing, Mrs. Crabb?"

"I'll tell you. Old age isn't for sissies."

"I don't guess it is." She hadn't seen anybody prowling. Nor had she seen Jo.

At home I downed a bowl of cold cereal, determined that tomorrow, creaky neck or no, I would get some exercise. As I was drifting to sleep, I heard a noise in the kitchen, someone fiddling with the lock on the door at the head of the stairs. The hinges screaked as the door slowly swung open. Footsteps. Then someone breathing softly in my kitchen. A silhouette tiptoeing across the kitchen floor, heading for my bedroom, one hand outstretched.

For a moment she was limned in the backlight from the kitchen windows, the dull city nimbus X-raying her nightgown.

She didn't bother to switch on any lights or advertise her presence. She dragged her own comforter along, wrapped herself in it, and lay down on top of the covers beside me. My drowsy voice startled her.

"Cheryl, sweetheart. Come give the big guy what he wants."

"Quit kidding around, Thomas."

"People get shot sneaking into bedrooms."

"Not me sneaking into yours. You lie up here awake nights waiting for me."

"Hah!"

"You don't even know anybody named Cheryl."

"What if I'd had a woman?"

"You never have women. Besides, it's nice that I can come in here without knocking. I know it's nice because all of my friends tell me it is."

I smiled. "What do you want?"

She stared at me in the dark a minute, then said, "Oh-ho. Don't get your hopes up."

"I'm not getting anything up." Kathy was lying on her side, facing me, her blinking eyes just visible in the nether light, her loose dark hair poufed out above her face. "You haven't done this in a long time. Since before the F-person showed."

"I saw one of them."

"One of who?"

"Whom. One of the hangmen."

"Which one? Where? It's who. Tell me."

"Don't get out of bed. We won't find him tonight. I was riding the bus from work, going up the Ave. from downtown, and I saw him coming out of the post office. He wore a gray suit and a navy tie with a paisley design like that one I bought you. You took yours back. And it's whom."

"It had a run."

"You didn't like it. Anyway, he looked as if he'd just gotten off work and was mailing something."

"Which of the three was it?"

"The one who drove us out from Myrtle Creek up into the hills. The sweaty guy."

"You sure?"

"When I saw his face in Oregon, I thought I'd seen him around someplace. I must have seen him here. On the Ave. He's soft-looking. Not at all the way he seemed in Oregon."

"Maybe he has a box at the post office."

"He didn't have anything in his hands except car keys when he came out."

"You saw him get into a car?"

"He walked across the Ave. heading west. I got off at the next stop, but by the time I ran down the street, he'd vanished. I hung around two hours, thinking I might see him drive by or something. It was crazy. The longer I waited, the jumpier I got."

"He wouldn't have recognized you without your clown shtick."

"I'm sorry, but I don't think I have a prayer of identifying the other guys. Not reliably enough for a court. This one I got. But not the others."

"One is enough. And we don't need reliable. We just need a little luck."

"Maybe he works in the U-District somewhere. Thomas. When I got off that bus, I was so scared I was shivering. Some college girls even stopped and asked if I was sick. I just wanted to . . . I don't know what I wanted. I wanted to do something really mean. Like . . . kick him in the shins. Hard."

"Me, too."

"I was so wobbly."

"His shins are in for considerable trouble."

"I was waiting in my rocker for you to come home, but you took so long I fell asleep listening to Tracy Chapman. And then I came up here. You don't mind?"

"What?" I feigned outrage. "You want to sleep here?"

"Just on top of the covers."

"I suppose you think you can trust me?"

"Trusted you before."

"Before was then. What about Dooright?"

"Nobody's going to tell Philip, but if someone is cheeky enough to go around bragging about it, he'll understand. He knows you're my friend."

"Yeah," I said, laying my head down. "Go ahead and stay. But you better be good."

After a minute she said, "How did the big date go tonight?"

I yawned. "Eartha Braintree arrived all coked up and could hardly sit still. She got her money and took off with her boyfriend."

"Poor Denny. How did he take it?"

"He thinks it went swimmingly. Even thinks he's going out with her again."

"You're *kidding*?"

"Wish I were."

After a while I started to drift off. Kathy's low voice brought me back. "Thomas? You awake?"

"Now I am."

"I had this feeling when we were in Oregon . . . you know . . . when they were kidnapping us."

"Let's not air this."

"It's just that I had this feeling we were standing next to our graves. Do you understand what I'm trying to say? As if the next thing they were going to do was hand us shovels and tell us to dig. We were that close. You know I get these feelings, and you know they're always right. When you started throwing punches, you saved my life. And you knew it, too. Don't deny it."

"I just want to find the bastards," I said, pushing her off. She'd rolled partially onto me, and the body heat was beginning to make me sweat. "So I can kick their shins."

"Joke, but I owe you. And I'm sorry. I've been so busy with Philip. I've just . . . I've been trying to hide from what happened. By staying away. I don't like that sense of mortality. I'm too young to be thinking I'm going to die. The Sandpiper? That offer to go to the ocean still open?"

"Thanks, but I don't feel like it anymore."

"I'm just sorry I got you involved in this, Thomas."

"I kind of like the case. Except for getting hanged."

At three minutes after two the phone rang. It was Elmer "Snake" Slezak, the agent I'd hired to track down Rex Ronquist's pornographic pinup. It wasn't tough to tell he was in his cups.

"Thomas! Gotta get down here tomorrow. I got this woman, man, the one from the photo. She's a class broad if you like bitches who spit fire. Backup. That's what I need, man. Backup."

"What about Freddy?"

"Him and me had a blowup in Frisco, and he lit out. I need backup, pronto. Like tomorrow morning." I could hear a woman in the background, cooing into Slezak's ear. Snake was a grizzled old coot, but for some reason he captivated the ladies. I think it was the blue eyes. And the blarney. He was the most magnificent liar I've ever known.

"So where are you?"

"San Diego. Stayin' at a place called the Westgate. Posh, but I ain't payin' for it. I'm on the tenth floor, and I can see out to the ships in the harbor. Hell, half the navy's down there on the street looking for a ten-dollar hooker."

"They'd have an easier time finding her if she wasn't already up there in your room, eh?"

"Janelle? Janelle's a class dame."

"You sure you found the woman from the photo?"

"As much as admitted it. I showed her the picture."

"Tell her what the deal is, and go from there. You've got ten grand to play with."

"She don't want to talk to the likes of me. Besides, I want you to bring me a piece. I want a nine millimeter with a fourteen-shot clip. I can't never get mine through the airport. I know you got some sort of technique. I think we might be needing a ton of ammo, but we can buy that down here."

"Snake, you're drunk."

"You want this squaw or what? I ain't down here for a tour of Balboa Park. Much as I like the palm trees and tequila and *señoritas* and shit. Now, you either trust me and get your ass down first thing, or I fax you a bill and you find this tomato again by your lonesome."

"Snake, I'm gonna be pissed if you're conning me. Stick around the hotel, and I'll call from the airport."

"You comin' in?"

"No army lingo."

"Damn you, Thomas, say it."

"Fuck you, Snake."

"Okay. I'll say it *for* you. You're coming in. You're coming in fast. And you're coming in low. And you're bringing steel."

"Try to sleep it off, Snake."

Elmer Slezak ran a miserable private-investigation service out of Tacoma, messy stuff, tracing runaway wives and checking out prospective bridegrooms for financial stability, documenting adulteries, skip tracing bail jumpers, defending fat cats confronted with various types of blackmail. At times, he had the morals of a rabid bat. At other times, I would have given him the shirt off my back. Now in his late sixties, Elmer had fought and been decorated in Korea. He had saved my life once. It had been my fault, a foolish mistake, and he'd delivered me without a qualm. I figured I owed him, tried to tolerate his foibles, and bounced him an assignment when I could.

"Who was that?" Kathy asked, half-asleep.

"Snake."

"Huh?"

"You know. Elmer."

"You're not still doing business with that lunatic?" I dialed the airport and made a reservation for 7:00 A.M. on American with a transfer to American Eagle. I clicked the bedside lamp off and settled in.

Before long Kathy became very still, and I think she stayed that way until long after I was asleep.

16

"How you doin', Thomas?"

"I'm exchanging air."

"Ain't much of a measure."

"It's all I've got left."

Out of Sea-Tac we had punched through the overcast and floated in sunlight to California. Near Shasta, the clouds began to disintegrate, and you could see a smoggy California summer below. After deplaning, phoning Snake, and boarding the commuter in L.A., I tried to lie back and relax, wondered what it would be like to be sailing along on one of the yachts in the whitecaps below.

Snake Slezak was a bandy-legged man who wore cowboy boots and almost always had a Stetson close by. In the headband of the hat you could generally find a two-shot .44 magnum derringer with rosewood stocks. His gray-brown hair was shaggy in back, and his grizzled beard would have been termed mere overgrowth on some. His piercing movie-star-blue eyes were always bloodshot, and you didn't have to get too close to smell beer. He was maybe five foot six, 125 pounds, and looked like what he was, a spent ex-bull-rider. I'd once heard a woman say he looked like a guy waiting for the right time to kill himself. When he wasn't laughing outrageously, a morose view of life radiated from his face.

"Got 'em?" he asked.

"What?"

"The iron, man. The shooters. I read about a terrorist smuggled 'em inside pineapples. What's your gimmick?"

"Snake. I hate flying, and I had a million things to do today."

He gave me a hurt look, scratched the raggedy fur under his chin, and said, "Abigail Hayden is her name, and she's a hotshot society bitch. Twenty years ago she's flashing beaver in a dirty magazine, and now she's flashing it under the table at the opera society. Owns a bunch of dress shops and about three different businesses in the Horton Plaza. Couple of restaurants in Old Town. A bookstore in Seaport Village. One apartment complex that I know of."

It was almost 90 outside, breezy, and sunny with just a few bright puffy clouds here and there. I took off my jacket. Palm trees rustled above us outside the terminal. "You spoke to her?"

"Once. Thought I was panhandling. Pulled out this here two-dollar bill and tried to hand it to me all folded long and stuck out so she wouldn't have to go skin on skin with this old dog."

I laughed at the miserable look on Snake's face. I couldn't help myself. I laughed out loud. Snake looked as if he'd just munched a mouthful of cotton. When the commuter van pulled up, we rolled open the side door and sat in the back. "How'd you find her?"

"The magazine you got from your friend."

"Rex Ronquist."

"Published in West Hollywood in '67. Outfit called theirselves Medusa Trio Publications. Put out a battery of tittie mags. Me, I got a rented garage stacked high with it in Tacoma. Anymore the stuff ain't even good for whacking off. Medusa Trio? A lot of black and white tits with the crotches covered. I mean, this is when the real beaver mags only came in from Europe. Medusa published *Jugs. Mothers in Heat. Black Bombers. Sex Starved. Bitches in Boots.* Remember all them?" Snake said, fondly.

"No. But they sound like classics."

Snake took a clipping out of his inside jacket pocket and

unfurled it, a nude on glossy magazine stock, Ronquist's dreamgirl. Maybe twenty years old, impossibly thick dark hair down to her ribs, full eyebrows, heavy, upright breasts, and a look of intense concentration on her face. "Know what she did when I showed her this?"

"Denied it?"

"Spit in my eye. Just like a camel. Blinded me for a minute. Had me a giant albino Chinaman in New Jersey try to piss on me once. Almost seven feet tall. Fought like a hellcat and then . . ."

"Why'd you show it to her? The picture."

"There are sixty-one points on a face, and each one tells me something. Tell more about a man than he knows about himself. She's into something heavy. Watch the zigzaggy lines under her eyes."

We rode in silence to the Westgate Hotel. Elmer tipped the driver a quarter, and when his back was turned, I rectified the slight. We went in and I checked into a room on the tenth floor, then met Elmer in the Imperial Lounge. I ordered a soft drink. He had something he claimed would blister a bobcat's behind.

"So let's start from the beginning," I said.

"See, I traced this Medusa Trio Publications down to West Hollywood. It was one a' them rackets set up to bag girls heading out to Tinseltown. Medusa went out of business on the record books around '71. Guy ran it was a joker named Risener, Harry C.

"Found his widow in Oxnard and sweet-talked my way into her basement where she'd ratholed Harry's old papers. Harry was eighty-eight when he died. This tush must'a been all of forty when I seen her. Hooters like fire hydrants. Used to model for Harry. Took me three days to sift through all his papers, photos, and letters and notes and old sandwiches. What I found was some names of employees. A scalp counter named Leaptrott in Los Altos was able to fill me in on how Risener operated."

"Tell me about Leaptrott."

"What happened to your neck, by the way? Some gal squeeze her thighs too hard?"

"Got lynched."

"I got lynched once. Leaptrott tells me they had a regular studio set up in West Hollywood, Harry doing the layouts, Leaptrott with the camera, and a woman named Maude doing the books. They'd do a shoot in thirty minutes, pay the bimbo a hundred bucks and down the road with her. Some of the models came back and posed for other publications. Once she'd hit three or four of their editions, she was bounced. I couldn't get nothing out of Maude's records. Besides. The gal in the pictures called herself Tiffany Stiff.

"So I fly up there and interview Leaptrott. He doesn't recognize her, but he has the address of one of the other photogs, some faggot living in Frisco near Candlestick Park. Frasier is his name. Turned out the guy was dying of AIDS. Looked like a concentration camp victim.

"Frasier didn't think she was anybody'd posed for them. Maude kept a separate filing system for free lances. It was in a little red two-drawer cabinet. When I got back to Risener's house, the widow was down there with some stud loading all the crap from the basement into a truck. I must'a got her thinking about what a mess it was. Grabbed that file cabinet from her in the nick of time.

"Fella named Rich Krohn sold Medusa Tiffany Stiff's photos. In '67 Rich Krohn had an address in Pocatello, Idaho. Couldn't find no Krohn living there, but on a hunch I called up to Idaho State University, told 'em I was Rich and wanted my records. Rich was from Bozeman. Still lives in Montana. Runs a hardware business with his father. Called him, but he got a little catlike on the phone, so I flew up. Face to face, he talked. She'd been his sweetheart. One night they had partaken of some wine and some grass, and he snapped the pictures, telling her he didn't have any film in the camera, then when he got 'em published, he showed her the layout. She blew her stack and jilted him. He paid me two hundred bucks to give him her address when I found her. Abby Huntington was her name. Hailed from St. Louis. Called her folks. Dad was a high school teacher. Told me she was living out here now."

"Where do I find her?"

"In La Jolla. Beautiful place overlooking the water. Did a site evaluation and it's got security, but we can bust it."

"Snake, we're not trying to launch an assault here. Got a phone number?"

He passed me a slip of paper. "First two are home numbers, then her office. She ain't around much. It's a disorderly life, runnin' crime."

I used the phone in the lobby, sat on an antique sofa. A maid with a heavy Spanish accent answered the home number, told me Señora Hayden was not home, that she wouldn't be back later because she was chairing a benevolent committee for the San Diego Zoo that night, then attending a black-tie social event for same. I called the business number. A man answered, "Hayden Limited."

"Abigail Hayden, please."

"Your name and the nature of your business?"

"I'm afraid this is private."

"The best I can do is to give her your number and name."

I left my name and the number at the Westgate. Snake said he was going up for a nap. I used the lobby phones to call a researcher in Seattle.

"Cassie? Thomas here. Martha Binstead? Lives at 805 Thirtieth Avenue. Her phone's been disconnected, and I'm out of town today. Find out anything you can about her." I gave her the number of the Westgate, then walked three blocks to the Horton Plaza, and strolling the pastel-colored ramps and walkways I window shopped and daydreamed.

On the way back the air was breezy, the streets sunny, perfect shirtsleeves weather of the nature the Northwest hadn't savored all season. As in Seattle, they were slapping up new buildings everywhere, dump trucks, cranes, noise, construction workers, dirt clods squashed on the sidewalks. A phone message was waiting for me at the desk.

I went up to my room, washed up, and dialed. A woman answered on the first ring. "Abigail Hayden."

"My name is Thomas Black. I'm a private investigator from Seattle. I'd like to talk to you. It shouldn't take longer than ten minutes."

"For the life of me, I can't imagine what a detective would want. Is it bad news?"

"Not in the least."

"I suppose I may be able to fit you in. Do you know the Bazaar del Mundo? Old Town Plaza? Let's make it easy. Grab a cab and tell them the Guadalajara Grill. Thirty minutes."

"Fine."

"By the way. What do you look like?"

"You can't miss me. I'll be in the maroon neck brace."

The Guadalajara was a rowdy joint with heavy wooden rafters, friendly help, and plenty of Mexican paraphernalia on the walls. I set Snake up at the bar and told him to remain scarce, then took a table and nursed a basket of chips. They said Mexican food in San Diego was better than it was in Mexico, and I was famished.

Twelve minutes late, she showed up with a man who had the burly, brooding look of a chauffeur/bodyguard. He took a stool at the bar three spots over from Snake.

"Mrs. Hayden?"

"Mr. Black." We shook hands, and she sat across from me. She wore an exotic billowy white linen skirt, sandals, a sleeveless white blouse, and a huge white belt. Also a wide-brimmed white hat. She was busty on top and trim everywhere else. I had the nude photo in my pocket in case I wanted to get one of my eyes lubricated. Her only jewelry was a big pale clamshell bracelet on her wrist. Her eyes were dark brown, liquid, set off by all the white. She was pale. It was rare in the San Diego population to worship tan skin the way people did in Seattle. I guessed it was because their servants and bellhops had tan skin.

"I'm assuming you're here for the same reason that slimy little man at the bar approached me yesterday?" She was good. I hadn't seen her notice Snake. "Which, by the way, he never got around to mentioning."

"Let me apologize for whatever Elmer did that was in bad taste. Your name was at one time Abigail Huntington?"

"My maiden name, yes. Hayden is my second husband's

name. Your man breathes through his mouth, always an unmistakable sign of the lower class.''

"Yes, well . . . You're not married presently?"

"You've evidently researched me at some length.''

"I represent a man who carried your picture through a tour of Vietnam. Claims it was the only thing that got him through. He would like to meet you. That's all there is to it. He wants to fly you up to Seattle, put you up in a nice hotel, and have a chaperoned dinner. It's a free trip, a free dinner, and a chance for some cordial conversation.''

"I don't understand.''

"It's what you might call a blind date.''

"I don't know anybody in Seattle.''

"He knows you.''

"You mean he became infatuated with wood pulp and ink. A picture in a dirty magazine. How utterly charming.''

"He means well.''

"Those pictures were taken twenty years ago without my knowledge.''

"He's an economist. Works for a think tank near Seattle. From what they tell me, he's quite brilliant.''

"Sounds brilliant all right. You say he's held the pictures all these years?''

"That's right.''

"I don't know what to say.''

"Say yes.''

"Mr. Black, I am not proud of those photographs. I don't make a habit of displaying my body in public. I'm sorry you've gone to so much trouble, but the answer is no. Emphatically, no.''

"Besides the trip and the hotel, there's money in it. Ten thousand.'' By the looks of her, ten grand was chump change, but I had to make the effort.

She was standing now, a woman accustomed to running her own show, nearing forty but looking thirty. A woman with stage presence. "I might have considered giving the money to charity, but I don't think so.''

"Fair enough,'' I said, standing and offering my hand. She ignored it. "Have a nice day.''

I watched them get into a stretch limo. White, of course. She in the back behind smoked glass. Ronquist's eyeteeth would have loosened if he could have seen it. He'd had this vision of rescuing a waif from the mundane sort of tract-house subsistence one might lead after being a porn princess.

Snake ambled over, and I said, "The lady knows what she's about."

"She didn't give you that crap about open mouths and the lower class, did she?"

"She said a lower class guy is a guy who puts slugs in parking meters, trips crippled people, and wears a baseball cap backwards in church."

"That lets me out."

"I figured it did."

"I don't go to church."

We both laughed. "Sit down," I said. "Let's have some hot Mexican food."

"Then we can take the trolley to Tijuana and get us some hot *señoritas*, eh?"

"Not tonight. I'm flying home in a couple of hours."

17 CASSIE HAD LEFT A TERSE MESSAGE AT THE desk. *Martha Binstead died July 8th.* I phoned her from my room, having disowned Snake on the street after he'd made a wager with some sailors that he could execute more successive push-ups than they could. In order to advance the dispute, they had adjourned to a nearby gin mill.

"Cassie?"

"Your phone bill is going to be monstrous if you're doing all your business from down there. How's the weather?"

"Sunny. Smoggy. What'd you get on Binstead?"

"Died three weeks ago. She was ninety. Survived by her daughters, Vivian and Louise. Louise lives in Tennessee. Vivian's husband, William Bleister, is the executor." Cassie gave me a number for him. The prefix, nine-three-two, I recognized as West Seattle. "Thomas?"

"What is it?"

"Is there something wrong?"

"Not a thing."

"You sound morose. Whatever you're working on must mean a lot to you, huh?"

"Yeah, I guess at least part of it does. Thanks, Cassie."

I dialed long distance and reached West Seattle on the fourth ring. William Bleister sounded like an old man smoking a cigarette. After introducing myself, I said, "I understand you have something to do with a house over on Thirtieth and Columbia."

"Yuh. Mother-in-law's. Passed on a few weeks ago. Been water'n the grass. Guess you'd call me the caretaker. Can show it to you if you're interested in makin' an offer. Excepting, with this real estate market, I ain't so sure. They say things're hot. I get maybe two calls a day on it from agents, but I'm not goin' to list it with swindlers."

"You'd show it to me?"

"Right now, you want to drive over there."

"I wouldn't want to disturb whoever's living in it."

"No one in it. All shut up since Martha passed on. Let me go find the key and meet you."

"That won't be necessary."

During a stopover in the San Jose terminal I phoned Nanette Corelli in Yreka. Jo's mother. "No, she hasn't telephoned or been here, but I did what you said, Mr. Black. Let that person get through to Jo Brown. I lied, Black, lied and said I was Jo Brown. The operator switched her through, but she knew I wasn't her before I could say boo.''

"She?"

"The voice. It was a woman."

"You positive?"

"She said, 'You're not her.' There was this here long hush, and then she hung up in my face. I remembered something else, too. A couple of years ago I was visited by a man. Never associated it up until after you called, but he must have been looking for some smell of Jo. Can't recall his name, only that he came prying around. Anymore I can't even recollect what he looked like. You get old, your mind goes out the window with yesterday's newsprint. If she would just come home. Been roamin' the house every night since you first called. Where is my Jo?"

"I wish I knew, Mrs. Corelli."

"Her daughters. They're all right, ain't they?"

"They're all right," I said, hoping I was right, and feeling suddenly a million miles from home.

Killing time at the newsstands, I discovered a tabloid with an article on genetic defects. The article mentioned people with two different eye colors. I paid for the paper, ripped out the article, stuffed it into an envelope, addressed it to Kathy at the office, and had another malingering passenger in the airport promise to mail it from Toledo.

In Seattle it was a few minutes past midnight by the time I inched the truck up the driveway, unlocked the kitchen door, and dropped my bag on the floor. Feeling run-down from the trip, I snoozed until eight-thirty Saturday morning, which was some sort of record for me, gulped a breakfast of dry cereal, skim milk, and toast, scanned the morning paper, and walked my Miyata through the backyard to the alley.

Horace, my elderly neighbor to the south was perched in a lawn chair watching his huge marmalade cat, who in turn was hunched in front of a dirt pile. The fact that I didn't have any moles in my yard drove Horace almost to psychosis. He grimaced at the interruption when I popped my cleats into the bicycle's clipless pedals.

It was gloomy weather, cloudy and too cool for anything less than tights and a long-sleeved jersey. I took a thirty-miler down through the University, across the Montlake Bridge, past the Museum of History and Industry, into the Arboretum, and then dropped down to Lake Washington Boulevard. The turn-around point was in Renton near the airport. On the ride back, I cruised around Green Lake to warm down. I hadn't ridden in a while and it felt fabulous, though my legs were rubbery when I got off the saddle.

I trundled the bike up the driveway and found Kathy squatting on the back porch in shorts and bare feet, blowing her way through an extra-large container of Mr. Bubbles, magic wand poised in front of her lips. It was eleven. The walk and yard were fouled with her earlier exploded volleys. Horace was still next door keeping an eye on the marmalade cat. "Thomaaaaaas," Kathy said, giving my name a peculiar elongated accent.

"Kathyyyyyy."

Lugging the twenty-one-pound bike into the kitchen, I slanted it against the wall and went back out and sat beside her. I doffed gloves and shoes and began sweating in the afterglow of my workout.

"Know what, Thomas? I think I'm beginning to get real serious about this man."

I skinned my jersey off and heaved it over my shoulder onto the porch. It was the first day since the hanging that I hadn't worn the cervical collar, and my neck was feeling stiff. It took a moment for me to crowd the words out. "The F-person?"

"Philip is the first really sweet man I've ever known."

"You said that about me once." I submitted my best puppy-dog look.

"Thomas. Give me a frigging break." She laughed gaily. "You are sweet. And you always will be." She dropped an arm across my shoulders and bussed my cheek so that I felt her wet lips on my unshaven face and her soapy, wet fingertips on my bare shoulder. "You know I'll always love you. But this is different. It's time to think about the rest of my life. Women have that biological clock you fellows don't have to deal with. You? I'll always have you." It was a sensibility I'd helped foster. Indeed, I'd labored to establish the protocol of strict friendship.

"I don't know, Kathy. A guy who wears black socks with Birkenstocks should be married to a lady fire fighter, maybe a woman lumberjack, not one of the hottest lawyers in the state."

"If I was so hot, I'd be rich."

"People with ethics take longer. Besides, he's from California. Part of the great invasion. And you're practically a charter member of the KBO. Lesser Seattle and all that."

"I'm all for Keeping the Bastards Out. But I think even Emmett Watson would agree that we can give visas to special exceptions. By the way, how was your trip?" I explained about Abby Hayden. "Sounds to me," said Kathy, "as if this dreamgirl needs ten grand from Rex the way a kangaroo needs a briefcase."

"Yep."

"How's your neck? Gawd, it looks like hell."

"It's okay. Hey, two bubbles inside another. Nice."

"I know you're up to your ears in this thing, but Linus Stegman turned up yesterday. He got looped and beat up some guy in a convenience store out in Fall City. Unfortunately they recorded it all on videotape. Seven minutes' worth. I got him out on bail and played it for him Friday. Sal gave me a copy. They're using it for entertainment in the precincts in place of Big Time Wrassling. Know what Linus did when he saw it? Broke down and wept. He needs professional help, but I can't talk him into it."

"He doesn't need anything a baseball bat upside the head wouldn't provide."

"He was so miserable when he saw what he'd done."

"Probably not as miserable as the guy he jumped. All seven minutes' worth. How is *he*?"

"At least he's out of the ICU. They expect him to stay in the View for a week." Linus Stegman had been a professional boxer and was one of Kathy's regulars. A heavy drinker, he was still in good shape and, from time to time, went on a bender, usually to the detriment of some sod buster's bridgework.

"What do you want from me?"

"Linus claims this other fella was dealing drugs out at the Snoqualmie Campground where they've both been living. Linus is sleeping in the back of his van again. That the drug dealing incensed him. If you could find something tangible. We need to muddy the waters a little. That tape is loathsome. People who think violence is glamorous should be forced to sit and watch it. When he was through hitting him, he kicked him, and when he ran out of energy for that, he began bouncing canned goods off his skull."

"I'll think it over. How much time we got?"

"A couple of months."

After showering and shaving, I took a sack of fruit with me to the CD, a quick lunch, feeling guilty for not having hit the streets at dawn. Nobody answered at 805 Thirtieth, and there were too many neighbors out on this Saturday noon for daylight larceny. I might phone Bleister and get the key, but somehow I wanted to squirrel that option away for later. I cruised the neighborhoods for forty minutes, and ended up at Thriftway. I bought an orange pop and a bag of frosted animal cookies from a toothy cashier. I drank the pop and left the cookies on the bench seat beside my binoculars. I checked Judkins Park, then toured back through the neighborhoods.

Martha Binstead's house wasn't as well-guarded this time, the neighbors having gone inside for tuna sandwiches and Mentholatum.

Locking my truck, I walked up the alley, vaulted Binstead's back fence, and dropped into a basement stairwell, the one I figured the girls had issued from earlier in the week. The cement stairs were cracked and slanting, the door unlocked. The stairwell smelled of must and freshly laundered cotton dresses.

I knocked, yahooed, then burgled the joint.

It was a dark, low-ceilinged basement piled high with cast-off furniture, ancient appliances, a tub-and-wringer washing machine, a TV with a picture tube the size of a slice of bread, wooden ladders with cracked rungs, dusty, ancient encyclopedia sets, bashed-in lamp shades, and enough cobwebs for an episode of *The Munsters*. I closed the door and made my way through a makeshift path someone had shoveled through the junk. If the cops came, I'd tell them I was looking to buy the house.

The shelving alongside the wooden steps was stacked with double rows of preserves in Mason jars: peaches, pears, and gruesome-looking stuff that might have been pickled lips. The door at the top of the stairs led to the kitchen. Rapping my skull against the lintel, I came close to knocking myself out and staggered against the stove.

"Hallo," I said. "Hallo. I know you're in here. I'm a friend of your mother's." It was only half true, but the vacant house didn't call me on it. Eventually my skull ceased beating with my heart.

It was a tiny dwelling with one bedroom down and a sewing room up, dusty everywhere except where the girls had been. They'd been sleeping in the double bed where mismatched flashlights lay on either side of the pillows, along with heaps of reading material on the floor. *Mad* magazines and a stack of local newspapers on the far side. The Berenstain Bears, *Salty Dog,* and several Steven Kellogg picture books from the public library on the other. On the refrigerator I found a list of chores they had divvied out.

Morgana fixed supper. Amber set the table. Morgana cleaned up and washed the dishes. Amber dried. Amber had the morning pickup. Morgana the afternoon. The last chore on the list was "evening prayers for Mother," a joint venture.

I found a stack of child's drawings similar to the two I already had. An unrepentant artist, Amber was remarkably talented. Most of these drawings were pen on lined notebook paper. Drawings of her mother mainly. A few of a tall black woman. Her sister as a high-fashion model? Several were of a bloated ogre with a gun in his hand.

Next to what I assumed was Morgana's suitcase I found a strange inventory list. Under a printed "I Owe Thriftway" were two long columns of prices and items: Crayons, sanitary napkins, and eight different brands of cookies. Martha Binstead's home, now filled with shoplifting squatters. Crammed with fear.

In the living room next to an armchair centered in front of the television, I spotted a framed photo of an elderly black woman with the Brown family, Jo, Morgana, and, in the woman's lap, a younger, smaller Amber. Auntie's. A haven safe enough for a crisis, except that Auntie had passed away.

Forty minutes later I sighted the two girls and several boys at Judkins Park, killed the motor, and shambled toward the playground. Judging by the aggressive body language of the group and the speed at which their mouths were moving, the gents were giving the oldest girl a hard time.

Stiff, gawky Morgana was doling out two jibes for each one she absorbed. Nobody involved was older than fourteen, and none of them were half as streetwise as they tried to look in this neighborhood where the stars were pimps, wigged-out streetwalkers, and gun-toting dealers. As I drew close, two of the boys glanced furtively in my direction and then to their cohorts. From what little I heard, they were teasing Morgana about how tall she was, about her stick figure, about her little white sister, except they weren't using any phrases I'd heard in a drawing room lately. Amber played high on a nearby pipe-and-cedar-post apparatus.

"Hey, Morgana," I said, cheerily, startling everyone involved. "Hey, dudes."

One of the boys shied off into the sand under the climbing apparatus. I stood tall and close to Morgana. Soon they defected en masse.

The thirteen-year-old girl turned to me, white teeth gleaming against brown skin. "Do I know you?"

"Thomas Black. Private investigator. I'm trying to help your mother."

"But don't I know you?"

It bruised me to watch her ingenuousness. She was five-nine or -ten, with a long neck, endless arms and legs, and not an ounce of excess flesh, just bones and sinew and an untutored openness. At her feet I noticed two angry bumblebees imprisoned in a jar, purple clover stuffed in to appease them.

Given her large-featured face, she would never be regarded as a raving beauty, but the flawless skin and the dignity with which she carried herself would count for something. Amber scuffed through the wood chips and tucked up against Morgana's hip, Morgana's large hand dropping down protectively around the smaller girl's shoulders.

"I saw you the other day in the parking lot of Thriftway." Morgana eyed me, distrust logging into the equation. She'd been so grateful to see the boys driven off, she'd waived caution. Now it was returning.

"You really know my mother?"

"I met her. She's been hurt. Whoever hurt her hurt me, too. At least I think they were the same people." They looked dubious, Amber cinching one tiny arm around Morgana's thigh like a belt. I pulled down the black turtleneck shirt so they could see the scars on my neck. Both pairs of little-girl eyes glued themselves to the mishap.

"Ick. Randy did that?"

"Three guys in Oregon. One of them was named Randy. I'm guessing it's the same Randy. That's where I saw your mother. I believe she was on her way to visit your grandmother."

Morgana fondled her little sister's shoulders, cupped her ruddy white cheek with her bony hand, and eyeballed the horizon to the east. Amber toed the wood chips at our feet. "Randy," Morgana said. "Randy hurt her."

"Who's Randy?"

"My daddy," said the little one. "He's a bad man." Morgana put her hand on her half-sister's head and patted her hair, which had been painstakingly plaited into braids.

"Mr. Randolph Schwantz," said Morgana. "He was my stepfather, but Mom and us divorced him."

"Divorced him good," said Amber.

"Hush," said Morgana.

18

"You're Amber?" I squatted and peered into her cornflower-blue eyes.

"We go by Brown," said Morgana, her voice so rich it could easily be mistaken for that of a grown woman, as Nanette Corelli had done. "Brown's *my* last name. My dad is dead. Amber's name is Schwantz. I'm Morgana." She stuck out her moist hand, and we shook.

"Are you going to take care of us now?" said Amber.

"Hush," said Morgana. "Don't you know anything? I'm the grown-up here. You hush."

Amber tucked her lip under her incisors and gave me the eye. She was small for her age, and about two shaky heartbeats beyond adorable, decked out in patent-leather shoes, white socks, two dirty knees, a frilled saffron dress with a tiny flower motif, plump cheeks, and eyes as blue as my mood.

Morgana became distracted, watching the boys clown in the rocks near the johns. "They were teasing."

"Lucky I happened along."

"You didn't *happen* along," said Morgana. "You've been after us."

"Look, girls. You've been phoning Grandma every night to see if your mom's there. So have I. She hasn't seen your mom, but I have."

Amber began crying, and, after ten seconds of straining to read me, Morgana knelt and hugged her, all knees and elbows. "Come on, honey. It's going to be okay. Momma's coming. I know Momma's coming."

"I wish he was dead." Amber sniffled. "I wish Randy was dead."

"Momma said we can't wish anyone dead. You know that. Think kind thoughts."

"Mommy's all hurt."

"She'll be okay," said Morgana, glancing at me. "Won't she?"

"If we find her," I said.

Morgana squeezed her little sister for a few moments, then stood, knees cracking, and walked her to a park bench. I followed and sat beside the child. Legs akimbo, Morgana stood in front of us, folded her arms over her chest, and stabbed her knuckles into her biceps. The look on Morgana's long face belonged at a hero's funeral. Amber's tears starred the graveled pavement at my feet.

"What's your name again?" Morgana asked.

"Black. Thomas Black." I handed her one of my cards. She tried not to smirk at the machine gun.

"How do we know we can trust you?"

"You're staying at Martha Binstead's house. I could have grabbed you there if I meant you any harm." Morgana's eyes blinked hard at the word *grab*. "Trust me. I'll find someplace for you until we can get you back with your mother." Morgana shifted her weight from foot to foot, bony hips teeter-tottering this way and that.

"Supposin' I trust you . . ."

"I'm supposin' you already do. Tell me what happened, we'll go pick up your things, and I'll take you out to my place by the University until I can arrange something better. But I need help to find your mother. Also your father."

"*My* father's dead," said Morgana. "Amber's father . . . we're just tryin' to keep clear of that good-for-nothing."

"I think he did this." I gestured at my neck. "I want to talk to him about it."

"He's pretty mean."

"Tell me what happened."

"He found us last week. So he found us and started pounding on the front door and trying to get in. So then Mom was talking to him through the door, but he went around the back and kicked it in, and so they had a fight, Mom and him."

"Randy was hitting her," said Amber, looking up at me, then returning her swollen eyes to the gravel.

Morgana wore a white blouse with mustard stains on the body and tight blue-striped cycling shorts that extended almost to her knobby knees. "Randy's got an order. From some judge. Wants us to go live with him. He's been trying to find us ever since we divorced him two years ago. The judge wouldn't listen to us."

"Know where he lives?"

"No."

"Tell me about the court order."

"So when we got divorced, the judge made us say where we wanted to live. So me and Amber both said with Mom. But the judge gave us to Randy anyway. So we went home where we were staying in Wallingford, and Mom packed up all our stuff in the middle of the night and we moved to Tacoma."

"I had to leave my swing set," said Amber. "And Fluffy."

"Fluffy was her retarded turtle," said Morgana.

"He was not retarded," said Amber.

"He only walked in circles and attacked the cat."

"I didn't want to leave him."

"I'm sure somebody is taking good care of him," I said.

"We left a lot of stuff," said Morgana. "One of Mom's old girlfriends lived in Tacoma out by the university. So we moved in with her. Mom got a job in a restaurant."

"But you couldn't go to school," said Amber.

"I had to stay out for a while or he would have tracked us."

"I wasn't old enough for kindergarten," said Amber.

"You in college now?" I asked.

"Second grade, dummy." Amber's grin was wide and gap-toothed. "Going into second. Except we don't know which school we have next year. Do you know where I'm going next year?'' Amber looked up at me, and I suddenly felt like I'd inhaled a pine cone.

"Wish I did."

"Where are we going to stay?" she asked, expectantly.

"With a lady magician. She's going to watch you until I can find your mom."

"Can she disappear a quarter up her nose?" Morgana asked.

"A rabbit. Maybe even a horse. And she can pull a dollar out of your sock. We'll have her do it first thing."

Amber said, slyly, "Can she pull a dollar out of *my* sock?"

"Two dollars. Tell me the rest of it. You were in Tacoma . . ."

"After a while Mom got scared Randy was going to find us. One day there was a man asking questions. So we moved to Twenty-fifth. Randy was just . . . he went crazy, Mr. Black. So he just started hitting Mom. Just started pushing her into the wall and hitting her. Amber tried to stop him, so he knocked her down."

"He did find us," said Amber, scooting along the bench until she was snug against my thigh. Morgana watched, neither approving nor disapproving.

Morgana said, "What happened to Mom?"

"Near as I can tell, she tried to drive to your grandmother's in California and couldn't make it. I guess she was going to send for you?"

"We got bus money," said Morgana. "She should have called Grandma and left a message. Dad's got her."

"No, he doesn't," I said. "The smartest thing for her to do right now is to lay low and heal up. Let me get you two safely undercover, and then we'll talk." Amber hopped into the truck in front of me, but Morgana stood hipshot, sizing up the situation.

"You're not going to hand us over to DSHS, are you? 'Cause they'll just give us to Randy. We'll run." Amber looked up at me quizzically, her short legs horizontal on the bench seat.

"I promise I won't do that," I said.

Morgana turned and shambled across the playground to pick up the jar of bees. We drove to Martha Binstead's, and all three of us went in the basement entrance to collect their gear. Thinking I hadn't seen it, Morgana secreted the list of items shoplifted from Thriftway under the leg of her cycling shorts. After locking the house, I drove to Thriftway.

Amber, who'd been toying with the unopened bag of animal cookies on the Ford's bench seat, said, "Who're these for?"

"You guys. After Morgana and I go in and settle a debt." Morgana gulped and stared at the dashboard. I handed her a fifty-dollar bill.

"All we had was bus fare. We couldn't spend it or we'd never see Mom again."

"I know. You did great, Morgana. Your mom can pay me back later. Now let's you and me go inside and clear this up, then we won't have to worry anymore, huh?"

The rest of Saturday was spent at my place, inspecting roses, releasing bumblebees, and putting up a swing under the apple tree. Trading frosted animal cookies. A pink bear for an ivory lion. Nobody wanted a crab-apple war.

I phoned the office and Philip's place, looking for Kathy. I was beginning to brood. I thought it might not look proper to keep two girls at my place without a chaperon, yet it might be hours before Kathy arrived.

While we hiked to the Ave. for our dinner, I wheedled information from the girls, any hint of where their mother might be. The friend they'd stayed with in Tacoma two-and-a-half years ago had since married and relocated in Connecticut. I got her maiden name, located her mother in Tacoma, then phoned her in Waterbury, Connecticut. She was alarmed, and after speaking to Morgana to ascertain the validity of my request, told me she did not know where Jo was.

We were dancing wildly, the three of us, had been for almost an hour. Bruce Springsteen. *Born in the USA*. The same album over and over. Their favorite was the title cut. Morgana was magnificent, loose-limbed, uninhibited, rhythmic. Amber was tight and erratic. And I was reckless, getting into the flow of it.

When she got a chance, Amber sneaked around behind Morgana and cycled the turntable speed to forty-five, so that Bruce sounded as if he were on helium, Amber making all of her subsequent moves so quickly and jerkily that Morgana and I cracked up laughing.

The walls were shaking when Kathy and Philip let themselves in.

This was going to be good. Now Kathy would discover he was a stuffed shirt. It took something Philip didn't have to let it hang out with a couple of kids. We would launch into another dance sequence, and he would sulk off in the corner as if he had a stick up his ass.

I shut off the stereo, and the girls grew quiet, smiles easing off their faces.

"Amber and Morgana Brown, this is my friend Kathy Birchfield. You're going to be staying with her for a few days." Kathy's eyes went wide, but not as wide as Philip's. He wore stylishly baggy trousers, loafers, and a checked shirt that looked as if it had been through a Chinese laundry twice. "Kathy can stuff a rabbit up her nose and make it disappear."

"Well," said Kathy. "A dime. Maybe a quarter. I think I can make a quarter disappear." She produced a coin, appeared to push it into her nose, displayed both empty hands, both sides, and then, with a flourish, withdrew the coin from Philip's mouth. He seemed disgruntled. I knew it. He hated kids. A teacher who hated kids.

Kathy went to the stereo and turned the sound back on. Before I could blink, Philip took Kathy's hand and pulled her into the middle of the open floor. Kathy kicked off her shoes and began moving to the music. Morgana resumed dancing. Amber bounced on the sofa, then wiggled like a monkey on a stick. Soon Philip was dancing with Amber and Kathy with Morgana. They danced until the temperature in the house seemed to soar twenty degrees.

After the record's first side played the last cut, "I'm on Fire," Kathy came over and catered to me while Philip catered to the stereo. "What's the matter? Neck hurting?"

"Just don't feel like any more."

"Better get with the program, brother."

"I don't think so."

"You know what you look like?"

"I just don't feel like it."

"You look like you're standing over here with a stick up your ass."

"Cute phrasing."

"You do."

19

SUNDAY WE SPENT FIVE HOURS ROVING around the Woodland Park Zoo. The new pachyderm exhibit had been recently inaugurated, and the girls got a kick out of touching the elephants. Morgana, we discovered, was fascinated by snakes, so the four of us dawdled in the reptile house.

Leg-weary and footsore, we headed back for the truck, derailing into the public rose garden near the main entrance, a vast expanse of established roses, of hedges, lawns, and the latest varieties of experimental plants from the Seattle Rose Society. I made a point of touring it twice a year and took notes on varieties to mail-order from Fred Edmunds, Inc.

Morgana spied a rabbit and gave chase, while the goldfish in the shallow concrete pond enthralled Amber. The girls had no idea what the future held, and it was a little depressing to watch the false calm they wore in public.

In the rose garden I goosed Kathy's bottom and grinned.

She gave me a wry smile and batted my hand away when I tried a second pinch. She said, "If a judge really gave custody to their father, perhaps we can get it overturned."

"Schwantz has her scared out of her wits. She's not going to prefer charges."

"What about that Seattle cop? Gary Glenn. Are we ever going to find out what he was investigating Jo for?"

"I doubt it. I've tried. He's one of the toughest sons of bitches you'll ever hope to meet." I jotted *Climbing Handel* on my notepad.

"Why would he have been questioning Jo's doctor? You better make sure I'm along when you see him," said Kathy.

"I take you on all my fun trips."

We fed the girls spaghetti at Stella's off Forty-fifth N.E. next door to the Metro theaters, plotting to take in a flick, but Amber was conking out and Morgana was yawning. They'd been under an immense amount of pressure the past two weeks, and it hadn't been until I took them in that they were able to unwind. It was catching up with them. We took them home, stuffed them on Goo-goo Cluster ice cream, and had them asleep in minutes.

Kathy wandered upstairs and plunked on the sofa beside me. I was trying to catch up on the Sunday paper. Kathy picked up the editorial section but didn't read.

"Morgana's a good little mother," I said, shunting the paper aside.

"It makes me want to cry to think about those two scared little girls hiding out in the house of a dead woman."

"They did just fine."

"But where are they going to stay?"

"Downstairs."

"Forever?"

"Nothing's forever. I can drop in a couple of times during the day to see they're okay. You can call from work."

"But shouldn't they be in a state foster home? What if Jo's looking for them?"

"I've been in touch with Missing Persons. Nobody's looking for them. Not officially. When Jo is ready, she'll call her mother in California and leave a message. Give her time to recuperate. When the bureaucrats get in on this, so does their father.''

"It makes me uneasy."

"It's okay to put your faith in the law, but, remember, justice is wearing a blindfold."

Kathy tucked her legs up onto the couch and thought about it for a few moments. "I'm so scared about what you might do to those three when you find them."

I bobbled my eyebrows. "Me?"

"You know, when we came home last night and saw you dancing, I thought it was the funniest thing. You looked absolutely demented. It was just too bad we had to bust in, because the spirit of the thing just seemed to die away."

"I don't know about that."

"If I were to get together with Philip, you and I would never be the same."

"That a statement?"

"Question."

"I'm just a little ornery after what happened in Oregon."

"You loathe Philip."

"I worry that your children will be born in little black socks and Birkenstocks."

Kathy laughed and leaned close. "You're not going to go wanting for female companionship. Not you. There are always women after you."

"Usually of indeterminate age but somewhere in the ten-to-twenty-years-older-than-me bracket. They wear expensive perfume and lots of it. They wear jangly jewelry from some exotic locale where they bought it in an open-air bazaar. They are attractive but sun-wrinkled. Clearly past their prime. They are held together by a god-knows-what arrangement of stiff lingerie. They want to smother me in mother love."

Kathy giggled. "You talking about Mrs. Hanover?"

"And others."

"Women love to mother you, Thomas. It's because you're cute."

Suddenly she draped an arm around my neck and yawed across to kiss my cheek. I turned, and to her surprise we kissed on the lips, a soft, gentle thing lasting a little too long for a couple of friends. She hadn't expected it, pulled away, stared into my eyes for several beats, all blue-violet surprise fused with a hardy dose of panic, then stood up and strayed distractedly out of the room.

As she thumped down the stairs, the echo of her footsteps was almost as loud as the heartbeat in my ears. She wasn't angry. I knew what she was like angry.

The thing of it was, the kiss had been electric.

Without knowing it, Kathy Birchfield had become the axis around which my life revolved, and, I suspected, the same thing had happened to her.

Philip was the only hitch.

The F-person.

Mr. Wonderful.

A wealthy man who, in humility and altruism, had devoted his life to schoolchildren. The breed of man who never forgot an anniversary. Who knew exactly which wine to order. A man who was at home in any capital of the world. Who dressed better than the models in my J. C. Penney catalog. Not the sort of chap anybody would try to mother. Certainly not a guy anybody would call cute.

20

THE NEXT SEVEN DAYS ENGINEERED themselves into a hell of a week.

I kept in touch with Nanette Corelli, who I thought was fast heading for a nervous breakdown and who was beginning to sound like a canary stuck in a soda-pop can.

First thing Monday morning, acting on an urgent request to fetch a stuffed pig named Bacon, back issues of *Mad* magazine, ballet shoes, roller skates, and a favorite hairbrush from Jackie Brown's house, I burgled the place and loaded up two duffel bags with provisions. Lest the house was being staked out, I took elaborate precautions. Nobody shadowed me. The girls were ecstatic when I left them to sort through familiar plunder and headed for the office in Pioneer Square, bypassing the daily accident on I-5 by taking Aurora. I sorted through my own mental tidbits as I drove.

We knew that Randolph H. Schwantz had beat up Jo Brown.

We knew that Schwantz was Jo's ex-husband.

We knew there probably weren't two Randys in this case, that Schwantz and cohorts had probably tracked Jo to Myrtle Creek and probably were the ones who had assaulted Kathy and me.

We knew Schwantz or one of Schwantz's buddies lived or worked in or near the University District. Kathy had been making ceaseless treks to the Ave. but so far hadn't spotted him a second time.

We knew the Seattle cop, Glenn, had been inquiring about Jo Brown.

I got a brainstorm and called Anthony Hallinan to get a look at Jo Brown's lease application, except Hallinan and his wife were out of town on an automobile holiday along the Washington and Oregon coast. One of Hallinan's law partners told me he wouldn't be back until the end of the week, if then.

"Tony doesn't think it's a vacation unless it's indeterminate in length. Three days. A week. Depends on how much fun he's having. Don't worry. He gets cooped up in the car with Maggie, they'll be squabbling like cats in a sack. He'll be back."

Noon Monday, Kathy called Randolph Schwantz's attorney during the divorce, a ruffian named Kopek.

"I called him, but he wouldn't talk. Got to be the dirtiest lawyer in town," said Kathy, sitting on the edge of my desk. "Literally and figuratively. He doesn't bathe. He shows up in court tipsy. Even the judges around here hate him. If a guy wants to snatch his kids from his wife, he goes to Kopek. A guy wants his wife committed? He'll use anything in the book. He's got a staff of investigators who specialize in bedroom fiascoes. They don't show their dirt to the judge, though, they show it to the kids. They want to alienate them from Mom. I've heard they've even gone so far as to set up lonely divorcing women with gigolos.''

"Snake used to work for him.''

"Snake and Kopek eat from the same trough.''

After more phone calls, some report writing, and an interview with a prospective client who had just suffered through a three-month affair with her soccer coach, Kathy and I walked to lunch at Trattoria Mitchelli around the corner. Soup. Rolls. Fettuccine con Pollo. The waitresses knew me, and I'd carved my name into the wall in the john. It felt like home. I told Kathy about my prospective client's affair with her soccer coach. Friday evening they had decided each to go home and dump their mates, then move in together Monday while the spouses were at work. She loved her husband and felt sneaky about dumping him, but she lusted after her soccer coach.

After a weekend of feuding, plate throwing, and recriminations, after she had finally convinced her husband the marriage was over, she phoned Coach Bertrand at ten Monday morning. To her surprise, Bertrand answered and said, "I really don't think we should see each other again.'' Then hung up. My prospective client called again, bawling, saying she couldn't believe he'd changed his mind. Bert's way of convincing her was to put his wife on the line.

"Poor baby,'' said Kathy, looking into my eyes. "So what did she want from you? An affair?''

"Wanted me to find out what Bert's wife has on him and get him off the hook so he could marry her.''

"It never occurred to her Bert loved his wife?''

"Blackmail is what occurred to her.''

A call from Cassie, my independent researcher, was waiting for me after lunch. She'd wrapped up an elaborate paper trace of Randolph Schwantz and discovered he was living in

Whatcom County, about twenty miles outside of Bellingham in a berg called Deming. Almost within rifle range of the Canadian border. "Been phoning his house all morning, but nobody answers," Cassie explained.

"You happen to know where he works?"

"Simpco Insurance. They have a small office in Bellingham, which he heads up. Thomas? What's the matter?" It took me a moment to remember which of my four clients worked for Simpco Insurance. Jimmy Canfield. The Bellevue office. Conspiracy or coincidence? We hadn't yet found Canfield's dreamgirl, a woman named Rhonda Lastusky, a cheerleader at Woodrow Wilson High the year Canfield and the rest had graduated. When you were looking for circles and found zigzags, you had to wonder if you weren't being gulled. "Thomas?"

"Nothing. Just thinking. You tried Schwantz at work?"

"His secretary says he's on vacation."

"Everybody's on vacation."

"Yeah, I know. Paco and I are driving down to see the Grand Canyon next week."

"Still with Paco?"

"The ten-year romance from hell. He ain't much, but I'm thirty-eight, I want a baby, and I need a sperm donor."

"Watch out for Gila monsters. I heard last week one of 'em down there ate a woman's foot."

"Oh, you."

After making a quick call to see that the girls were all right, I told Kathy I'd be late for dinner, gassed up the truck, and steered north. It was 140 miles to Deming. I left town before the afternoon traffic congealed and drove through Bellingham at dinnertime. Whatcom County was heavily forested, hilly, and magnificent. Deming was situated on the dead-end highway to Mount Baker, a half hour east on Highway 542, a piss-poor little community of about 250 souls. Deciduous trees. A few clearcuts. The odd logging truck barreling down the two-lane highway.

Randolph Schwantz lived up the road just off the blacktop in a three-bedroom rambler with several outbuildings on the acreage. Everything was green, and the low late-afternoon sun was scintillating. I wondered if it had been that way all summer. Seattle had been overcast when I left. A horse grazed in Schwantz's back pasture. His ugly dog tried to bite me, and a towheaded neighbor kid who was feeding the animals informed me Schwantz hadn't been home for two weeks. The ugly dog nipped my calf and I sent him reeling with a kick. The kid sniggered.

"Know when he's coming back?"

"At two bucks a day, I don't really care," said the kid. He wore rubber boots and manure-spattered jeans.

"Want to make twenty-five?"

"Cents or dollars?"

I gave him one of my business cards and five dollars on account. "Just call this number and tell me when he gets home. And don't tell him I was here."

"You carry a machine gun?" he asked.

"Not usually."

I had pizza at a joint called Smiley's, flirted with the waitress, and dozed off early at the Coachman motel after playing channel tag on the TV. It had been a long time since I'd felt this alone. Nobody in this town cared if I lived or died, and I was tempted to pick up the phone and call Kathy, just to hear a voice I knew, but she would have thought I was getting dingy.

The next morning I checked out, breakfasted, scanned the papers, and drove to Simpco Insurance. This was a company used to dealing with private investigators. They said only that Schwantz had taken a leave of absence. It was obvious they weren't going to give out information. I tried to bribe several employees at the first morning break but struck out.

When I got back to Seattle, Kathy was in the office researching on the computer, using Lexis. "I've got a surprise for you," she said. "Sort of a thank-you for taking this dumb dreamgirl case."

She had arranged a blind date with the bus driver on the number 18, a woman I'd been trading long, hot looks with for over a year, a busty, cherubic vision with satiny-blond Breckgirl hair. Sometimes we made gun signs of our fingers and shot at each other. Twice I had flicked a fresh-cut rose through her open passenger door.

"A what?" I gasped.

"Blind date."

"Forget it."

"Too late. It's all set," said Kathy, apologetically. "For tonight."

"Tonight!"

"I knew if I gave you more time, you'd weasel out of it. Your own personal dreamgirl. Don't you want to see what she's like? You have a thing for women who drive buses and have huge boobs. I thought you'd die for a chance to take her out."

"Hell, no."

"Why on earth not?"

"Because she's perfect the way she is. If I go out with her, it's going to collapse all my delusions."

"But you don't know her. You've hardly spoken to her."

"That's why it's perfect. What if she has a Dan Quayle poster in her bedroom or collects college mugs?"

"I'm afraid you're stuck."

"*You're* stuck. I'm not going."

She looked as though she was about to cry. "Oh, Thomas!"

At six-thirty when I picked up Tiffany Jones in Ballard, she wore a snug sweater and a tight smile. Up close she was even prettier than on the bus, and I began to wonder why I had balked. Kathy had already filled her in on who I was and what I did, explaining that she was doing this as a surprise favor, that I wasn't actually a moron. Tiffany gave this all to me in the first few minutes. Clearly she had pegged me as a social retard.

Tiffany Jones. Next to her I was uglier than a homemade shoe. I was dying to ask if that was her real name. If that was her real hair. If those were her real breasts. If she hadn't been flawless, she might have been perfect.

Looking back on it, I could see the date was orchestrated inch by inch by a crew of cackling jokesters from beneath hell's back porch.

We ate at an atmospheric place called the Poor Italian on Virginia between Second and Third, where Tiffany feigned an attitude of hanging on my every word. She was good. When the waiter approached, she spoke fluent Italian with him long enough to make me feel suitably deficient. She claimed to fly a light plane to relax; said she had a commercial license she rarely used. She spoke of a Ph.D. in literature from Dartmouth but said she was going back to school to become a medical doctor. The coup de grâce was the year she'd spent sailing around the world alone. Her adventure had been featured in *Time* magazine and on *Good Morning America*.

The woman dated judges, professors, politicians, actors, and famous writers. Lord only knew why she drove a bus or why she would agree to spend an evening with me. I wore a turtleneck, but it didn't completely hide the scarring on my neck, which I ended up having to account for.

"You really should take a self-defense course," she said, helpfully, then went on to tell me about her tae kwon do and karate tournaments.

After taking in *The Fabulous Baker Boys* at the Guild 45th, she favored me with an in-depth psychoanalysis of each of the movie's characters, supplemented by a detailed critique of the film's script, direction, and editing. We drove to her home, where she invited me in and we chatted. We were on her couch when she said, "Are you eating enough greens?"

"What?"

"You seem to squint."

"I don't squint."

"It's from not eating enough greens. I could fix you up with a diet. People who look like they've just come out of a cave need diet advice. I was thinking of writing a book on it."

"Yeah. I'll bet."

Then she was kissing me. She was a self-assured woman, not afraid to take whatever she wanted, and at that moment, I guess she wanted me. I was going to play it by ear and see what developed. We kissed for a while before she straddled me on her knees. I was stretched out with my feet on the floor and my head on the back of the couch. She smiled at me and slowly unbuttoned her blouse, unhooked her brassiere, and let her enormous pale breasts fall free. She stared at me quizzically. "Well?"

"Huh?" I asked.

"Aren't you going to say something nice?"

I thought carefully, but the best I could manage was, "They're real big."

She frowned, kissed me, then sat high, nudged my cheek with one breast, then the opposite cheek with the other. She was playing with me, slapping my head with the monsters. If my neck hadn't been bothering me, it might have been amusing. One side. Then the other. Slapping harder each time. She was laughing. A severe jolt of pain suddenly shot down my neck to my knees. She whacked me harder and harder, on opposite sides, five, six, ten times in a row. She was laughing louder.

"Oh, Lord," I moaned.

"You like that, don't you?"

"I have to go." I slid out from under her clumsily and headed for the door, neck rigid, knees buckling.

"Don't go now. We're just getting started. I'm terrific in bed, you know."

"I might have to call a cab. Maybe an ambulance."

"What's your problem, Thomas?"

"I'm not feeling so hot—probably haven't been eating enough greens." I escaped through the front door, neglecting the standard promise to call.

Every man in the world has a dreamgirl.

At least one.

The perfect woman. Perhaps it was just someone he saw walking in the rain one summer afternoon, splashing in the puddles, a woman he never was able to shake from his daydreams.

Dreamgirls. Songs are dedicated to them. Poems are written about them. Books are created around them. Every guy has one. Me? She drove a bus, intentionally surpassed me in every arena, and I took her on a blind date from hell.

Not a second of it pleased me. It was my sorriest debacle in years.

When I slunk home, the house was dark, upstairs and down. Bridget Simes was waiting outside in her car. Bridget was wearing black slacks and an ivory blouse, her auburn hair pinned up. She looked rather fetching. "Jesus," she said. "What the hell happened to you? You look like the cat dragged you through a hundred miles of backyards."

"Real good guess."

"Thomas, I got her. Rhonda Lastusky. The cheerleader from Woodrow Wilson High class of '69. Her name is Yellowknife now. Rhonda Yellowknife. Married three times and lives alone in Philadelphia. See, her dad's dead, and nobody could find her for the high school reunion because her mom's remarried. Different last name. I traced her mom's credit records and found her in Olympia. It's five-thirty in the morning back there, so we can't call. You sure you're all right?" She handed me a sheet with names, addresses, and phone numbers.

"Nothing about a month of sleep won't cure. Thanks, Bridget. Nice work."

Figuring I'd catnap on the plane, I made a reservation for a Delta to Philadelphia the next morning. The hour layover was in Cincinnati. I got into Philly at 4:15 eastern time without a wink of sleep in the air. I'd flown next to a talkative outboard-engine salesman who splashed coffee all over himself. I was wearing light-colored slacks and hadn't brought another pair, didn't dare nap.

I phoned Rhonda Yellowknife from the airport and got no reply. I took the limo service to the Sheraton near the river, checked in, and phoned again. Still no answer. A nap only lasted thirteen minutes. Jet lag.

Philadelphia was a town I could grow to like. A walker's town. The traffic problems at four-thirty had been a turkey trot compared to Seattle's. The row houses, block after block of them, were something I hadn't seen anywhere on the West Coast except San Francisco. There weren't as many fair-haired people on the streets as in Seattle, nor as many Mediterranean types as in New York.

Hailing a cab in front of the Sheraton, I got a whistle-stop tour of the city from my emaciated cabbie. Admiral Dewey's flagship. The Liberty Bell Pavilion. Independence Hall. Benjamin Franklin's grave—buried with Deborah. He took me to Brewery Town, which was miles from the Sheraton.

Rhonda lived at 853 Twenty-fifth Street near the corner of Parrish Street. It was a town house, a stoop and a door opening right onto the sidewalk, the buildings brick, neat, clean, the area run-down. I knocked, but Rhonda wasn't home. I paid the cabbie and strolled to the corner.

A fire hydrant across the street was missing a cap. Half a block away a car had been stripped by vandals. A young woman in a purple raincoat scooted home from work along the sidewalk. The sun was sinking fast. Except for Seattle, it had been sunny all across the country.

Beato's Pizza on the corner of Parrish and Twenty-fifth. I ordered half a hoagie, which I didn't eat, some root beer, and settled in with sections of the *Philadelphia Inquirer* a previous customer had junked. Two undercover cops huddled near the door wolfing down food. I tried 853 around the corner twice before I hit pay dirt at quarter to seven. I had to keep translating. It was quarter to four back home.

She answered the door by peeking through the gap over the chain, a Japanese print robe swaddling her generous body. She'd just stepped from the shower, a towel screwing down her face. Though colorless, it was a lovely face, twenty years beyond cheerleading. "Can I do for ya?"

"I'm looking for Rhonda. I flew in from Seattle to speak to her."

Her eyes brightened, and the breach in the door fattened. "You did? Fancy that. *I'm* Rhonda. From Tacoma. Born and raised. What can I do for you?"

"Maybe a half hour of your time. I'm a private detective." I handed her one of my cards. "Had dinner?"

Squinting at the small print, she said, "What's this concerning?"

"It's long and complex. I'd rather do it over a meal, if that's convenient."

"I got a date, but sure. Where're you stayin'?" I told her.

"How about Downie's. You can walk there from the Sheraton. Meet you in an hour?"

"You're on." Before the door closed she gave me a look that seemed to be a brew of flirtation and mistrust. She was perfectly proportioned, but that cheerleading uniform was going to bust out all over if Jimmy Canfield tried to stuff her into it.

21

I HIKED TO DOWNIE'S ALONG BRICK and cobbled streets, past rows of expensive-looking condominiums with fancy alarm systems and wrought-iron gates, past old-fashioned shuttered shops.

The sultry Philadelphia summer air was laden with pollution. Occasional vehicles inched along streets blueprinted over two hundred years ago, boulevards broad enough for a horse and carriage and maybe a man with a walking stick, not much else.

South Street was *the* walk in Philly.

All the stores and shops were buzzing. Youngsters with radical haircuts and preposterous clothes mobbed the shops and swarmed the sidewalks. I gave a wide berth to a seven-foot-tall lunatic who spit high on the wall, then gave a bellow and jump-kicked at the dripping. By the looks of things he'd been sleeping in his clothes about a year.

On the corner of Second and South, Downie's was a raucous, standing-room-only Irish pub with plank walls bedecked in old-time posters and photographs, dozens of antique radios attracting dust on shelves overhead. I sat at a table for two against the wall.

She sauntered in, gathering looks, her wide hips canting this way and that, wearing a black-and-white houndstooth-check shirt and a tan skirt with brown belt. A watch and earrings. She was one of those redheads with milky skin that always appears a bit flushed. Robust as a field-hockey player. She wore her weight proudly. Faultless features and a smile that turned her eyes into merry slits.

"Young place," I said, looking around.

"What's the brace for? You in a car accident?"

"I hurt it a few weeks ago and then unfortunately reinjured it last night."

"You should be more careful."

"Last night was what you'd call a natural calamity."

"So," she said, after we'd ordered. "What's this about?"

"It's complex, and I'm suddenly starved. How about we eat and then talk?" I thought she might be more receptive after she'd been fed.

"No problem." She ordered white wine, while I drained three water glasses. She talked. After high school she'd gotten a degree at the University of Michigan, then married her first husband in Ann Arbor. An ineffectual stockbroker. It lasted a year and a half. He ended up in prison for fraud. After the divorce she flew to New York to work as a part-time model and designer. She met her second husband there and moved to Philadelphia when they married. He owned three restaurants on the Main Line, where she worked with him for ten years until a linebacker with the Eagles named Jack Yellowknife wooed her, prompting a second divorce. Jack, it turned out, was a drunk, a philanderer, and a steroid junkie with "knuckles that sounded off like castanets and balls the size of green peas. Six weeks it lasted, and then he shanghaied our Siamese cat and ran out on me," she said. "And here I am slaving for Harold again, taking orders from the man I jilted."

"You two thinking about . . . ?"

"He was pretty hurt when I went off with Jack, especially

after he found me and Jack taking a bath together and tried to bust Jack in the chops. Jack tied him into a bathrobe, backward, you know, like a straitjacket, and taped him to a chair in the corner. We were drunk, or I wouldn't have done it. I feel ugly even telling you. Harry's married now, and I think it's the best thing ever happened to him. Wendy's real devoted. I just never could get into that. Being devoted. I need to have a life of my own. Girls' night out, and so forth. Harry couldn't see it. I was supposed to be there every minute of the day in case he needed me to locate a stray sock or clean out his ears with a cotton swab."

We both dug into our deep-dish seafood pie, Rhonda had more wine, and then we splurged on chocolate-chip cheesecake.

"So what's it all about?" Rhonda asked.

It took ten minutes to lay it out in a light that wouldn't sketch Canfield as a dimwit. That was the stickiest element of this case—aside from getting hanged—keeping my clients from sounding like bugs. "It's really quite a romantic notion," I concluded.

Amid the noise and candlelight, green-eyed Rhonda gazed at me for several long beats before she spoke. I had the feeling she wanted to be amused, but wasn't sure it was suitable. "So these guys all went to Wilson High? What are their names?"

"Jimmy Canfield. He's the one who wants to date you. Floyd Boyd. Rex Ronquist. And Denny McCallum."

"And who are their dreamgirls? These other ladies. Tell me their names."

"They won't mean anything."

"Then you won't lose anything by telling."

"Jo Schwantz Brown. Yourself. Eartha Braintree. And a woman named Abigail Huntington, now Abigail Hayden."

"Not Susie Capshaw?"

"Who's that?"

"Just somebody from school."

"Why would she be included, do you think?"

"No reason. She was cute was all. A lot of guys liked her. But wait a minute. I knew a Jo at the University of Washington. I wonder if it's the same one? About my age? I only went there a year before I transferred. She go to the U?''

''Jo Corelli would have been her name.''

''You're kidding! That was it! That's whose dreamgirl now? Jo Corelli? I can't believe I knew her. Oh, this is weird.''

''Boyd's.''

''Can you believe this? Now, a couple of these guys I remember. Denny McCallum, huh-uh. I think he was a nerd in high school. Was he? Floyd was on the student council with me. Jimmy Canfield used to hang around with Floyd, you know, just to be with one of the cool guys. Except he never quite made the grade. He used to do things like see how much beer he could drink at a school dance or park one of the teacher's cars in the girl's locker room. Fell off the ferry on our prom cruise. A little wild. I remember afternoons he was forever going off to the golf course by the drive-in for fistfights. I wonder how much he's changed.

''Ronquist was real quiet, went out with one of the other cheerleaders for a while. Marsha Vaughn. There was a big deal for a few weeks during our senior year because everybody thought he knocked her up and they were going to get married. The rumor was she got an abortion up in Seattle. 'Course, they were illegal and dangerous then.

''I saw Marsha in New York a few years ago for lunch. She said high school had been the highlight of her life, that it had all been downhill after that. Can you imagine life being downhill from the age of seventeen? Christ, I didn't figure out what I was about until my mid-twenties. She married some guy who sold electronics and wore this little rug down low on his forehead. Still in Tacoma, ten blocks from where she was raised—had come out here for a convention. I don't know. High school was okay, but things have definitely gotten better. I mean, I'm not even going to the reunion. Would have been this year.''

''Early June. Jimmy was disappointed you didn't show.'' Her cheeks flushed with color. I was beginning to think she cared more about the past than she wanted to admit.

"What about the others? Did they go to the reunion?"

"I believe so."

"I should have, but what was the point? I've kept in touch with a couple of girlfriends, but that's enough. So who's Floyd's dreamgirl?"

"You thinking about accepting the offer? It's Canfield, you know, who wants the date with you. Not Floyd."

"Floyd and I dated in school. I thought he was a little self-involved then, and I don't imagine he's improved much. Selfishness isn't a trait you customarily outgrow, do you think?" She pondered what she had said. "He was actually quite the cad. He'd try to have sex with you, and if you wouldn't, he'd tell everybody you did anyway. It wasn't that big a deal though, because I'm not sure many people believed him. God, the teachers adored him, though. He could certainly snow the old farts."

"So what do you think about Canfield?"

"Ummmm. I don't know. You're right. It is kind of romantic. I mean, this should be a 1938 Fred Astaire flick. Will I do it? It's kind of nuts. What do I tell Mom? I'll be flying out for a few days because I got a scholarship to avalanche-control school?" She laughed.

Rhonda was crinkling her eyes at me, and I was having a hard time telling what that meant. She was a healthy woman. Full of joy. A fast talker. Quick on the uptake. Generous with her emotions. Yet her history belied the calm, sensible presence in front of me. When confronted with that sort of dichotomy, I usually went with the history. "You're lucky you came to Philadelphia tonight. It's practically my only night off." She laughed. "So these guys are all well-off? I mean, to be hiring a private detective and having him zip all over the country to arrange dates."

"They're doing okay."

"Who's Denny McCallum? I'll have to get my high school yearbook out when I get home and look him up. No. Tell me about Canfield. He's the one who sent for me, right?"

"Canfield works for an insurance company. Keeps himself in shape. A softball fanatic. Was married once. No kids. He wanted kids and she didn't. That was part of the reason for the breakup.'' I shrugged. ''He's got a great laugh. It's high-pitched and sounds like a society matron who just had a drunk fall into her lap. It kind of sneaks up on you.''

''What about Floyd? What's Floyd up to these days?''

''Boyd's running for state representative. What they call a shoo-in.''

''I wonder if he remembers me?'' She gave me a look. ''Darn. Maybe I should have gone to the reunion.''

''He was married and lived in Utah for a while. He's got one daughter around eleven who lives there with her mother.''

''And these guys must all have some sort of wager going to see who nails his dreamgirl first, correct? I mean, Thomas, I don't want to fly out there just to tell some lunkhead I'm not going to be a piece of Kleenex.''

''They do. I don't know about it. Honest.''

''Come on. It's in the Guy Manual. Of course they have a side bet.'' She looked me over earnestly. ''Don't they?''

''I don't think so.''

''One last date as the high school cheerleader? It could be kind of romantic. 'Course, I'm not what I was then.''

''I seriously doubt Jimmy will be disappointed.''

She smiled until her green eyes collapsed into slits. ''Let me think about this.''

I paid up, left a tip, and, Rhonda clutching my arm, elbowed through the noisy crowd onto South Street. When we got to the sidewalk, she said, ''Walk you back to the Sheraton?''

''Sure.''

We were strolling north along dark, cobbled streets. ''I was just wondering. How many of these women have agreed?''

''One.''

''I hate to say this, but it sounds like fun. Would I meet the others?''

''They're dying to meet you.''

''There's just one thing. I want to bring my own chaperon. It sounds like a blast, and I'm sure nothing outrageous is going to happen, but my cousin. He's into martial arts. I'd just like him along."

"That can be arranged."

"So what are you getting out of all this?" Rhonda asked.

I smiled. "Fees I don't want. Headaches I don't need. Conversations in the night with beautiful strangers."

We had drinks in the spacious atrium lobby of the Sheraton, Rhonda more white wine, lemonade for me. We sat beside a huge planter and talked gibberish, about the differences between Philadelphia and Seattle, the East Coast and the West, about high school and life. She stared at me with bedroom eyes, I thought, but then, sometimes white-wine eyes looked like bedroom eyes. After last night's adventure, I wasn't ready to venture into the world of casual sex so soon, or ever.

At eleven o'clock I said, "I thought you had a date tonight."

"Canceled it after you dropped by. My cousin, you know. There's something you should know about him. His name is Tony. He's a cross-dresser."

"You mean . . . ?"

"Spends most of his time in women's clothes. Been going through the operations. Is he okay to be my guardian?"

"No problem." It was just after midnight when I hailed her a cab and gave the driver a twenty. She kissed my cheek.

Ten minutes later, lying in bed in a dark room, I picked up the phone and dialed.

"It's me, sister."

"Thomas? Why the call?"

"Just wanted to talk."

"We talk every day."

"Not this day."

"Why did you really call?"

"I just said."

She thought about that. "Good. Then I want to talk, too. You find her?"

"Coming out Saturday. Bringing her cousin in drag."

"Weird. What's she like?"

"She kissed my cheek."

"Is she absolutely gorgeous?"

"Not as gorgeous as you."

"So why was she kissing your cheek?"

"No idea."

"Like hell. What time is it out there?"

"Twelve-thirty. How are the girls?"

"Chugging along. Morgana's learning magic tricks from some old books I had. Keeps trying to fool Amber. So far, it's been no go. McCallum approached me today. He wants some of his money back because his date didn't work out. I said no soap."

"Good for you."

"Thomas? Anything wrong?"

"Not a thing."

"Later, Cisco."

"Hasta la vista, Pancho."

22

WHEN I DEPLANED, THE THREE OF them were lined up in the terminal in pigtails and whiteface. Amber galloped higgledy-piggledy through the crowd and rocketed into my arms. "Did you find my mommy?" Amber asked without hesitation.

Kathy and I exchanged looks. "Not yet. But I will."

Kathy had canceled all her appointments for the day except one, which she told me about as she scoured her face in my bathroom sink. I was across the hall on the bed, watching her sinewy backside.

"Don't you think it's about time we have a meeting with Gary Glenn?" she asked, burbling into the sink. "I'm curious about why he was getting information on Jo from her doctor. Aren't you?"

"Yeah, but I don't think he'll talk."

"And if he knows anything about those three pigs in Oregon."

"Well, let's see him then. Feel him out."

"Four o'clock. I made the appointment already. He thinks it's some civil case he worked on." She plied her face with a towel and examined me with only her brilliant eyes showing above the raspberry-colored fabric.

"You want to go like that?" I asked. She was wearing pigtails, no makeup, silver Lycra tights, and a top in hot pink. "You look like you're ten years old."

"Catch him off guard."

Still in whiteface, the girls were glued in front of my television in the front room, which I thought was a bit peculiar since they weren't TV leeches. They were watching the dusty tapes Floyd Boyd had loaned me of their mother doing the PBS pledge drives. Sitting cross-legged, hands folded as though at a prayer service.

The meeting was to be in a sandwich shop in Gilman Village in Issaquah. Glenn lived on the Plateau in one of those moribund projects that were decimating the forest. On the way Kathy said, "So what's the scoop on your blind date?"

"Tiffany and I made it through the evening without throwing sharp objects."

"I spoke to her yesterday. She was fairly noncommittal when I asked how it went. Thomas? You're blushing. You never blush. What happened? You blew it, didn't you?"

"Don't let your imagination get away from you, little sister."

She laughed a laugh that assured me I would never have any secrets from her.

The Garden Sandwich Shop was a thoroughly unpretentious little eatery with tiny tables, pink accoutrements, overhead fans, and a row of square windows at the north end overlooking the parking lot. Shrimp sandwiches and seltzer water. A watercolor print of Marie Antoinette's Summer Cottage on the wall.

At twenty-five minutes past four Kathy bustled over and met him at the entrance. He had two friends with him. All three of them were cops. You could tell.

When they drew close, I could see the karate calluses on his knuckles hadn't gotten any prettier. All three of them were muscled, and all three had calluses. Any one of the three matched the third man in Oregon. I looked Glenn over carefully. He was wearing a bullet-proof vest. I wondered if he always wore it off-duty, but then, Glenn had been nearly murdered off-duty by armed robbers at Salty's on Alki, so I guess he wasn't taking any chances. He was bigger than I remembered, almost my height but carrying an extra forty pounds.

Gary Glenn almost smiled when he saw me.

He was the kind of guy who would break his grandmother's fingers during a handshake, so I was as happy as he to skip the amenities. Kathy said, "Sit down?"

"Not going to stay that long." Glenn peered around the room. He was wearing slacks, loafers, and a windbreaker. His gun was in the back of his waistband. The creases in his slacks were about as subtle as neon tubes. I could see hanger marks. His two friends hung back and pretended not to be interested in the proceedings, though I sensed this was a facade.

"Not working today?" I asked.

"Wednesdays and Thursdays off."

"How're they treating you?"

"Pretty damn good. Should have stayed on."

"Not bloody likely."

Kathy said, "The reason we wanted to meet with you has to do with a woman named Jo Brown. You might know her under the name of Schwantz. She was beat up pretty severely by her ex-husband a couple of weeks ago and is apparently hiding out from him now. We're trying to contact her regarding a legal matter."

"Who told you that?"

"Which?"

"That her ex beat her up?"

Kathy glanced quickly at me, pigtails whipping her face with the swiftness of her movement. I said, "Witnesses."

"Better check your facts, ladies and gents."

"Why? What do you know about it? Did you investigate the beating?"

"Just check your facts."

His face was puffy, the shock of black hair thick and well-groomed, his eyes little blue nuts. He spoke with a slow, cold, deep authority, as if he'd never been mistaken about anything in his life. He kept reconnoitering Kathy's body in a way that made her fidget.

"You were asking about her at her doctor's office, weren't you?" I said. "We just want to know what's going on."

He glowered, shifted his weight, and glanced at a weary young waitress wiping tables. It was past closing, but she was too timid to throw us out. "An exchange of information. Is that it?"

"Why not?"

"Because you don't have anything to exchange."

Kathy shifted. "What makes you think it wasn't her ex-husband who beat her up? We have unimpeachable witnesses who say it was." Glenn turned to her and grew silent. Nobody could hold his peace better than a cop.

"It's true," I said. "We find him, we'll pin it on him. Noooo problem."

"You lure me here under false pretenses and then you expect me to feed you information like some rookie with wet diapers. Get lost." He turned for the door.

"You don't have anything to lose here, Gary," I said.

"Look," said Glenn. "I've got my ducks lined up in a row, and you'd better not scare them away. Don't spoil things."

"You know anything about a hanging in Oregon a few weeks back?"

Without replying, Gary Glenn and his friends strode out of the shop to a late-model Chevy Blazer. Kathy said, "It's possible he was the third man. We had the talker. The guy who was all nervous. And the guy who did the shooting. It could have been him."

"Him or one of his friends."

"He was looking at your neck, Thomas."

"That makes us flush. I was looking at his."

In the truck Kathy said, "When you were gone back East, I checked out Glenn with Ralph Crum. There wasn't anything that would have officially tied Glenn in with Jo Brown. No case that he might have been working."

"Didn't think there would be. Did Crum mention how much trouble Glenn was in?"

"From what I hear, he's on the verge of being thrown off the force. And I thought somebody said he was a loner. So who were those other two guys with him?"

"Cops."

On the way home I stopped and made some calls. Anthony Hallinan, Jo's landlord, still wasn't back from vacation. Cassie had taken a trip herself, but had left a message for me that she hadn't had any luck tracking Randolph Schwantz.

We stopped at a video store before returning to my bungalow. Neither girl had ever seen a western, and I was determined to rectify their misfortune. We started out with *Red River*. Morgana dragged out her little notebook and scribbled memorable lines, tongue dabbing at the side of her mouth as she penciled. From John Wayne: "There's quitters to be buried. I'll read over 'em in the morning." From Walter Brennan: "Funny. Funny what the night does to a man. They're all right during the day."

Later, putting the girls to bed in Kathy's apartment, I caught Amber uttering a prayer. "Dear God," she said. "Help me seem better than I really am. Okay?" Then she unclasped her hands, looked up at me, and winked. "Pretty slick, huh?"

23

JIMMY CANFIELD WAS TRYING ALOOF on Rhonda.

He wasn't meeting her until that night.

He had sent a limousine to the airport to pick her up and take her and her escort to the Four Seasons Olympic downtown, was planning to dine that night at Ray's Boathouse at Shilshole Marina, where they could watch the evening fishing boats under the sunset. Jimmy reasoned that a sampling of saltwater and a smattering of seafood would help sway Rhonda into moving back to the Northwest. Jimmy was in insurance, and liked to work the odds.

I dusted off my suit and slipped on a yellow tie Kathy had given me.

The Four Seasons Olympic had been erected in 1924, the Italian Renaissance lobby graced with magnificent chandeliers and a second-floor balcony all the way around. Out-of-towners used the entrance on University Street next to Abercrombie and Fitch. Native Seattleites used the older and more direct entrance a block south on Seneca.

It wasn't until I went through the lobby of the Olympic that I knew I'd been followed. Gary Glenn. I thought I'd seen his Blazer behind me on the street. He spotted me spotting him and ducked back outside. When I got out to the street, he was driving away.

Only Floyd Boyd had skipped the meeting, off at some political fund-raiser.

I rendezvoused with them at six-thirty downstairs in Shuckers. Rhonda Yellowknife, Jimmy, Denny, and Rex. Also in attendance was her cross-dresser cousin, Paris London, otherwise known as Tony. Jimmy Canfield was in a tux. Denny McCallum, still grousing about getting reimbursed for his failed date, nodded grudgingly at me, as did Rex Ronquist, who was half-swacked. All the men wore suits save Paris London, who wore a slinky red skirt and ivory silk blouse combo. Paris had a pretty face and about ten pounds of blond hair brushed off to one side. He gave me an endless, lingering look. It would have made my teeth tingle if I hadn't known there was a pecker under the skirt.

Rhonda was huddled at the end of the bar with Jimmy Canfield. Denny and Rex were flirting with Paris London, who was sitting on a barstool exhibiting enough rounded thigh for a Volkswagen full of fan dancers. Paris was softer and prettier than I would have thought, an accomplished coquette, and I could see by the aggressive flirtation that was taking place neither Denny nor Rex had guessed the undeclared.

Taking me aside to a table in the corner, Rhonda said, "I don't think I'll need Tony with me at dinner. He's having a pretty good time right where he is. And you don't have to bother either. Really. It's the first time he's been out of town as a woman. She, I mean. This is not what I imagined. The other day, I don't know, I suspect I got a little paranoid. I tend to do that. Thinking of all the ulterior motives this could be about and blah, blah, blah."

"Such as?"

"Oh, nothing to bother your head over. I was wondering . . ." She wore a simple black dress with a scoop neckline, the color setting off her skin tones and red hair to a breathtaking effect. "They were saying you're an ex-cop?"

"Um-hmmm."

"Any reason you didn't tell me that in Philly?"

"I didn't tell you a lot of things. That I never eat the brown

M&Ms. That I never wear mittens. That my dentist is a woman.''

"I've got a couple of questions I've wanted to ask a cop for a while. Or a lawyer. Mind?''

"Nooooo problem.''

"There's no statute of limitations for murder, is there?''

"Nope.''

"What if it's a death, and it might be murder but it might be manslaughter? I'm writing a short story about something, and I need to find this out.''

"I'd have to know the circumstances.''

"But people don't get much time these days, do they?''

"Manslaughter? A typical sentence might average thirty-one to forty-one months.''

"What about running over somebody with a car?''

"Now you get into vehicular homicide. Maybe even first-degree murder. Depends.''

"Well, let's say it was an accident.''

"Reckless driving. Maybe vehicular homicide.''

"There a statute of limitations on vehicular homicide?''

"Now, that, I doubt even a filing deputy in the Prosecutor's Office would know off the top of his head. You're not writing a story.''

"Sure I am. Well, not really. It's something . . .'' She glanced around the room. "Something Tony got mixed up in. Don't worry. He didn't do anything.''

"I work with a dynamite defense attorney.''

"Naw. This was all back there. Besides, he found out I told you, he'd kill me.'' Rhonda crinkled up her nose, nudged my shoulder with it, squeezed my biceps, and was off with Jimmy Canfield. Her hair had fallen across my arm for a moment. She smelled like a good time.

Denny McCallum had lost count of the bourbons by the time he sashayed over to my table. With my escort assignment canceled, I was at loose ends. Kathy was out on the town with Philip, and the girls were staying overnight with some neighbor kids they had quickly become pals with. I was in a suit on Saturday night with ten dollars in my pocket, no ring on my finger, and not a thing to do. Denny was in the same predicament, except he was half-juiced.

"How about you and me kind of sneak around and pick up some girls?" Denny said.

"Maybe tomorrow night."

"Tomorrow's Sunday."

"Better make it next week, then. What's the matter with Paris over there?"

"Rex seems to be more her type. I'm not anybody's type. You ever get that feeling? No. You wouldn't. I don't think I'm anybody's type. I think maybe I should go back to the wife. What's your opinion?"

"Up to you." I sipped a Shirley Temple Rhonda had bought me. She thought it sweet that I didn't drink.

"Penny calls twice a day, did you know? Just to see how I am. Doesn't want a divorce. I know she doesn't."

"What do you want?" I was watching Paris London and Rex Ronquist at the bar, giggling, their noses moving closer and closer over their drinks.

"I don't know what I want," said Denny. "We got all sloppy at the last Yellow Dog Party. All of us. Talking about what it's like to have different women. You know what it's like. You're single. Been married?"

"Actually, no."

"A guy like you. I bet you had your share. That lawyer lady. Others."

"Let's leave my sex life back at the ranch with the polo ponies, okay?"

"Know how I met Penny? My best friend's sister. Floyd's sister. Floyd Boyd's my brother-in-law. Think about it. I never went out with hardly anybody except Penny. I been to bed with two other women. Both hookers. I don't know. I guess there was really nothing wrong with our marriage, it just seemed like I should be doing something else, know what I mean?

"Floyd screwed everything. Me? I couldn't touch a chair a girl had been in without busting into a sweat. Once, back in high school, me and Rex saw some girls in a Mustang, us driving my old man's Pontiac Lemans, and Rex started making signs at 'em and stuff, and they waved and took off, so we followed 'em, chasing all over town. Ended up in a ditch down off of Bantz Boulevard. Scratched the car up good. Had to get towed out. Man, did I catch hell, my old man waving a deer rifle in my face. He wanted to make me swallow the keys. If my mother hadn't stopped him, they'd still be in my intestines.''

"I didn't realize you and Floyd were related."

"Nobody talks about it much since the split with Penny."

Out of the side of my eye I watched Rex and Paris London leave the room together.

"Know how many dates I had before Penny?" McCallum asked. He'd dragged out a comb and tidied up his thinning hair. "Penny was the only girl I'd ever been around didn't make my guts all knot up. A guy like me just needs some experience under his belt, don't you know? That's a funny one. A guy like me, thirty-eight years old and only been to bed with the one woman. Twice with them hookers, but that doesn't count. In my whole life, the one woman!"

"A lot of people would call that idyllic," I said.

"Besides my mother-in-law, name one."

"Me. A lot of people."

"But you've been to bed with a lot of gals?"

"I'm not single because it's more fun. I'm single because it's what I'm stuck with."

"You know, seems like that Yellow Dog Party *always* stirs something up. Rex and Jimmy both got divorced after one of our parties. And now me. I couldn't believe how strange it was being with another woman. I mean, I love Penny, but it was just that the experience, I don't know. And now Penny calls me up every day. And you know what?"

"What?"

"We talk for hours. She misses a day, I get lonely. But don't you think it's kind of embarrassing to go back? Like I made a nincompoop of myself?"

"People split up and get back together all the time. Besides, don't you know what you just said? You said, 'I love Penny.' ''

"Did I?"

"Sure did."

Denny sipped his drink, dabbled with the tumbler on the tabletop, then peered around the room, blowing air through his gapped front teeth. "That Eartha woman from the King-dome really didn't work out. I didn't even like her. Didn't think she'd be like that. I thought she looked like Princess Grace, as if she never peed in her life. You should have heard her mouth. It was 'fuck' this. 'Fuck' that. Penny would have died. Know when I think about Penny most?"

"Nights."

"Did I already tell you that?"

"Stab in the dark."

"You think I should go back to her, don't you?"

I shrugged. "I think if you love someone, and they love you, you should be with them."

"It'd sure as heck save a bunch in expenses."

"How long have you been separated?"

"The day after you said you'd take this case." McCallum swigged the remainder of his drink. "Pretty dumb, huh? I don't know what I thought was going to happen. You know, Penny spends about fifteen minutes a day crying on the phone. Maybe she really loves me. Do you think? You know, like in the movies. That kind."

"Uh, maybe it's even better than that kind."

Forty minutes later Rex Ronquist strutted down the steps into Shuckers, spotted us, and sat down at the table. His smile would have lit up the White House Christmas tree. His tie was missing, lipstick down the side of his mouth, over his collar, on one cheek. A man smeared by wantonness.

McCallum was grinning. Ronquist was grinning harder. I was smiling so hard I thought my lips were going to rip.

"Man," Ronquist said, adjusting his glasses. "That Paris is some hungry broad. Took me upstairs to show me this Cascade Suite Jimmy put them up in. A thousand and ten dollars a night. There's a vase in there Paris says costs more than my Jag. So we're in there and before I know it, she's got my unit in her mouth." He laughed. Jealous as hell, Denny McCallum guffawed, too. I laughed until I thought I was going to rupture every hollow organ in my system.

Finally Ronquist and McCallum caught on that I was finding more humor in this situation than was appropriate, their laughter skidding to a slow halt. Still smiling, Denny and Rex had to ask, "What's the matter?" three times.

Backhanding tears from the corners of my eyes, I said, "I apologize. I shouldn't be amused by this. I don't know what's wrong with me."

"I don't either," said Ronquist, butting his glasses higher with one finger and running a cupped hand across his skull. "I just got the best blow job of my life." He grinned widely.

"Don't be shy," McCallum said, wickedly. "Tell us how she was."

"Ferocious. That's how she was."

We all laughed again. I said, "You mean that's how *he* was."

Ronquist's smile began to decay as he gulped down his bourbon. "What do you mean, *he*?" Ronquist tried to knot his tie, found it missing, then took a napkin and began skinning lipstick off his face. "What the hell are you trying to say? That's all woman up there. All woman."

"How much did you see?"

"Well, she's got knockers out to here. Man, she's beautiful. Looked like a goddamned *Penthouse* centerfold."

"Modern science."

"She gave me a blow job. . . ."

"So you said."

McCallum made a retching sound and laughed experimentally. Rex could have been back in Vietnam staring over the sights of his M-16. "I'm going up there and see. God, she told me to come back after I'd recharged my batteries. Said she'd be waiting with nothing on but the radio. I know she swiped the line from Marilyn Monroe, but she had me going."

"His name is Anthony, and he really is Rhonda's cousin."

"Come on. Gimme a break."

"No, really. He's a karate artist. You don't need that kind of aggravation."

McCallum said, "What? Did he just unbuckle your pants, or did the two of you talk about it for a while? I want to know how these things work. Were you guys talking dirty? Just normal? Fess up."

"I should have known," Ronquist said, disgustedly. "Paris London? Who's got a name like that except . . ."

"Now, now," I said.

He gave me a long, slow look, his head almost on the table. "Man, you just wrecked my whole week."

All three of us contemplated the predicament, then burst into laughter, Rex included. We had dinner at Shuckers. Before we finished our oysters, I said, "Who really started this dreamgirl stuff? I never have figured that out."

"Why, it was Jimmy," said Ronquist. "He wanted Rhonda Lastusky so bad he could taste it. No, wait, then Floyd started talking about the woman from PBS. Then Denny here did. We each had a dreamgirl. Actually I had about four picked out. Then Denny boy here was saying we should find them. We should all find them."

McCallum left Shuckers early without paying. He'd done the same thing at one of our earlier meetings. Half an hour later I said good night to a somber Rex Ronquist on Seneca in front of the cabstand.

"When you going to find my girl?" Ronquist asked.

I thought about Abigail Hayden in San Diego, on the Parks board, the concert steering committee, the Zoo review. I thought about Abigail Hayden taking Rex apart bone by bone.

"You know, you got me reduced to having my unit serviced by a guy?" He grinned until I laughed. "So where is she?"

"Soon."

I walked to the downtown Metro cinemas and watched a Woody Allen movie, *September*. Gary Glenn wasn't following me anymore, and I wondered if he was just playing the suspicious cop, or if he was linked somehow to the three pigs. Back at the hotel, I took the escalator up from the University Street entrance and used a house phone to dial 1120, the Cascade Suite. When nobody answered, I spoke to an attractive black woman at the desk who told me someone had gone up to the suite not long ago.

I took the elevator to the eleventh floor and found 1138, the adjoining bedroom, at the northeast corner of the building.

The carpets were thick enough to muffle trotting horses. Nobody answered.

I went around the corner to the deep-set entrance to the Cascade Suite. Music leaked out through the cracked-open door. Mendelssohn. The door was unlatched. I might have knocked except there were dark, smudged fingerprints on the cream color of the door. As if someone had reached around from inside. Blood.

I pushed the door open with the toe of my shoe.

24

I FACED A LARGE ROOM CHOCK-FULL of antiques, oil paintings, and rugs from exotic climes. To my right ran a long corridor, a row of closet doors flanking one side, and on the other side a single closed door. Possibly a bedroom. Dark droplets tracked the expensive carpet in random splotches.

The staff at the Olympic was not going to be pleased.

As far as I could tell, I was alone.

I sealed the front door and began wandering through the suite. I passed through the foyer and into the palatial sitting room. A formal dining room with a rosewood table and chairs for twelve abutted the south end of the room. The paintings on the walls were English landscapes and portraits of Dutch gentlemen. A kitchen nook led off the dining room. I pulled open a pantry door, empty, then drifted into the nook, flipped a light switch. A door in back of the kitchen led back around into the corridor where the droplets had stained the carpet.

Searching for bedrooms or bleeders, I went back the way I'd come. North of the main doors was a small area with a writing desk and a pair of love seats. Dual coat closets, each vast enough for children to camp in.

The smudges on the entrance door were heavier on the inside. I tried to trace the droplets, but they didn't seem to form any path. I tried a door on the left. Another closet. I tried the next door on the left. More hangers. The next. It was the other side of the door to the back of the kitchen where I had been a minute earlier.

I proceeded down the corridor and opened the only door on the west side of the hall. Tile and mirrors. A bathroom.

I found the switch, flipped the light, and my heart skipped.

Her hair was splayed out on the floor as if for a fashion layout. Except for off-white garters, red stockings, and the red stiletto heels, she was nude. One of her shoes was half-off. Her torso was twisted, legs to one side, spine flat, her gray-blue eyes staring up at me. Her breasts were aimed at the ceiling, as full as science and cockeyed chromosomes could accomplish.

The male apparatus between her legs hadn't been altered yet.

The bullet hole in her breastbone was downright depressing.

I was standing on her hair. Just the three of us. Mendelssohn, me, and a dead man who had wanted to be a woman. I stepped out and peered down the hall, walked back to the front door, pulled it open, and glimpsed empty hotel corridors.

Back in the bathroom, I knelt and took Paris London's pulse at the carotid artery. His narrow gray eyes were fixed. The tiny trickle of blood on his pale breastbone appeared to have dried a while back. I didn't expect much and found less. He was warm, but tacos were warm.

The shower had been running earlier. And I smelled an odor of smoke. It took a while to find the smattering of ash at the base of the commode. Kneeling, I lowered my face to study it. Charred bits from an old newspaper clipping. Mere fragments. Someone had flushed the remnants down the toilet.

I closed the bathroom door on Paris, but not without staring at my own face in the mirror. The blank expression reminded me of another time in my life, when I was a uniformed cop and discovered three bodies in a vacant house. I'd stared into a mirror that day, too. I hadn't known what I was looking for that day, and I didn't know now. Maybe I was just checking to be sure I was still on the convenient side of eternity.

Was Rex Ronquist angry enough to have doubled back and shot him? Down on the street Ronquist had seemed resigned, laughing about it. I switched off the bathroom light. Since entering the suite, I hadn't heard a sound except the Mendelssohn and my own breathing. An occasional heartbeat in my ear. But there were a thousand hidey-holes in this maze.

At the dark south end of the corridor I found a door that led into a closet-sized room with nothing in it but another door of the same size. The adjoining bedroom, wherever it was, had, until now, escaped me. This had to be it. I turned the knob, stupidly prepared to duck bullets.

All the lights were blazing. I pushed the door open.

A four-poster bed stood against the opposite wall. An armoire had been rifled, the drawers hanging out like loose teeth. I searched quickly, and found nothing but one huge bathroom with a five-man tub and a shower enclosure. A phone on the wall. It looked as if Rhonda and Tony were sharing this bedroom, and Rhonda had packed and bolted. The clothing I saw was clearly Paris's. But there was only the one bed.

I opened every door and cupboard in the place, adrenaline pumping through my veins so urgently I was ill with it. I hadn't been ready for this. It wasn't until I got all the way back into the enormous living-room suite and was popping closet doors one by one that I stumbled upon the other one. Paris in the bathroom. This clown in the closet.

He was balled up inside a small pantry at the north end of the suite's sitting room. He'd been shot, probably at the same time as Paris/Tony. Or within minutes. Probably in the bathroom, too. There had been more blood on the tiles than Paris London's wound would have produced.

My guess was he'd started to exit, then reconsidered, leaving a couple of fast-drying crimson handprints on the front door. Maybe he had seen somebody in the corridor. Heard something. Perhaps he'd just panicked, the way a child who has been hurt and who is alone panics. Looking for a burrow.

His plump body was heaped into a corner of the otherwise-empty closet as if the cleaning lady had stored him there. He wore black socks with dress garters. Undershorts on backward and inside out, streaked with bloody fingerprints.

Denny McCallum.

His hair was neatly combed. As usual. I thought he had been going back to Penny. He must have detoured upstairs. First a free blow job, and then patch up the marriage.

I counted four bullet holes. One over his right nipple. One beside his navel. That one had bled. His hands clotted with it. One through his left biceps. And one that had punctured his cheek. Blood had trickled out between his lips. It had been a small-caliber handgun. Or maybe McCallum was just tougher than a widow with six kids. His clothes were knotted under one leg, as if he'd dropped them when his strength gave out.

His eyes were closed. I touched him for pulses and found nothing.

In the main drawing room I located a phone and slumped down on an expensive divan. Then the clouds of officialdom began raining down. The medics to ascertain death. The uniformed cops. The hotel dick. The night manager. A janitor. More cops. The medical examiner's investigator. Finally they posted a guard, and the stream of gawkers thinned.

Before they hauled the bodies away, one of the detectives came to me with a tiny device he'd picked up from beneath a lamp. "Recognize this?" he asked.

"It's a bug."

"Know anything about it?"

"I just got here."

"How long have they been in the suite?"

"This was their first night."

"Probably somebody from before. A lot of important business meetings take place up here. Millions of dollars change hands. Industrial spies would go to a lot of trouble to hear what goes on up here.''

"Got to be,'' I said. "I don't see how it could be related to this.''

Jimmy Canfield and Rex Ronquist were both at home, but both willingly drove back to the Olympic to field questions. Jimmy said he had dropped Rhonda off half an hour before I discovered the bodies. Tomorrow they were planning a car trip to the San Juan Islands. He had left her at the outer door to the bedroom. One chaste kiss. Hadn't been inside the suite since before six when he, Paris, Rex, Denny, and Rhonda had all been up here for a few minutes.

Rex Ronquist was a different story. After leaving the Olympic, he had killed time in a neighborhood tavern in Kirkland. No, he hadn't driven there directly, had cruised around the lake for an hour first, brooding about what had happened to his manhood. He admitted to me that the incident with Paris London had shaken him. The police found out about it not from me but from Ronquist himself, who falsely assumed I had told them everything. He started making alibis, and ended up revealing the entire episode. They thought about holding him that night on suspicion of murder, but they realized they were going to need a stronger case first. A motive was one thing, but this one needed buttressing. I noticed London's death didn't seem to upset Ronquist in the least.

In the lobby Ronquist said, "I don't think they're going to be leaning on Jimmy that hard, do you?''

"Jimmy? It's you they're going to go after. After you ratted on yourself about getting the blow job.''

"Well, it's just, I thought with his record, the cops would be on him. But that's not necessarily true, is it? I hope it isn't. I mean, he was with Rhonda when it happened, wasn't he?''

"Record?'' I felt like a castaway who suddenly heard a slow leak in his air raft. If this ran in the same groove with my recent luck, Canfield was a serial killer.

"I thought you knew about it.''

Ronquist looked up at me innocently. We were standing in

the lobby of the Olympic in a corner near a grandfather clock. It was 3:00 A.M. Ronquist said, "Just a couple of years in Monroe when he was a kid. Some guy cut him off on the exit at Roanoke, and they got out of their cars and had some words."

"Must have been more than words."

"Yeah, well, the other guy took a poke at Jimmy with a tire iron. Jimmy never should have served any time. 'Cept the guy had a car full of eyewitnesses, and they all told it different than Jimmy." Ronquist grinned. "Couple of broken ribs. Knocked out two teeth. Jimmy was a scrapper when he was younger. Had himself a little temper, too."

I said, "You're aware *you* don't have an alibi for the probable time of death."

"I need an alibi?"

"You haven't been paying attention, have you? We all need alibis. For every day of our lives."

"I got nothin' to worry about."

A few minutes later I spoke to Jimmy Canfield next to the clock, the two of us watching couples straggle in, a leggy escort hurriedly leaving the hotel and flagging a cab.

Canfield: "I only want to know where Rhonda is. She has to be around. I left her upstairs. She was going to bed. She was bushed with all the flight time. And what the hell was Denny doing there? One of the cops told me he was naked, for chrissakes. That doesn't sound like Denny. Unless he was making a move on Rhonda. But he was a pretty quiet guy. They *made* him take his clothes off. Hadda be. Somebody was robbing the place. Don't you guess? It had to be some punks setting up what they figured was an easy score. It was just Rhonda's bad luck she was the one staying there."

"You saying you think she's been kidnapped?"

His voice was whiny. "Where else could she be?"

"Hiding."

"Now, why the hell would she do that?"

"It was Rhonda's room. There was a murder in it. Now she's missing. A lot of people are going to think Rhonda killed those two."

"No way. She wouldn't shoot anybody."

"Let's hope you're right."

"I better be right. Hell. I'm going to marry the broad." It wasn't until he was gone that I recognized the fragrance he was wearing. Calvin Klein for Men. The same thing I'd smelled in Oregon just before I got hanged.

Kathy was still stirring downstairs when I got home, lonely because the girls were staying overnight at the neighbor's. She missed little people hogging the bathroom, asking questions, and dripping toothpaste on the sink rim.

She sneaked up the stairs and caught me in a sleeveless T-shirt and dress slacks. The house was warm. Kathy wore only a slip. "Talk?" she said.

"I was hoping you would be awake."

"Were you?"

"We need to say some things."

"Shoot."

She lit some candles, and we sat on the sofa in the living room in the semi-dark. Her hair was still pinned up from a date with the F-person. I watched the angle of her chin in the candlelight. A car passed by outside and brightened the room momentarily. Other than that, the world was asleep.

"I've got things to talk about," she said. "I want advice."

"Want to hear about the murders first?"

"The what?"

I told her what had happened. We discussed contingencies. What could be taking place. "Murder?" Kathy said. "I don't believe it. Do you think this is related to what happened in Oregon? Or the girls?"

"I hope not. I sincerely hope not."

"The lynching? Those were rough guys down there."

"This dreamgirl gig never has seemed right. There's a kink in this thing that I haven't been able to uncover."

Finally the topic cooled, and I said, "What do you want advice on?"

"Just something weird. I don't even want to bring it up now."

"Bring it up."

She shifted, tucking a piece of her slip around one knee. "Philip asked me to marry him."

"Oh?"

"Don't be like that."

"Like what?"

"You know what. This really means a lot to me. Don't ruin it."

"Of course I won't, Kathy. Of course I won't ruin it. He asked you to marry him. I thought he might be working up to that. What did you tell him?"

"I didn't know what to tell him. I told him I needed a week to think it over. He said fine."

"A guy gives you a deadline over a thing like that. I don't know. Sounds pretty damn cocky."

"He didn't give me a deadline. I didn't say he gave me a deadline. *You* said deadline. I asked him if I could have a week to think it over. It was my idea. The week. 'Sure, fine,' he said. He is not cocky."

"What are you going to tell him?"

"You don't like him, do you?"

"Sure. I was going to ask him to join the lodge as soon as he reached his full height."

"Somebody mailed me a clipping about people with two different eye colors, all about genetic mutations. From Ohio or someplace like that. You were behind that, weren't you?"

"Me?"

"Just come out and say it. You don't like him."

"I do, actually. I do like him."

"Mean it?"

"No."

"Damn you."

"I just don't like him with you."

"So I need your permission to date a guy?"

"You're the one who asked."

"Why not? Why don't you like him with me?"

"Because it won't be the same between us if you go off with him."

"You mean this all has to do with you and me? Not me and Philip?"

"You could say that."

"You think our relationship will be different?" She

thought about it. "Well, it might be. And that's important to you?" Kathy stared at me in the semi-dark. Her violet-blue eyes were all pupil. Black as sin.

"You're my best friend, Kathy. I've never known anyone quite like you."

"We won't lose that. You know we won't ever lose that."

"Don't kid yourself."

"I think I love Philip. Thomas? Don't sulk."

He arrived just then, Philip, always showing up at the wrong time. He hadn't dropped her off too long before. Maybe he forgot one of his earrings. Kathy heard his car in the drive, that distinctive purr of a large BMW. I heard it, too. Pretended I didn't. She reached back, flipped open the curtains, and waved him up. Then she arched her body and unlocked the front door without getting off the sofa. That's how big my house is.

It took Philip a few seconds to digest the candles, Kathy in her slip, me in my undershirt, and then to come to terms with it. Too arrogant to be jealous, he smiled at me, touched a finger to his mustache, and nodded weakly at Kathy, who sprang up and gave him a peck.

"I . . ." he said. "I needed to tell you something. I'm sorry. I didn't realize you would be up here with . . ."

"Don't be silly," said Kathy. "You're not interrupting a thing. Is he, Thomas? Thomas?"

"Not a dad-blamed thing."

"Come downstairs, Philip. 'Night."

"Good night, Kathy."

Lieutenant Crum was on duty. I phoned and asked him to check DMV and tell me what vehicles Gary Glenn owned. Also Randolph Schwantz. He called me back a few minutes later. Glenn owned an '86 Blazer and an '83 Corvette. Also a '76 Dodge pickup. Schwantz owned a Chevy van, a Mazda RX7, and an '89 Lincoln Continental.

25

IT WAS OVERCAST. A WARM BREEZE.
We got no further than the sidewalk in
front of the house when Floyd Boyd pulled up in his leased
Chevrolet. He owned a Mercedes 380, as well as a Maserati
convertible, but some whiz on his staff figured that until the
votes were tallied this autumn, Detroit metal.

Kathy, Morgana, Amber, and I waited on the sidewalk
while Boyd got out and straightened his trousers, adjusted
his tie, and palmed the slightly graying hair at his temples.
His daughter, Echo, eyed Morgana curiously through the
closed car window. Morgana returned the look with an
expressive impassivity, if there is such a thing. Morgana
had a way of looking at people.

"Thomas," said Floyd, approaching me in rapid strides.
"Got a minute?"

"Got all day." We stepped aside, and he clasped my
elbow. He smelled boozy, a condition I presumed was left-
over from his campaign party last night.

"Jimmy called me early this morning. Damn it. Denny
was working on my campaign. It's bound to come out in the
newspaper reports."

"Maybe."

"Look, I don't want to seem callous, but Denny is dead,
and nothing we can do will bring him back. I know the last

thing he would want would be for me to lose this election because I got dragged into some slimy sex scandal. I only know what Jimmy told me about this other person who was killed . . . Tony? It was all real sketchy. He was a queer?''

"A budding transsexual.''

"Whatever. What I'm asking isn't all that much, Thomas. I want you to keep my name out of this. All this dreamgirl business, it wouldn't look good.'' He stopped to let that sink in. "No matter how we intended it when we started out, I don't think we'd have the sympathies of the general population. Especially not after last night. And it's not fair. Because you may end up having to lie to the police. But there it is. Circumstances. What are you going to do? Go figure.''

"For starters, I'm not lying to the police, Floyd.''

He gave me a power stare. "I'm not asking you, Black. I'm telling you. Keep my name out of it!'' He started to walk back to the driver's door.

"First, you don't talk to me like that. Second, your name hasn't come into it.'' He came back to me, pretending to be angry. He knew he couldn't cow me, but he had to try. "And neither has this job I'm doing for you four. Come into it. As far as the police are concerned, Rhonda and Paris London were here visiting friends. Flew in from Philly and had drinks with myself, Denny, Rex, and Jimmy. And then Rhonda had dinner with Jimmy. As far as hiding this from the public? That's fine with me, but Rhonda might talk if she shows. And she might be dead. If her body turns up, they'll be digging harder than ever.''

"Those guys that hung you. They did it.''

"Give me a reason, and I'll believe that.''

Boyd began stepping backward off the curb, then back up, looking over at Kathy and the girls who were talking with his daughter. I thought it ironic that he didn't know the girls belonged to his dreamgirl. He was looking at Kathy's white dress.

"Black. For godsakes. Have some pity. We're talking the rest of my career here, over something that started off pretty silly. I mean, they're considering bringing me back in two years and running me in the gubernatorial campaign. And higher if that goes well. I'll be in a position to make some sweeping reforms, Black. And you could help out. Don't think your cooperation wouldn't be appreciated. We don't forget our friends.''

''Supposing the cops get a whiff of what was really going on and I keep mum? Supposing Eartha Braintree sees this in the papers and steps forward and says she had a peculiar date with Denny McCallum, that maybe Denny was having another kind of a funny date with Paris London? What if she tells them she thinks maybe a certain Thomas Black was setting up these funny dates? Or what if Rhonda shows up and spills the beans? These other two guys could implicate you. Jimmy. Rex. It could happen any number of ways. I mean, how many people know about this, between you and Rex, Denny, Jimmy? All the people each of you told. Does Penny know? She'll tell. I'm not going to get caught trying to herd cats.''

Boyd clamped his jaw muscles hard and gave me a hollow-eyed look. Obviously I was bringing up points he had yet to consider. His eyes were puffy. I noticed a patch where he hadn't shaved. ''My daughter's going home in a couple of weeks,'' he said, distracted.

''Echo's a nice kid.''

''Wish I could spend more of my life with her. That your little girl?'' He nodded toward Amber.

''I wish. Wish they both were. We're taking care of them for a friend.''

''Listen, Black. What the hell was going on in that hotel last night?''

''I'm as much in the dark as everyone else.''

''What was Denny doing up there? I can see where this eccentric Paris Whatshisname could get into trouble. Probably picked up a trick in the bar downstairs. Who knows whatall was going on? But Denny? I don't get it.'' I shrugged. I didn't need to defame a dead man. The evidence was there for anyone to kick around. ''Jimmy said Denny was half-naked when you found him. Hiding in a closet? Shot two or three times. God. It's incredible. Did he say anything to you before he died?''

"He was dead when I found him."

"But he must have . . . what? Was he shot in the closet? Why would somebody put him in the closet and shoot him? It just doesn't make any kind of sense. Jimmy and I went over and over it last night on the phone. Denny wouldn't swat a fly. I mean, the guy was scared of his own shadow. Why would anybody shoot him?"

"He was shot in the bathroom with Paris. They were both shot there. All the hits Denny took, if he lay still, it would be natural to assume he was finished. My guess is, the shooter thought they were both dead and was somewhere else in the suite. Denny got up and tried to get away, maybe heard the shooter coming back, and crouched down in the closet intending to wait until the coast was clear."

Boyd considered me. "It must have been terrible for you. This whole weekend."

"I've had worse. And not too long ago."

"It's funny," said Boyd, his tone changing. Floyd was a master of changing gears to get the most mileage out of any social engine. "Everything in your life seems so ordinary, and then all of a sudden your best friend is on the front page in something as bizarre as this. Go figure."

"Go figure. By the way. You knew Rhonda in high school, didn't you?"

"We all knew her."

"You took her out."

"I took out every good-looking girl in high school, Black. It was a thing with me." The breeze seized a tuft of his sandy hair and wagged it down over his brow, making him look, with his horsy mouth and honest, square-jawed face, like a member of the Kennedy clan.

"What happened?"

"I was a kid. Kids don't know what they're doing. I'm sure I talked about myself all night and I'm sure she tried to pretend she was interested and then I tried to get her panties off and then we went home. Typical school date."

"Denny thought you were something. We had quite a long discussion last night after Jimmy and Rhonda went to dinner."

"I thought he didn't say anything to you. I thought he was dead when you found him."

"He wasn't dead at dinner."

"Tell me what he said."

"That he wasn't much in high school. That maybe Penny still loved him. That maybe he should have gone back to Penny. That you had been pretty cool. It made me wonder why you wanted into the dreamgirl shtick in the first place. This dreamgirl stuff was more like what a high school nobody would be doing after he found out he was an all-right kind of guy."

"Nobody's ever certain they're an all-right kind of guy, Black. Nobody."

"You must have been pretty self-possessed in school."

"To Denny it might have looked that way. Underneath it all, I was just another scared kid trying to find himself. You look back and you wonder if you were even the same person. Seems like someone else entirely. Look. I went along with this because I could see how much it meant to Denny and Rex. All right? I can't speak for Jimmy. I guess he could have lived without it, too. Maybe. But Denny and Rex thought something was going to come of this. They really did."

"Look," I said. "I promised the girls we'd go roller-skating this afternoon. Anyway, it just occurred to me that Echo might want to come along. We'd pick her up and drop her back. Around twelve-thirty, one?"

"Sure, Black. Fine. Perfect. One more thing about Denny. A few days ago he said he was beginning to think there was something fishy going on. You know, he was dreadfully disappointed in the way his date turned out."

"I'm not carrying a little bow and arrow. I find the lady and secure the date. The rest is out of my hands."

"I tried to tell him that. But you know how Denny was about money. He figured he'd wasted big bucks on this thing, and he was looking around for someone to blame. Then, too, I think he was getting at a little something more. Did he say anything like that?"

"You mean he thought one of you was doing this for some reasons other than the obvious?"

Floyd Boyd stared at the pavement for a moment. "The thing is, you got hurt, and I have a suspicion it had something to do with the woman from Channel Nine, didn't it? And now this. All connected, isn't it?"

"Doubtful," I said, remembering Rhonda had known Jo at the University of Washington. Perhaps we *were* stacking coincidences a little too high.

Boyd said, "But if Denny was involved in something weird, maybe that's why he was up in the suite. I mean, you guys thought he had gone home, right? Maybe he was up there because he was involved in something clandestine himself."

I made a face. "Like what?"

"Beats me."

"Maybe we should ask her."

"Who?"

"Echo. Ask her if she wants to go skating."

"I guess. Yeah. Sure."

I didn't think Floyd Boyd's world was going to topple, but a politician's career was a ship built with toothpicks and sugary spit, especially a fledgling congressman on the express route to the presidency, which I had a hint was where Floyd thought he was headed. Good for Floyd. Somebody had to be ambitious. It took the pressure off the rest of us.

"Echo," I said, moving to the front of the car. She was hanging out the window, her hair a cute mop, talking to Morgana, who was toeing a weed in the sidewalk. "You like to roller-skate? There's a great little rink out in West Seattle."

On the way to the Ave., the girls walking ahead, Kathy said, "Floyd wanted you to keep him out of it, didn't he?"

"Yeah. What did Philip want this morning?"

"He didn't stay, if that's what you're asking."

"He stayed ten minutes and forty-five seconds."

"What? Thomas! You timed him? That's no fair. A girl should have some privacy."

"This from a woman who escorted a tour group through my bathroom while I was in the tub."

"Don't be silly. That was just Myra and Helen. And they didn't come in."

"Helen came in."

"Well, I didn't tell her to."

"You didn't stop her."

"Yeah, and I think she wants you to ask her out."

"Philip didn't seem at all jealous to find you sitting in the dark on my couch in your slip. Guys that broad-minded piss me off. Nobody should be that tolerant. You sure he's still got both balls?"

"I know he does."

"Ever think there might be something wrong with one of them?"

"Sometimes I think Philip is your Kryptonite."

"You're my Kryptonite, sister. Always have been. Always will be." Kathy smiled. She liked that. Being my Kryptonite.

26

SUNDAY, WHILE THE RADIO STATIONS belabored the murder at the Olympic, we went skating, Kathy, myself, Amber, Morgana, Echo, and the F-person.

Amber made a rolling hop onto the rink as I was helping Echo, took a lap at top speed, whizzed around behind me, and barreled between my legs in a tuck. A cannonball on wheels. All cheesy grin. Braids flying. It was unnerving to see someone that vulnerable and, at the same time, that forceful. Morgana, with her height and long limbs, was as fluid on wheels as she was awkward off. They darted in and out of traffic like gnats while the monitors in black-striped referee shirts tried to whistle them down, then recognized the skill level they were operating at and disavowed the effort. No way were they going to knock into anyone.

Philip wore black pants, a long-sleeved white shirt, and a natty little vest he had probably borrowed from the national champion he was taking lessons from.

We'd been there an hour when I spotted a dead ringer for an older Abigail Huntington of the nude photo. I pointed her out to Kathy. "Thomas. You can't."

"I'm fed up with these guys. Rex finds out and he doesn't like it, let him sue."

"He *will* sue."

"It's too good. Call it a practical joke."

"Call it fraud."

"Let's see what she calls it."

The woman was towing a four- or five-year-old boy around the rink, and, despite her girth, she could skate. After one of her boy's spills, I stopped and helped her pick him up before the rabble rolled over any little fingers. Amber appeared from nowhere and bossed traffic around us, which got the woman laughing.

Minutes later I skated over to help again. "He's like a yo-yo," she said. "Thank you." She had long, frizzy black hair and was dressed in worn jeans and a red T-shirt. I noticed she wore no ring.

Tina Hosty had been divorced three years, clerked in a convenience store in South Park, and took night classes in court reporting. She was intelligent, witty, had a sense of humor and a boy who looked as though he needed a puppy. As I talked to her, Amber and Morgana swooped down and began skating him around the rink, each holding a hand.

After relating the situation, I asked Tina if she didn't mind having a temporary tattoo applied to the top of her left breast to match one that was visible in the nude photo of Abigail Huntington.

"Buddy," she said. "For two grand I'd tattoo the *Encyclopedia Britannica* on my ass. Heaven knows, I got the space.'' She laughed energetically, got me laughing, too. She was a pistol.

During a couples-only session, Amber, Echo, Morgana, and I all sat at the rug-covered benches in the changing area. An old Beatles tune. In the rink Philip was trundling backward in front of a shaky but game Kathy.

Said Morgana, ''I read in the newspaper where something went wrong with this airplane, and a big piece just fell off. A stewardess and one passenger got sucked into the sky.''

''Just sucked out,'' said Amber, fiercely. ''S-u-c-k-e-d o-u-t.''

''What happened?'' asked Echo, all ears.

Morgana said, ''So there's pressure inside a jet, see. Lots of pressure. So on account of the higher you go, the less air there is. So they pump all this air hard into an airplane the higher it goes. Otherwise your head would swell up and your tongue would pop out. So when a door opens up or a window breaks, that pressure just rushes out.''

''Like a balloon,'' said Amber, who had obviously been through the story before.

''I knew that,'' said Echo.

''So a piece of the engine blew up, and it hit this emergency door on the plane and knocked it off. About thirty thousand feet, see. So all this air rushed out, and this stewardess and this passenger got sucked out in the sky.''

''What happened?'' Echo asked.

''They fell,'' said Morgana.

''And they didn't have parachutes,'' added Amber.

''I knew that,'' said Echo.

''It took them sixteen minutes to hit the ocean,'' said Morgana. The girls thought about it, sipping Cokes and chewing hot dogs.

''I knew that,'' Echo repeated.

Later that day I phoned Anthony Hallinan at home and got him to drive down to Pioneer Square to dig out his lease applications. When Jo rented his house, she had been given a glowing recommendation from Esther Hope, her former boss at Papa John's in Tacoma. I looked Esther up in the Tacoma phone book and gave her a jingle.

"Not here," Esther said, as soon as I mentioned Jo's name. "I don't know where she is. And if you come around, I'll have my husband after you with his .30-06."

"Nobody's coming around, Mrs. Hope. If you see her, tell her I'm the private investigator who visited her hospital room in Oregon. Tell her I almost died for her, and that her daughters are staying with me. They're fine. We went roller-skating today. Tell her she can stay in hiding as long as she needs. I just wish she'd call her daughters. I'll give you my number where she can reach them. They're so worried they've stopped growing."

Esther Hope said, "You've got Jo's kids?"

"They miss her and want to talk to her. I know what her husband did to her. Tell her that."

"I just couldn't say where she might be, Black."

"Yeah, well . . ." Perhaps Jo wasn't tucked away in her spare room popping aspirins and watching soaps, but Esther knew.

At home that night while the girls and I sat in front of *Shane*, Alan Ladd chopping on the stump with Van Heflin, the phone rang. "Thomas Black here." Someone was on the line listening to the movie with us, but they refused to answer, and then they were gone. Two minutes later Nanette Corelli from Yreka, California, telephoned.

"She just now called. Wanted to know about the girls. Wanted to know if you really had them. And were they okay. Black. It was my daughter." Nanette Corelli was weeping.

"You just call me a minute ago?"

"I was talking to Jo a minute ago."

"She tell you where she was?"

"Can you believe I didn't even think to ask. You think she's here in town?"

"Probably not, Mrs. Corelli. What did you tell her?"

"I tried to give her your phone number, but she was gone before I could."

When I hung up, the girls were staring at me. "Your mom called Grandma," I said. "She's all right."

"Why didn't she call us?" Amber asked, in a tiny voice.

"You'll be hearing from her. Very soon, I think."

Nobody said another word. They were on a long fall from thirty thousand feet. By ten o'clock, when their mother still hadn't called, they tumbled into their sleeping bags. Neither child looked too cheery.

27

MONDAY MORNING'S CALL FROM KATHY was unexpected. The girls were in the backyard with a magnifying glass canvassing ant routes and waiting for the sun to come out. Judging by the skies, I expected tendrils of smoke by midmorning. Not a good day to be an ant.

"Thomas. I'm off the bus. At a phone booth."

"The sweaty guy?"

"He looks so normal. I know it's him, though. Looks like he's on top of the world. He was walking fast up the Ave., probably late for work, since it was about two minutes past eight, but I managed to keep him in sight. He bought a bagel and went into a building across the street from the Neptune. On the west side of Brooklyn."

"Get his floor number?"

"Six. He was the only one on the elevator."

"You're beautiful, Kathy. Meet me?"

"At the Neptune. Thomas?"

"Eh, Pancho?"

"I don't think you should bring a gun. I just don't think it would be good. You're going to lose your temper around this guy, and I don't think that's something you want to do with that big old .45 in your hand."

"I'll bring cookies. You bring tea. We'll scrounge cups and saucers."

I grabbed a roll of cookie dough out of the freezer and drove the six or seven blocks, parking in the lot behind Pay'n Save on Brooklyn. Kathy met me at the corner of Forty-fifth and Brooklyn in front of the Neptune Theater. She wore a navy pinstripe jacket and skirt. Her dark hair was pulled back, ran down the center of her back in a handsome plait. The diffused light from the clouds worked on the tone of her pale skin. Her eyes were brilliant violet lamps of fear.

"What the hell is that, Thomas?"

"Chocolate-chip cookie dough." She touched it to see if I was telling the truth.

"You're not going to use that. Look," she said. "I don't know what sort of security they've got, but don't you think we should be the tiniest bit discreet?"

"Cookie dough won't bother anyone."

Kathy gave me a look. "Thomas. He doesn't know what I look like. It's you he'll recognize."

"Right."

"I had a few minutes to buy props." She peered into the brown paper sack in her arms, then stooped, untied and partially unlaced my shoes.

"What're you doing?"

Kathy pulled a chocolate éclair out of the bag and jammed it into my mouth. I took a mammoth bite, but she kept pushing, backed me up against the kiosk at the Neptune Theater, and got it on my face.

"What the hell?"

"It'll be perfect. Don't you see? Nobody on earth can do this quite the way you can."

"What are you talking about?"

She tugged a baseball cap on my head backward, pulling tufts of hair out from under the brim, then looped a pencil-

thin necktie around my head and knotted it. She yanked a
handful of shirttail out of my belt, ripped two buttons off,
fastened the rest crookedly, then unzipped me. I tried to grab
her hands, but she was like lightning. She fed a piece of
shirttail out the opening and slammed the zipper on it, then
stuck a crooked pair of woman's tortoiseshell glasses onto the
bridge of my nose. The lenses were so thick I had to peer over
the tops to get across the street. She slapped a Band-Aid
across my nose.

"What do I do best?" I asked, as we walked. "What are
you disguising me as?"

"A blockhead."

"What?"

"You make a perfect blockhead."

"Me?"

"Open your mouth. There. Let your tongue hang off to one
side. Make it all swell up. Good." She dabbed more chocolate
from the éclair onto my shirt. Touched my ear with it.

"I don't want to be a blockhead."

"Next time you say your prayers, ask the big guy. Maybe
he can fix things."

"I'm too mad to be a blockhead. Damn it, Kathy! You be
the idiot for once. I'm just going to bust in there and . . ."
I made a move, but she grabbed the shirt herniating through
my zipper and held me captive.

"Now, now. That's why I want you playing a part. Maybe
you'll forget yourself. It's better to sneak up on this guy, and
you know it. Otherwise the police'll be on you in two shakes.
Good. Distort your jaw. One side. Good. You look like my
high school math teacher."

"I was trying to look like Philip."

"You'll have to grow a mustache and get debonair for
that." Kathy dragged me across the street. One of my hands
was wedged stupidly into my jeans pocket, the other weighed
down by the batch of cookie dough. I stumbled, balked, and
finally let one arm swing unproductively. We were some
sight. Two young men in a Camaro stopped to gawk.

"So I'm a blockhead," I said. "How are we going to work
this? You've apparently given it some thought."

"I'm the rich widow Birchfield. IQ one forty-five, in case you're wondering. No, let's make it one sixty-five. There are a lot of counselors and a couple of psychologists on that floor. I'm hoping he's one. You're my brother. Hit in the head at the age of twelve by a brick that fell off the side of a building while you were peeping into Mrs. Chisolm's shower. Poor dear. You never were the same after. We tape boxing gloves on your hands at night."

"Mrs. Chisolm must have been something, to make me lose my mind."

"It was the brick, dummy."

"What if this bozo's in investments or writes software programs?"

"You should be so lucky. What if he's a karate instructor?"

"The sweaty guy? I watched him in Oregon. He wasn't any karate instructor."

"We'll wing it. You're good at winging it."

"Not as good as you, sister."

We rode the elevator with a majestically coiffed woman in her late forties. I managed to create a minor disturbance and get some of the chocolate onto her tailored suit before she escaped on the fourth floor.

"I'm so sorry," Kathy apologized to the fleeing woman. "I'm just terribly sorry. Will you ever forgive us? I've just checked him out of the hospital for this one visit. I really should have him in a jacket." She slapped me across the face just to show the woman who was in charge. "Gawd, Thomas," she said, when the elevator doors encapsulated us. "I haven't seen anything like that since the *Three Stooges Go to Mars*. What's the matter with you?"

I reached for her, but she slapped my hand away, secretly pleased that I had taken such a keen interest in the part.

Dragging my hunched-over frame by the tie, Kathy peeked into several offices on the sixth floor before she found it. A place called Merit-Corp. I figured they bought small countries from dictators. Or estimated the costs of drilling pipelines in national forests.

We sailed past the receptionist and three women working

at desks, and headed for an office at the back of the room. The sweaty guy was on his feet and moving to throw us out when Kathy smiled. He considered her up and down, then, just a bit testily, said, "May I help you?"

"My name is Katherine Birchfield. I just need a few minutes of your time. I apologize for bringing my brother along. He's not been well." He considered me for a moment. From a hunched position I gave feverish, cringing looks through the Coke-bottle glasses.

"This about the Camden closeout?" he asked. "I was expecting somebody to drop by. But that shouldn't be until tomorrow."

"I've heard you're very good at what you do," Kathy said. The engraved nameplate on his desk read EARLE ROBB. Earle had been the name of one of our assailants in Oregon. "Mind if we close the door?"

"I have a meeting in twenty minutes."

"Tell you what, Earle," Kathy said, in her most seductive voice. "If we can't conclude things this morning, perhaps dinner? Just the two of us. I'll put this idiot back in the home." I shuffled and slobbered. "Calm down, Thomas."

"Sure. Sure." Earle Robb offered her a chair and gave me a contained look. I drooled, breathed heavily, and kept my eyes as jittery as chickadees on a wire.

"Don't mind him," Kathy said. "I got stuck with him for a day."

Earle Robb perched on the lip of his desk, one leg cocked, studying Kathy. Robb had several good-sized moles on a fleshy, sensual face. His suit was new and expensive, and he wasn't sweating the least bit. The flesh hanging below his chin wobbled when he moved. He was about my age. Early thirties. Waiting patiently for his first coronary.

It was a large room with a view to the west, a sofa, a huge desk, and on one wall a map of the world with colored pins in the shape of miniature freighters. I hobbled over between the two of them, scrabbled in her purse, and retrieved some chewing gum. "That him?" I whispered.

She nodded. The dough felt cold and wet now in my grip

as my fingers dug into the cylinder. Nothing made a better
sap than a roll of frozen cookie dough.

"Be sure," I whispered.

"I am sure."

"What are you saying?" Robb asked.

"Mr. Robb. It has come to my attention that you were in
Oregon with some friends a few weeks back."

"What?"

"You kidnapped a couple of people."

"Get out," Robb said, without inflection. "And take the
moron with you."

"You and two other men," said Kathy, calmly. "You
held a clown and a private detective named Thomas Black at
gunpoint for half an hour. You lynched the detective. One of
you tried to take shots at the clown."

Earle Robb burned up a few seconds digesting the change
of direction, then spoke. I couldn't make sense of another
word either of them said. I was back in the murky dusk
outside of Myrtle Creek, pleading for my life, dancing on a
slippery stump while a rope twisted itself around my neck.
And then I was off the stump and swinging, knowing this was
the end. Not guessing. Knowing. I could feel my legs kicking
wildly. Swinging like a pendulum. Tick-tock. Expecting the
pain to go away now that the blackness had come, and the
pain not going away. Tick. Growing worse. Tock. And then
the spinning stars behind my eyes turning colors. And slipping into another kind of delirium, the hurt of knowing my
body was no longer fighting for air.

I turned abruptly and felt out of control as I began to bring
the cylinder of dough down on Earle Robb. Unaccountably,
I switched targets at the last instant and shattered a ceramic
bust, which exploded into hundreds of pieces on his desk.
Even though I hadn't touched him, the suddenness of my rage
knocked him against the edge of the desk, where his knees
gave way and he dropped into a squat.

"What the hell!" he shouted, slowly rebounding off the
desk, still in a crouch. It was as if he was afraid to stand up,
lest I hit him.

"Why the hell did he do that?" he asked, staring up at us.

I took off the glasses Kathy had saddled me with and rubbed my eyes. "Christ!" he sobbed, dropping onto the carpet on his buttocks, overwhelmed by my fury and by the recognition of who I was. Tears trickled down his rounded cheeks. "God! I thought you were dead."

Kathy went to the door to see if anybody had noticed the ruckus. I turned and glanced at her. She was pale, but she nodded. Soundproof rooms. Plush carpets. Extra-thick walls.

"What do you want?" Robb asked shakily.

"What do you think I want?"

"Don't kill me." I knelt and jerked his tie, sliding the knot tight until his face began turning red.

"I was going to break your arm with that dough. Maybe both arms."

"What do you want?"

"Names, bastard. The other two. Now."

"You going to take me to the police?"

"What are the names?"

"I didn't know the one guy. He drove down by himself. I just saw him that night for a few minutes before we met you. I really don't know who he is. I was so nervous I'm not even sure I would recognize him if I saw him again."

"What was his name?"

"Randy never told me his name. Honest."

I tightened the tie. "Randy who?"

"He's my friend. Randolph Schwantz. Hey, fella. It wasn't supposed to be like that. He just wanted me and the other guy to go down there with him to help him get his kids back, and then at the hospital Randy saw you and some clown, so he asked around. He told me you were a private detective who specialized in dirty deals. You didn't look that bad to me. And then, after I thought about it, on the drive home, it didn't seem like you really knew what we were talking about. You didn't, did you?"

"I told you I didn't."

Tears swamped his eyelashes. "I thought you were dead. I really thought you were . . . What are you going to do?"

"There are authorities in Oregon waiting for you, Earle.

Kidnapping. Attempted murder.'' I looked around the office. ''I guess you can kiss this posh little setup adios.''

''Black. Listen to me. Randy told us you took his kids. He figured you were working for his ex-wife. He had a court order. I saw it. The kids are his. But the old lady had them. She stole them, and you were helping her. They wanted to be with their dad, but she was hiding them. He showed us drawings and letters he got from the little one. It would have broke your heart. And then things just got out of hand.''

''Tell me about it.''

''I drove down there with Randy. Randy said he might be needing help. His wife is nuts, you know. Crazy. And she's hired goons before. He tried to have her committed at the time of the divorce, but all he could get out of the judge was custody of the children. You know, that woman is all screwed up or it wouldn't have happened. I just went down there to help Randy straighten things out.''

''Is that where he is now? In Oregon?''

''We went to Yreka to check some old lady out, then came back right after. The other guy said if no one talked, nobody on earth would ever pin anything on us. He said guys get caught because they can't keep their yaps shut.''

''And you never heard his name? The other guy?''

''Randy knows him. That's all.''

''What happened to his wife? Jo? What did you guys do with her?''

''Nothing. Randy just saw her that one time in the hospital there in the middle of the night, and she started screaming, so he scooted out of there. The broad is certifiable, I'm telling you. If you're helping her with those children, you're breaking the law.''

''You know all about the law, don't you? Twenty years in a cell will give you plenty of time to learn the rest.''

''Don't be so sure,'' said Earle Robb, regaining some of his confidence. ''It's your word against ours. Three against one.''

''Three against two,'' Kathy said. ''You forgot the clown.''

Robb squinted up at her through his tears. "Oh, cripes. Look, I don't want to go to jail. It's not going to be a good place."

"Forget jail," I said. "Point to some of your favorite bones."

"State's witness. Isn't that what they call it? I'll testify to anything you want. But I don't need to go to jail. I read an article in *Esquire*. They'd like a big soft white guy like me."

"Where's Schwantz staying?"

"With his wife's folks. In Broadmoor. Copeland's their name. Black, you gotta understand. Randy loves those kids. He's got to get them away from that loony woman before she kills them. Don't you understand?"

"I think I do."

"Good. Then you can forget all that stuff in Oregon. Randy's obsessed with those kids. It's all he thinks about. He's taken a leave from his job to track them. He'll make it right with you. I know he will. You should hear some of the things she's done to those little girls. Randy's told me all about it. She'll work an eight-hour shift and leave them out in the parking lot in her car. Nailed 'em in the garage one time, and the house caught fire."

"That's crap. I've talked to her kids."

"I swear she's going to kill them one day, Black. We were trying to help. It just got out of hand."

"I'd saying hanging a guy is getting out of hand. Yeah."

"Are you willing to testify?" Kathy asked. "If we can get the charges on you dismissed?"

"Swear to God I will. I haven't slept for weeks. I'm just glad you found me."

"I'll bet you are," I said. "One other thing, Earle."

"Yeah?"

"You warn either of these two birds, and you might as well pack your toothbrush and your Vaseline. Got it?"

"Warn 'em? You kidding? I don't even know one of 'em. Besides, they'd murder me."

"They'd have to stand in line."

We went to the door. "Jeeezus. You're not going to call the police on me?"

"You're a big boy. Besides, I think it will hurt more if you do it alone."

"And if I don't, you'll make sure my life goes down the toilet."

"I've got my hand on the handle."

In the street Kathy said, "I was proud of you. I thought for a minute you really intended to hit him with that cookie club of yours, that you were really going to hurt him, but you were bluffing."

"I wasn't bluffing. I just pulled back at the last second."

She gave me a worried look. "I'm glad, Thomas."

28

WE DROVE STRAIGHT TO BROADMOOR and told the guard we were there to see the Copelands. He admitted us, but the Copelands were not home.

We could have staked the place out, but you didn't stake out a house in Broadmoor. Not in a pickup. In Broadmoor you didn't spit into the wind. I had already spotted two housewives monitoring us through Levelors. In another thirty seconds a squad of fashion police would swoop down and whisk me and my rumpled jeans out of there.

I drove Kathy to work. I went into the office with her and phoned the Copelands to see if they'd come home in the last fifteen minutes. They hadn't. I called the girls to see if they were okay and gave them instructions to ring me if their mother showed up. Morgana asked permission to dig a hole in the backyard for a camp.

Waiting was something I didn't do well. By noon the Copelands still weren't answering, and Kathy hadn't said more than
ten words, barricading herself in her office. When she hadn't
emerged by twelve-thirty, I took Beulah to lunch.

We ate at the counter at Trattoria Mitchelli. Beulah ordered
a salad. Drank water. I had ravioli and garlic bread. And
soup. And bean salad. I had Beulah's bread when she offered
it. And a thick slice of chocolate cake. "You and Kathy do
anything special this morning?" Beulah asked.

"Why do you ask?"

"She's in her office reading *Clown Quarterly,* and you're
in yours reading old issues of *Velo News*. I figured something
was up. Usually you'd be bugging each other."

"Look," I said. "What do you really think of this
F-person?"

"I think anybody who calls a guy named Philip the
F-person is jealous."

"Bull."

"The sooner you face up to it, the sooner you can tell
Kathy how you really feel."

"Kathy knows how I feel."

Beulah could roll a laugh for ten miles if she had to. This
one only lasted about three. "Gimme a break. How could she
know how you feel? *You* don't know."

I explored Beulah's Technicolor blue eyes for a minute.
"You're right. I used to know. I figured if we became anything but friends and it ended, the friendship would be scuttled."

"Sure, things sometimes die after you become lovers and
break up. But sometimes you never break up. Sometimes you
see an old couple in the newspaper been married seventy
years. So long they look more like brother and sister."

"I've had a lot of pressure on me the last few weeks, these
girls, the case, the F-person. Almost dying changes your
perspective."

"I'll bet it does."

"Besides, friends are forever. Lovers come and go."

Beulah squeezed my biceps through my shirt. The buttons
Kathy had ripped off that morning stood out like empty eye

sockets. "Kathy wanted to hurt you a little bit. Did you know that? Philip started off just being something to make you jealous."

"She told you she was dating that guy to make me jealous?"

"Don't ever let on that I betrayed a confidence."

"She really told you?"

"It was my idea in the first place."

29

WHEN KATHY CAME IN, I WAS NAP-
ping on the crummy sofa in my office,
dreaming about a succubus who looked remarkably like Tiffany Jones—the seemingly perfect woman who managed to make me feel lousy at every turn. I had four clients who were searching for the perfect woman, but I guess what they didn't know was that sometimes you just aren't ready to meet her.

Kathy was standing over me with another woman. Beulah was in the doorway. Kathy was shaking me awake. I'd been on the ragged edge for weeks, and cuffing Earle Robb around that morning had been a release. I didn't think I could ever nap like this again.

"Thomas? Thomas?"

I rolled off the sofa and thunked the floor on my hands and knees. The clock on the wall said one-thirty. Kathy was giggling.

"Excuse me just a minute," I said. "My leg went to sleep."

"Looks to me like your whole body went to sleep," Beulah snapped as she left. "You've got a box sitting in a room back here looks almost like a coffin. You should get rid of it."

"Having a bad day, Thomas?" Kathy asked.

"*Day*? I want a refund on my whole damn calendar."

The woman beside Kathy was Jo Brown Schwantz.

The bruising had gone down considerably, but there was still a sepulchral border of black and yellow besieging both eyes. She had temporary plastic caps on several front teeth. She wore a long-sleeved white blouse and loose-fitting paisley pants. Her left arm was in a cast to the elbow. To help conceal the mayhem, her brown hair was fluffed loosely around her face. Her upper lip was going to need surgery. Even now, three weeks later, she limped.

She was almost as tall as I am, and when I looked into her skittery hazel eyes, what I saw made me want to take her in my arms. Yet her deep voice did not betray fear, but rather a slow and quiet assurance.

"Mr. Black. I'm Jo Brown. Kathy tells me you rescued my girls."

"I'm not sure they needed rescuing, but I'm taking care of them." I couldn't get over the look of her hazel eyes. Even beat-up and bruised, the woman had a magnetic presence.

"Where are they?"

"They decided they needed to dig a hole in my backyard. I'll drive you."

Jo looked at Kathy, and Kathy said, "Jo's a little jumpy. It was real hard for her to come in, Thomas."

"Sure. Sit down. Let's talk." I picked up the phone and dialed home, let it ring, got Amber on the line, and handed the receiver to Jo. She wept immediately, feeding the girls every it's-going-to-be-all-right platitude in the book. It was only in listening to her with her girls that I realized how frightened she was, that half of her brain was telling her I was with Randy, that any minute her ex-husband would burst through the door.

She spoke to them a few minutes, hung up, and dabbed at

her eyes with a tissue. I touched her shoulder and said, "Take your time. We're on your side. Yours and the girls'."

"Has Mr. Schwantz talked to you? If Mr. Schwantz's talked to you, I'm leaving. He gives people a line. I'm really leaving if he has."

"I've been watching your girls for almost two weeks. I can see what you've done with them. You should be proud."

"I thought he would brainwash you. He has a psychiatrist who testifies against me. It's surprising what you can do if you have money and no morals."

"When I was in Oregon a few weeks ago to see you, your husband and two other men drove me out into the country and put a noose around my neck, hung me from a tree, and left me for dead. There's no way they're talking themselves out of anything."

When I started to move for the window, my foot brushed her black leather purse on the floor. There was something heavy and hard in it. Our eyes met, and we both knew what it was. We reached for it at the same time. She folded her hands primly in her lap while I opened the purse and pulled out a .22 caliber semiautomatic the size of a cigarette lighter. I popped the clip out and made certain the chamber was empty. In the bottom of the purse I found half a box of Federal pistol cartridges. Thirty-eight caliber. Paris London and Denny had been shot with a .38, and the weapon had not been recovered.

"Been in town long?" I asked.

"You'll have to excuse Thomas," said Kathy, giving me a look. "He has a thing about firearms."

"These are my personal possessions," Jo Brown said.

"Got a permit?"

"I had the gun . . . I had it in case I needed to defend myself. From Mr. Schwantz. If you've talked to the girls, you heard what happened. You see, he puts on this facade of respectability.

"Our plan was prearranged in case we got separated and couldn't get away together. I was so scared of Mr. Schwantz that this was necessary. My plan was I would get myself to my mother's and wait for them to call. Yreka was perfect because my mother hadn't heard from me in years. I knew Mr. Schwantz had all but given up sending people around to her. After they called me, the girls were supposed to take the bus down. Morgana could handle that. She's a good girl. Did you know she does the *Times* crossword puzzle by herself? When Dad was alive, Mom wouldn't talk to me. But I don't know . . . You can't hate your parents forever. Morgana was to phone Mother once an evening, person-to-person collect. Asking for me.

"But I was so sick. I stopped on the freeway every rest stop. Fell asleep at one and woke up with two raggedy-looking men looking in my window. I was so scared. I drove most of that night. And then I pulled onto the exit in Oregon somewhere and dragged myself into that hospital. I think I had a couple of seizures. They drugged me, and after that I dreamed Mr. Schwantz came in the middle of the night and put a knife to me and said I had to give him the girls. I can't even tell you the nightmares."

"He was down there. Schwantz was. In Myrtle Creek. We thought you knew. We thought that was why you ran."

"I thought it was a dream. He said he had friends and they wanted to kill me but he had talked them out of it."

Kathy said, "Does he really have legal custody of the girls?"

"I had a rather incompetent lawyer. And the judge was biased against me from the start."

"Who was it?" Kathy asked.

"Bollon."

"Him. He's notorious for being hard on women."

"I found that out later. They used the fact that my first husband, Morgana's father, was black to insinuate that somehow I wasn't a fit mother. Can you believe it? In this day and age? He was obsessive, Mr. Schwantz was. When we first got together, I misinterpreted all the attention, thought he loved me. But what he needed was to control. He views his family basically as a possession. Because of his own insecurity, he became authoritarian and controlling. I almost could have lived with that. It was when I discovered his trying to sneak into Morgana's room at night that made me pack our stuff.

"I was trying to be too nice about the whole thing. Stupid? Didn't mention it to my attorney. I didn't want to put something on Mr. Schwantz's record that would ruin the rest of his life, and I didn't want Morgana to know what he might have done to her. And Morgana wasn't touched. I got out of there too fast for that. Unfortunately Mr. Schwantz had no such compunctions about being polite. He lied on the stand and said I brought boyfriends into the house, that one of them had attacked Morgana. She told Bollon it wasn't true, but he assumed she was trying to protect me or that I had coerced her into lying. My lawyer said I would have been better off letting Randy do something to Morgana. That way we would have had physical proof. Can you believe that?"

"Bollon's a bastard," said Kathy. "He shouldn't be on the bench. And it sounds as if your attorney should be washing dishes at a Tijuana bus stop."

"If Mr. Schwantz finds me, he's going to kill me."

"Stick with Thomas," said Kathy. "He'll take care of you."

"The girls adore him. I could tell by the way they talked on the phone."

"Thomas has a way with kids," said Kathy. "It's because he is one."

"I can't thank you enough. If the state got their hands on . . ."

"We guessed that," said Kathy. "But why didn't you come back? Surely your ex-husband couldn't be everywhere? You could have slipped in, picked them up, and been gone. Couldn't you?"

"He couldn't be everywhere? He didn't have to be. All he had to do was run into me once. He would have killed me, and then where would my girls be?

"After you all found me in Oregon, I figured Mr. Schwantz would guess I was heading for Yreka. I mean, where else could I have been heading? So I made my way back to Esther's. She's been hiding me out for almost two weeks. Twice, I drove up here with her husband, Bill. He had a hunting rifle. The first time we tried to break into Auntie's, a police car came around and spooked us. I was afraid the police had already found them and turned them over to Mr. Schwantz. He doesn't really want them, you know. It's all to punish me. Then Bill and I came up two days later and drove past my house. Mr. Schwantz was there. Parked halfway down the street.

"I scooted down in the seat and hid while Bill got out of there fast. I'm just glad you found them, Mr. Black."

"Thomas," I said.

"This shows how paranoid you can become. Right up until I walked in here and Kathy was so nice to me, I thought you were with Mr. Schwantz."

I said, "Why don't you tell us what happened a couple of weeks ago?"

Jo Brown stared at the pistol on the corner of my desk. "He pounded on our front door. Said he had sheriffs coming right behind him and he was going to take the girls whether I consented or not. He went around to the back and smashed the door in. He was ranting and flinging things. Accused me of living with another man.

"He ransacked the house looking for whoever he thought was living with me. Anyway, when he took after Morgana, I grabbed a knife out of the kitchen drawer. What else could I do? He's twice as big as me.

"He got the knife away from me and started slashing at the girls. I thought we were all dead and gone. Then he buried it in a door and hit me. All I know is that at some point I told Morgana to take Amber to Auntie's. I guess Randy thought that was next door. Later he went next door looking for the girls, but of course, the neighbors didn't know what he was talking about. He came back and tried to get it out of me, but I was barely breathing. I don't remember much of the rest of it. I guess he got in his car and went looking. When I woke up, I grabbed my purse and keys, but it was hard to drive. I could barely see."

"And then you saw us in Myrtle Creek?" Kathy asked.

"I don't remember you. Who knows how I got that far."

"Would you like to see your girls now?" I asked.

Jo beamed. "Of course."

"One other thing. Did you know a woman named Rhonda Lastusky? Rhonda Yellowknife now. Lives in Philadelphia, but she went to the University of Washington. Came from Tacoma. Thought she knew you at the U."

"Rhonda? I wonder. I knew a Rhonda. But I can barely picture her. Mr. Schwantz knew that fellow, though," said Jo, glancing down at the open *Post Intelligencer* on my desk. In the lower-right quadrant of the front page was an article about the shooting at the Olympic Four Seasons. A photo of Denny McCallum headlined the article.

"You knew McCallum?" I asked.

"Randy did. I don't even know why I remember. Mr. Schwantz and I bumped into him at Sears once. We had coffee. He just left an impression. Randy didn't have a whole lot of friends. I tended to remember the ones he did have."

"Where did your husband know him from?"

"Near as I can recall, high school."

"In Tacoma?"

"That's where Randy grew up."

It took five minutes to explain why I was asking. When I'd finished, Jo said, "You mean you were chasing all over the countryside because some man wanted to take me out to dinner?"

"Crazy, huh?" She nodded. I asked her whether she knew any of the other three clients. Floyd Boyd was the only name she recognized.

"I think I met Boyd, too," she said. "At a fund-raising dinner Mr. Schwantz and I went to. I just saw him for a minute, but for some reason I remember him."

Jo went into the outer room while Kathy lagged behind and said, "Isn't she wonderful? So what are you going to do with her?"

"The spare bedroom until I nail Schwantz. It shouldn't be long."

Before we left the office, Kathy received a phone call from the Seattle PD. They wanted a meeting tomorrow morning concerning an assault report I'd filled out in Oregon. It seemed someone had come in and confessed. She told them she'd give me the message and passed along Aldredge's number in Myrtle Creek.

"Earle Robb contacted them?" I asked.

"Um-hummm. It sounds like they're going to arrest Schwantz. But they want to talk to you first."

"I'm glad Robb went through with it. Otherwise I would have had to kill him," I said, leaving the room.

"Thomas, you know you don't mean that," Kathy shouted at my back. "You know you don't."

30

MORGANA HAD ACHIEVED A MOON-crater excavation in the center of my back lawn. We caught the girls in a freeze-frame. Morgana knee-deep in the hole, shovel in hand, while Amber, smudged from head to toe, sat cross-legged on a heap of fresh dirt, kibitzing.

In a squeaky little voice Amber was the first to speak. "Why didn't you come for us, Mommy? Morgy called, but you wouldn't answer."

"Oh, honey," said Jo, rushing to pick her up, while Morgana leaped out of the pit. They webbed themselves together in reunion.

While they laughed and wept and finally went inside to scrub up, I leaned against my crab-apple tree and chewed over the coincidences that were banking up.

Four men had hired me to find four women.

The men had all been friends since high school.

They had wanted me to recruit an ex–high school cheerleader, a PBS-drive chairperson, a nude model, and a season-ticket holder from the Kingdome. Fine. The PBS chairperson was in trouble when we caught up with her. I could live with that. Being pursued by her ex-husband. Her ex-husband had gone to school in Tacoma with my four clients. Now Rhonda claimed to have known Jo back in their college days. That was possible. And Jo's husband knew McCallum in high school, according to Jo. If he knew McCallum, he knew the others, too. Which meant he probably knew Rhonda as well.

And none of my four clients was willing to acknowledge a hidden agenda, that there was anything more than simple-minded lust driving this investigation. Boyd had dated Rhonda in high school but had said nothing about it.

McCallum had died receiving fellatio from a transsexual he had known all of twenty minutes, an act more than one pundit over the past couple of days had advertised was not exactly in character for Denny. And Rhonda had disappeared. Had she been in the suite during the killings? Maybe her relationship with Paris London was not what she had led us to believe, and she had killed them both in a fit of jealousy? Or maybe she had witnessed the crime and fled. She could herself have been kidnapped or even murdered.

Then there were the charred newspaper scraps I'd discovered next to the toilet at the Four Seasons Olympic. Why would a murderer—if that was who had done it—stop and destroy a newspaper clipping? The remnants had looked old, yellowed. Perhaps it hadn't been a clipping at all but, instead, had been an object wrapped in newspaper and what I was seeing was just the remains of the wrapper. A stack of stock certificates? Photos?

Before her date with Jimmy Canfield, Rhonda had been asking about the statute of limitations. Was there any significance to that? I wondered.

After making sure Jo and the girls were comfortably ensconced with instructions to stay indoors and keep things locked, I hopped on my Miyata and pedaled East to Seventeenth N.E., through Greek row, traversed Forty-fifth onto the campus, and coasted down through the walking paths to

Suzzallo Library. It was a typical late-summer afternoon at the U. A warm wind tongued the leaves on the maples. Several shirtless males wrist-snapped a Frisbee through the thick air. A woman in a white smock and sandals lay on the grass, braining up a novel, a panting mongrel beside her.

It was just a hunch.

Boyd, McCallum, Ronquist, and Canfield had all graduated from Tacoma's Woodrow Wilson High School in 1969, as had Rhonda Yellowknife and apparently Randy Schwantz.

I went to the periodicals section by the front entrance in Suzzallo and got the *Tacoma News Tribune* in small square Bell and Howell microfilm boxes starting in September of '69 and moving backward from there. I sat at a quiet brown booth and threaded the film onto the spool under the white viewing table. I began working my way backward through the summer and into the spring of the year they had graduated. It had been a three-year school in those days, and I was prepared to go through '69, '68, and '67, if necessary.

After three hours I called home to tell Jo to go ahead and help herself to whatever she could scrounge up in my kitchen for dinner. I could hear Kathy in the background with the kids.

In 1969 a Chrysler sold for under three thousand dollars and proud of it. A four-bedroom home for $14,450. Women's nylon tops went for $1.44, with the suggestion "Charge it." *The Wild Bunch* was entertaining couples too preoccupied to care at the Autoview Drive-in. On television KTNT had a lineup of reruns you couldn't beat. *Sea Hunt. Batman. The Rifleman. Lucy. The Steve Allen Show.* The *Tribune* cost ten cents and was thinner than a tax man's obituary.

I was looking for something local. Rhonda had hinted at a crime involving a car. Had alluded to manslaughter. Said maybe it was an accident. All I could think of was a car crash during an illegal drag race. Something like that.

I slogged through the microfilm until my eyes hurt. Some guy wielding a sawed-off shotgun held up a service station on South Eighth at five in the morning, saying, "I need bread." There was a .22 shooting on South Yakima Avenue. The victim was hauled off to St. Joseph's, where he died. Men were arrested in both cases. I was looking for something where the culprit had not been apprehended. I began making a list that I could check against the court records in Pierce County.

Then I found it. A sizable article on June 29, a follow-up profile of a grieving family. The crime had happened months before. The caption under a photo of two somber people in a middle-class living room said, *No end to sense of loss for Agnes and Eugene Driscoll.*

I studied the columns, took notes, then wound up the film and opened the box from March 1, 1969, to March 15, 1969. The March 2 paper carried the story on the front page, replete with smiling photos of the victim. In those days items that wouldn't even make today's paper rocked the town, the topic of conversation across every back fence. I took more notes. Finally, eyes glazed, I scanned the rest of the front page of March 2.

TROOPS HURL GAS AT BERKELEY AS US CAMPUS TURMOIL SPREADS. GOVERNOR REAGAN ORDERS TROOPS IN. FORMER PRESIDENT EISENHOWER DYING OF PNEUMONIA. IKE WEAK BUT CLINGS TO LIFE. CLAY SHAW CLEARED IN JFK DEATH PLOT.

After double-checking the weeks beyond June 29 to see whether they had arrested a suspect, I ran off copies of the articles. My suspicion was that bits and drabs from the charred newspaper clippings at the Four Seasons Olympic could be traced to the March 2 *News Tribune*. I called the Tacoma Police Department, and after explaining who I was and what I thought I had, I conned a grumpy detective into looking it up for me. Twenty years was a long time, he told me, chewing food loudly in my ear. It took a while, but he finally said the case was dead. Unsolved, shelved, and forgotten.

Nobody had ever been brought to trial.

Nobody had ever been jailed.

I phoned the Seattle detective assigned to the Paris London/ Denny McCallum slaying. He told me there was no evidence of a struggle whatsoever. Paris and Denny had both died of gunshot wounds. A .38-caliber Colt. Blood had been found in a closet by the front door, and in the dining-area kitchen-ette in a cupboard next to the refrigerator. Denny had tried to conceal himself in as many as two other sites before collapsing in the closet where I found him.

I phoned Rhonda Yellowknife's home number in Philadelphia. She had an answering machine, and my guess was she would monitor it long distance if she could.

"This is Rhonda's machine. I'm someplace else. After the beep and all that jazz. Don't you hate these things?" The sound of a wet kiss.

"Thomas Black here. I know what happened in your last year of high school. I know why Paris and Denny McCallum were shot. You might as well meet with me and clear it up before more people get hurt."

It was almost seven when I wheeled the Miyata through my back door and into the utility room. Kathy, Jo, and the girls were just finishing the supper dishes at my sink.

"Look what the cat dragged in," said Kathy.

After greetings, a bite to eat, a general confirmation that Jo would stay tonight with the girls in Kathy's cramped apartment while Kathy would squeeze into my spare bedroom with my weights and bikes and extra wheels, Kathy took me aside and said, "I called. He's there. I told the woman who answered I was from the Heart Association and I wanted to talk to her about charity work. It clicked. Her husband's got a bad ticker. He's on an exercise program. She said she'd leave a message with the gate guard to pass us on through."

"Schwantz?"

"Yep."

"Let's go." I was already heading for the door.

"Floyd Boyd telephoned, too. He and the guys want to meet with you at the Olympic Hotel. Maybe one of them has something to confess." Kathy raised her eyebrows. "Jimmy Canfield has been hanging around there all day hoping Rhonda would show. Did you know this year's Yellow Dog Party is Thursday?"

"I thought it wasn't until late August."

"They decided that was too close to the election. Thursday."

"Let's call 'em. We'll hit the Olympic before we see Schwantz."

We took my truck. I was still wearing jeans, though I had taken advantage of one of my stops home to replace the shirt Kathy had desecrated, had tossed a sport coat over that. Kathy was all in black. A short, straight skirt with gold piping running down each side. A severe close-fitting jacket with matching gold piping. Black gloves, earrings, high-buttoned shoes, and tights. Her dark hair was pulled back into a chignon. Round-lensed black sunglasses. She didn't look like Kathy. But then, she rarely did.

We parked in the elevated parking garage across Seneca from the Olympic. The three of them were waiting in the mammoth lobby. Floyd Boyd in an oddly disheveled suit. Jimmy Canfield in a satin baseball jacket, tall, grass-stained socks, and baseball pants. Ronquist in cords and tasseled loafers.

The five of us took the stairs to the mezzanine. The St. James room held a long conference table, chairs, and not much else. We took our places around the baronial walnut table.

Boyd sat at the head. "Look, Black. What have the police found? I've been in touch with their public-information officer, but all they're giving me is bullshit."

"What I want to know," said Jimmy Canfield, resting his thick, satin-clad elbows on the table and knitting his knuckles together like crude zippers, "is how much danger we're in. And what the hell happened to Rhonda."

I said, "Look, I can't help you guys with information from the SPD. And I'm not pushing them on this. For one thing, it wouldn't do any good. For another, I do, they might start pushing back, and there's a lot they don't know that I don't want to tell them."

"For instance?" Canfield asked.

"That a certain congressional candidate hired me at the same time Denny McCallum did. That they hired me to find women. The cops don't need to know that, and I don't think it would do Floyd's campaign much good."

"Appreciate your discretion, Black," said Boyd. "But you've got to let us in on what's happening. I have a daughter staying with me. I don't want her endangered."

"I'm not scared," said Ronquist, banging a heavy chrome-plated .357 onto the table.

"Put that away." I pulled out the photocopied handbills from Myrtle Creek. "You three know either of these birds?" Randolph Schwantz and Earle Robb. All three studied the sheets and shook their heads. "How about this guy?" I had scissored out the picture of Randolph Schwantz from the group portrait I'd swiped from Jo's house. I passed it around. More negatives. "Anybody ever heard the name Schwantz?"

Nobody had.

"His ex-wife says he went to high school with Denny McCallum. If that's true, it means he went to high school with you three." They passed the photo around again while I tried to decide who was putting on a pose and who actually didn't recognize him.

"Lotta people in our high school," said Ronquist. "What was there? Six hundred in our graduating class? Seven?"

"Who is this guy?" said Jimmy Canfield. "I mean, maybe I recognize him. Didn't he play chess and walk around the school with this big old briefcase thumping against his knees all the time?"

"That was Kirby Finklestein," said Floyd.

"The question before us," I said, "isn't who is Schwantz. The question is what is going on. I think one or more of you four guys had an ulterior motive when you came to me to find these women."

They glanced at each other for a few moments. Boyd probed the bridge of his nose with a pair of mated index fingers and said, "Explain 'ulterior motive.' "

"Rhonda was asking some peculiar questions the night she went out with Jimmy."

"We had a good time," Canfield said. "I gave her a little kiss at her door, and that was that. We were going to drive up to the San Juans the next day. What are you talking about, questions? You keep looking at me. Everybody keeps looking at me. So I dated her. She was pretty. A guy'd be nuts not to want to see her."

"*Was*?" It was Ronquist. "She *was* pretty? You know something we don't?"

"Fuck you!" shouted Canfield, standing and knocking his chair over. He moved around the end of the table toward Rex. Floyd reached out an authoritative arm and said, "Calm down."

"He's accusing me," said Canfield. He'd been drinking, and it was evident in the way his movements seemed almost strobe-lighted.

"Sit down, Jimmy," I said.

"You think someone's in danger, Black?" It was Floyd Boyd.

"I do."

"Why, exactly?"

"Because when you hired me, one of you four was lying." They stared. "Maybe it was Denny, but one of you wanted to meet his dreamgirl for something other than the obvious reasons." I watched their faces.

"Wasn't me," said Ronquist.

"No," said Jimmy Canfield, bitterly. "But you practically twisted my arm to make me use up my wish on Rhonda. Remember? I didn't want Rhonda. I was going to choose Susan Engelking. She was dating a guy in my office before she moved to England to be with her dying father. I never did find out what became of her. She was gorgeous. Long blond hair. Big old Nordic teeth. Susan was my choice, but you guys egged me into picking Rhonda."

"You chose Rhonda," said Ronquist.

"Maybe. But I kissed her good night and left. Besides, what are we talking about? I don't even know what we're talking about."

"I think one or more of you was involved in some sort of mishap in high school," I said.

"Mishap?" Kathy turned to me.

"Something shameful enough that whoever was mixed up in it doesn't want anybody finding out twenty years later."

"You're saying Denny got killed over something that happened twenty years ago?" Boyd asked. "Isn't that a little far-fetched? I mean, think about it. We've been seeing each other at a minimum of once a year since high school. Rex and I see each other more often. And I used to chum around with Jimmy here. If somebody wanted to bring up something from the past, don't you think it would have happened a long time ago?''

"It happened Saturday night. I think Rhonda was chosen because she knew something. I think somebody wanted to find Rhonda so they could talk to her about a crime that happened a long time ago.''

"Basically,'' said Jimmy Canfield, eyebrows raising, "you're accusing *me*.''

"I just want to know the mechanics of how each of you chose your dreamgirl.''

"Somebody wanted to find Rhonda?'' said Ronquist.

"Boyd's choice, the PBS woman, was married to a man who apparently went to high school with the four of you. Although nobody seems to recognize him. There are a bundle of loose connections here, and I want your help.''

"You found her, Black?'' Boyd had both hands flat on the table, ready to stand. "You found the PBS gal again?''

"I did find her. I haven't had time to ask about getting together with you. What I want to find out from you guys is, who is the man in the photograph?''

Silence. "It was a big school, Black,'' said Boyd. "And it was a long time ago.''

31

BROADMOOR WAS AN EXCLUSIVE neighborhood molded into the middle of town around an eighteen-hole golf course. You bought a house there, the neighbors caucused and audited the wax job on your Mercedes, checked the polish on your teeth, and calibrated the part in your kid's hairdo, then balloted whether to let you put ink on the closing papers. At the entrance, visitors crossed a speed bump where they were cross-examined by the private security guard. He didn't have a gun on his belt, but I felt sure there was one in the kiosk.

Low brick walls between some of the houses. Columned homes. Elegant landscaping. They surely had ordinances against pickup trucks in the driveway. It resembled a movie lot, with street names like Windermere, Lexington, and Shenandoah. The children playing in the streets could have stepped out of a time warp from 1951. Cheerful. Polite. Leather basketballs and European bikes. The Sunday schools in this little burg were probably bursting, and the kindergartens had no bad-boy corner.

It was almost dark when we pulled in front of a brick house with two white columns flanking the main doorway. Somebody had spent weeks sculpting the hedges. The lawn was a putting green. The yard had some healthy marigolds, but both the Dolly Parton and the Red Devil were mildewed, black spot, too. In the open garage I spotted matching Mercedes 380s. One pink. The other pewter. It was the white Lincoln in the drive that started my blood pressure escalating.

"Now, you behave," said Kathy. "You almost lost it with Earle Robb. Try not to lose it here."

"What?" I was trembling, not a single tangible thought in my head. Whatever developed was going to be as much a surprise to me as to anybody.

"Thomas, this is a respectable neighborhood, and whatever Schwantz has done to you, remember this is not his house. These are his in-laws, and I'm sure they don't know a thing about what happened in Myrtle Creek. Keep that in mind."

"You act as if I should be on a leash." My lips were numb as I spoke. I felt dizzy, my head light and spinning. I was beginning to get an uncomfortable feeling that I might spend the rest of the week in a jail cell. Or the rest of my life.

"Just be civil. Remember. He had a gun in Oregon. He probably hasn't ditched it. By the way. Was it a .38 in

Oregon? Like the one that killed Denny and Paris? I never thought about that. Was it?''

''Nine millimeter. Sure he's home?'' I had already spanked the brass knocker twice.

''He was here an hour ago. At least the lady who answered the phone said he was.''

I swung the brass knocker again. A film of metal polish somebody had forgotten to rub off marred the base plate. When a matron in her early seventies answered the door, I ceased trembling, overcome by an easy and rather disquieting calm. I was beginning to get a feeling for what it would be like to lose my sanity.

''Yes?''

''We're looking for Randy,'' I said, grinning. ''He around?''

''Upstairs in the den.'' She half-turned and pointed out the direction with her eyes. Her curly gray hair was cropped close to her skull. Her face had given away an extra fifteen years from too much sunbathing, but her sparkly brown eyes took us in like a waif's. ''Is Randy expecting visitors?''

''I believe so,'' said Kathy, squeezing past the woman, who had left barely enough room for the strategy.

''Mind if we just go on up?'' I said, stepping through the tight opening and chasing Kathy up a lushly carpeted circular staircase. An evening newspaper was spread out under a chandelier at a dining table in the next room. You could have played catch with a football across the distance. I heard a parakeet cheeping somewhere. The carpets were the sort you felt guilty walking on.

''Randy's very particular about his quiet time,'' said Mrs. Copeland, courteously. ''He has dinner, and then he needs his quiet time.''

''That's okay,'' said Kathy, whisking her dark glasses off at the top of the stairs. ''We know just how he feels.''

''Second door on the right,'' said Mrs. Copeland, too polite not to assist our infraction. She clasped the carved ash banister and began hastening up after us. In motion she looked like a pile of moving sticks. Kathy was right. People could get hurt here. Innocent people. A harsh word would probably put this sweet old lady in traction.

I rapped on the second door upstairs, then opened it. An attractive woman I took to be the second Mrs. Schwantz was leaning over a man who sat at a large oak desk. They were reviewing some papers. She wore a dress and high heels and looked as if she'd once been a beauty queen. She wasn't heavy enough yet to have lost her sex appeal, with wide-spaced Elizabeth Taylor eyes and brunette hair clipped short and fluffy. Schwantz seemed to specialize in beautiful women.

"Yes?" she said.

"Just here to see your husband, ma'am," I said, stepping into the room.

Centered on his face was an immense, freakish gauze bandage, tented over his nose and taped lightly on all sides. The bleeding man from the Lincoln. The Talker. The one I had punched in the face.

When he recognized me, he surreptitiously opened a drawer under his right hand. This was the man from Jo's family portrait. Randolph Schwantz. No doubt about it. Dark hair. High forehead, furrowed with worry and success. Round face. A mean and intense look to him. The wife-beater. The hangman. My face was getting hot. My ears were on fire. I grappled with an impulse to leap across the desk.

"This is a delicate matter," I said to Mrs. Schwantz, trying to keep the adrenaline jitters out of my voice. "Perhaps your husband would like to talk in private?"

They exchanged looks, and Randolph Schwantz said, "Screw that, Beverly, stay here. I need a witness. Who let you in?"

"I did," said Mrs. Copeland, breathless with apology, sliding unctuously through the doorway behind Kathy. The room contained a desk, a computer, a fax machine, several electronic adding machines, and at the far end, a snooker table with a Tiffany lamp over it. "I'm sorry, Randy. They said they were expected."

"Don't worry, Mother."

Randolph Schwantz stood, and you could see by the methodical manner in which he did so that he was suffering. When he cleared the desk, he was holding the same Llama 9mm he'd toted in Oregon. The brunette sauntered past and took her mother by the arm, leaving me to flounder in a fog of provocative perfume.

"Let's forgo the tough stuff," I said to Schwantz. "I thought we could dicker and get you a lighter sentence, maybe spring you before you die of old age."

Schwantz was smaller than I remembered. Two-ten and about my height. His hair was greasy and slicked straight back, thinning. I imagined it was a bit awkward showering with a diaper taped to your face. If his tiny round mouth hadn't been exposed, he would have looked like a masked bandit.

"They had to drill it out," he said, when he saw me looking at his nose. "Twice. I've never felt such excruciating pain." He spoke as if he had a cold, nostrils tunneled out and tamped down, serviced with gauze and elixirs. "I'm not admitting anything, Black. You might as well leave."

"You know my name. Funny, I don't believe we've been formally introduced."

"Who's she?" Schwantz asked.

"The clown. She saw you without your disguise. She can finger you."

He eyed me over the diaper.

"That your Lincoln downstairs?"

"It's mine. So what?"

"You graduate from Woodrow Wilson High School in Tacoma?"

"Kind of losing track of your point, aren't you?"

"Something happened in 1969 in Tacoma, and you were either part of it or you knew about it."

Schwantz smiled smugly. "Black, you're close, but you're fishing."

"You got into trouble, didn't you? The whole town was looking for you."

"Let's hear the deal. Otherwise shove off."

I walked around the right side of the desk until Schwantz was only a pace away. Behind his desk, a row of thigh-high windows overlooked a Beaver Cleaver yard, and beyond that, the Broadmoor golf course. A heavy dusk was settling in. Just beyond the windows was a short, slanting roof, maybe ten feet long, and below that the outer lip of a swimming pool in the shape of protoplasm. An elderly man was doing sluggish laps—I could just see one slack arm and his semi-bald head—the surface choppy and shimmering from his exertions.

"I just want to know what you thought you were doing in Oregon, Randy. You could be facing a murder rap there."

"That'd be all right, except I never was in Oregon."

"Tell him the truth," said Beverly.

"So I was there. Big deal. I never saw you before in my life."

"You knew my name."

"He was tracking his former wife when we stumbled across him," said Kathy, looking at the women in the back of the room. "Lord only knows what he was planning. He beat the hell out of her a week before that."

"That's not true," said the elderly Mrs. Copeland, pulsating with fury. An individual who cloaked herself in a strict, old-fashioned morality, she had been giving me the evil eye since determining that we had lied to her downstairs. "Randy's never touched a woman. Her colored boyfriend beat her. Another pimp boyfriend. Don't you see? It's those little girls who need to be saved. Lord Almighty. After all Randy's been through, you come in here and accuse?"

Kathy gave me a look that said trespassing wasn't one of her favorite hobbies; nor was giving heart attacks to elderly women.

"You been to the Olympic Hotel lately, Randy?"

"What's that supposed to mean?"

"A guy was murdered there Saturday night. I understand you knew him."

"I don't have the faintest idea what you're blabbering about."

"Denny McCallum."

"From Tacoma? Yeah. Went to school together. So? You're about the most off-the-wall guy I've ever met. Can't you keep a straight train of thought? No wonder you're in a dead-end job. You were like that in Oregon, too. Everything off the wall."

I glanced at his wife. I had to fight to keep from throwing myself at him. "You admit seeing us in Oregon?"

"I'm not admitting squat. I just think you're nuts. What about Denny McCallum?"

"He was killed Saturday night at the Four Seasons Olympic."

"Maybe you had better leave," said Beverly Schwantz.

Randolph Schwantz said, "I haven't had time to read the papers. Denny's dead, you say?"

"Shot upstairs in the Cascade Suite, along with another man. Nobody knows who did it. When was the last time you saw Denny?"

"The police want to talk to me, I'm not hard to find."

"Randy often takes a day or two off when he needs to do some thinking," said Beverly Schwantz, defensively. "It's just his way. And I don't like your insinuations, Mr. Black. What makes you think you can burst in here and ask these questions? I believe we have grounds to sue."

"No, let him go for a second," said Schwantz. "How did you know I used to be friends with Denny? You're in touch with Jo, aren't you? Jo met him once."

"That's right. I'm in touch with Jo. And Earle." He had to think about that for a moment. "Funny thing is, Earle doesn't want to do any time. He's agreed to testify. Probably downtown signing a statement this very minute."

"You're full of crap, Black."

"Why don't you call him and see?"

Shaking his head, Schwantz said, "You know Earle can't do that."

"And why not? Because he was part of it?"

"I'm not admitting shit. Sorry, Mother. Earle went with me to Oregon. I don't know what he's told you, but you've obviously been misled.'' Schwantz exchanged looks with his puzzled wife and mother-in-law. "He's nuts.''

"Look, Randy,'' I said. "How about you sign away the rights to your kids. You do and I'll agree to go easy on you in court. You know you don't really want them. You're just trying to torture Jo.''

"I'm taking my kids. The woman's mad. She pulled a knife on me.''

"Only because you were knocking the girls around.''

"I insist you leave,'' said Beverly Schwantz, sternly.

"Sure,'' I said, turning and heading slowly for the door. "That's all I wanted. A little dialogue. I'm sorry, ladies, if I spoiled your evening.''

Beverly, still holding her mother's arm, turned her around and escorted her into the corridor. I could feel Schwantz coming up on my left. We were facing the same direction, heading out of the room.

I formed my left hand into a fist, and when he pulled even with my shoulder cocked my fist backward and up as hard as I could. A sucker punch Snake had showed me. It was the last thing Schwantz expected.

My knuckles connected with the soft diaper on his face.

The pistol plopped noiselessly onto the thick carpet. Schwantz staggered backward, lungs empty, eyes bleeding tears. The diaper was stained red. He clasped his face. Stooped. Backing away from me, in small, shuddering, almost comical steps.

I turned and advanced on him.

Seeing me advance, Schwantz sped up his shuddering retreat. He shook his head just a little, signaling surrender, both hands cupping his face. Then he took a huge, wheezing breath. He didn't realize hangmen weren't allowed the luxury of surrender.

"No,'' Kathy said. "Don't do it.''

I punched him again.

The blow smashed his fingers against his face and propelled him backward. He staggered three or four steps back before his buttocks broke the thigh-high window at his back. It sounded

like a sheet of ice cracking. Slow motion took over the rest
of it. He somersaulted backward through the shattered window, even as shards sprinkled down around him, clattering
into the room. He rolled through the sudden opening and
out onto the roof. Behind me I heard Beverly Schwantz
yelp.

Schwantz was rolling down the short roof, on his back like
a turtle, spinning slowly, dizzily clawing for a hold, sliding,
blood pumping from his face, fingers clawing for a handhold,
down, down, then his torso waggling precariously on the lip,
then off—backward—with a wail.

A huge splash and somebody below yelling, "What the
hell?"

More splashing. You could see blood spreading in the
pool. A shoe bobbing to the surface.

Beverly Schwantz and her mother had reached me in time
to watch him skitter off, yanking the aluminum gutter out as
he went.

"Don't worry," I said. "I'm paying for the window. I'll
pony up for a fresh Band-Aid on the smeller, too."

Beverly Schwantz pulled her left arm back and swung at
my face. The blow rang out in the room and jolted my still-
sore neck. My cheek stung. Good for her. She stared for a
few seconds to see whether she'd hurt me, then, when I
grinned sheepishly, said, "I suppose you're the one working
for that dirty little politician?"

"Huh?"

"A policeman warned us about you." She galloped heavily
out of the room, followed closely by her nervous mother.

"What are you talking about?" I shouted at her back.

"Thomas! What the hell is wrong with you?" Kathy asked.
"I thought you were above this."

"So did I." I rubbed the knuckles of my right fist. "But
I'm not."

"I wish you'd handle this according to the rules," said
Kathy. "At least give the system a chance. You're turning
into something mean and ugly."

"A guy gets hung, he does not just forgive and forget."

"But you're turning into . . ."

"I'm sorry. I've been crazy for weeks, but I think it's gone now."

"Well . . . I hope so. Did she mention a policeman? You think Gary Glenn's connected to these people?"

"I don't know, and I doubt if she's going to answer any more questions."

"He could have been the third person in Oregon. She also mentioned some dirty little politician. Floyd Boyd? 'Course, there are a lot of dirty politicians. I don't get it."

"Me neither, sister."

Kathy inspected the shards of window, the blood, the threads of torn clothing. A Rolex on the roof next to the wagging gutter. Beverly Schwantz bustled into view below for a second. I heard a man's deep voice. Mr. Copeland. I could see Schwantz floundering in the pool.

"God damn you, Thomas," said Kathy. "You promised."

"Jennifer James says keep in touch with your feelings."

"Is that all you wanted? Is that the only reason you came here? To punch him?"

"It's not as good as hanging the bastard, but it was all I could come up with on short notice. What with the crowd."

Kathy touched a finger to my forehead and traced it off the tip of my nose. "I still can't believe you did that."

32

FEELING DECEITFUL, EVEN SLEAZY, I arranged the date between Rex Ronquist and Tina Hosty for Tuesday night, paying Tina a stipend in advance so she could buy some clothes and pay for a sitter. Rex showed up in a tux, and they ate in the Georgian Room at the Four Seasons Olympic. I peeked in a couple of times. Rex didn't seem to notice Tina wasn't the girl from his pornographic pictures. They were doing a lot of laughing.

"She's fantastic," said Rex, after he'd located me in the lobby of the Olympic. "She's so funny." Wednesday morning Tina called me at the office.

"Thomas? Tina. I just wanted to ask you about Rex."

"Sure."

"Is he for real?"

"What do you mean?"

"I mean that date last night. I had a good time and all, but the way it was arranged . . . And who he thought I was. Is he eccentric?"

"Why do you ask?"

"Because he wants to take me to a show this weekend. And I want to go. But I'm skeptical. I mean, you've already paid me two grand of his money. Do you think . . . ?"

"If you like him and want to go, go. Otherwise, forget it. You're under no obligation."

"He seems very nice. And he acts like he worships me."

"I think he does, Tina."

At noon on Wednesday Randolph Schwantz was arrested and charged with the assault on Jo. On top of that, the Oregon authorities asked Seattle to hold him until they could question him about a lynching and kidnapping in Myrtle Creek. Earle Robb had already turned himself in and started talking. All we had left was to find the third man from Oregon. And, of course, the murderer from the Olympic. But I was beginning to believe we'd never get him.

Wednesday night we were at my place dancing again. A celebration of sorts.

It was late. The girls were reckless, Morgana teaching me a different move with each new cut on the album and me feeling pretty good because my neck didn't hurt anymore. And because I had been dancing with Jo, too. Despite her broken arm, Jo danced like a dream. Even so, I kept glancing over her shoulder at Kathy and Philip. Kathy wore a black skirt and a sleeveless black turtleneck. This seemed to be her black week. She was barefoot, dancing on tiptoe. The Boss again. The house was rocking. Amber was bouncing around like a cannonball fired into a dungeon.

When the doorbell rang, I assumed it was Horace from next door, come to bellyache about the racket.

Rhonda Yellowknife stood on my porch under the yellow bug light giving me a direct stare and a small, shy smile. She wore jeans and a windbreaker, her auburn hair wild and loose. She stood on the porch glancing up and down the street, as if she thought somebody was tailing her. A Yellow Cab was idling at the curb. The cool outside air felt good on my moist brow.

"May I come in?" She peered over my shoulder to see what the hullabaloo was about.

"Sure. Just friends."

She waved the cabbie away and stepped inside.

In my bedroom I pulled out a chair for Rhonda, closed the door, and sat on the edge of the bed. I was struck by how Irish she looked. Her pale skin. Merry eyes that closed down into slits when she laughed, which she probably would not do tonight. The wash of freckles across her nose. The tight waist, buxom hips and bosom. "They're having a good time," she said.

"Yep."

"I got the message you left on my phone in Philly."

"Figured you would."

"Well, I did."

"You all right, Rhonda?"

"Sure. Fine. Why wouldn't I be?"

"I thought you might have been hurt Saturday night."

"By Jimmy?"

"By the killer."

"So you don't think I'm the killer, huh? Everybody else seems to. It's all over the newspapers and radio. Rhonda Yellowknife missing. Implicated in vicious sex killing in Four Seasons Olympic. Blah, blah, blah."

"Calm down. I don't think you're the killer. Tell me what happened."

"Jimmy brought me back to the bedroom door. There are

two doors up there to that suite, you know? The bedroom and the one just down the hall, the big doors to the really big part of it. The suite?''

"I've been there. I found the bodies.''

"You? The papers didn't say.''

"I went up to give you a check for your expenses. The door was partially open and nobody answered.''

"Where was Denny? I just saw Tony in the bathroom. Did everybody think Tony and I were sexually involved? I was afraid of that. Of course we weren't. Tony was my cousin. I told you. Poor bastard. He was going to sleep on the couch in my room. He was afraid to be by himself. He said the hormone injections he was taking were screwing him up.''

"Did you see anybody?''

"I went in the bedroom and brushed my teeth in the adjoining bathroom. I thought about getting ready for bed, but Tony wasn't there. He said he'd wait up for me. So I went in the suite, and there he was on the floor in that other bathroom. I could tell he was dead. I've never been that scared. It just . . . the fear in me was like a drug. I thought I heard somebody else in the suite, and I started looking around. There weren't any lights on. And then I thought it must be whoever shot Tony. So I went straight back to the bedroom, grabbed the one suitcase I hadn't unpacked, and ran out. I walked to the Pacific Plaza right around the corner on Spring. I registered there under a different name. I figured they were going to find me by the next morning, but I guess I could have stayed there forever.''

"I guess you could have.''

"I had this suspicion I wasn't really there to date some guy from my old high school. I was afraid the killer really wanted me, so I was afraid to surface and go to the police. And then thinking about how Jimmy kept talking about the old days the way he did . . . I don't know. It just made my blood run cold. Because of what happened back then. We never mentioned it at dinner, but I was thinking about it. Then I was beginning to like him. I even agreed to drive up to the San Juans with him. Did he do it? Jimmy?''

"How could he have done it if he was with you?''

"We came back from dinner and had drinks in the Palm Room downstairs. Jimmy excused himself. He was gone for a long time."

"Long enough to go upstairs and shoot two people? Come back and clear the look of satisfaction off his face?"

"That's a horrible picture. But, yes. I've been thinking about that for two days. Yes. I think it was that long. Why did he really invite me out here?"

"You tell me."

Rhonda smoothed the denim over her knees, looking at her lap, letting the hair fall down around her face. "I wish I knew for sure."

"So who burned the newspaper clipping?"

"What?"

"There were fragments of burnt newspaper around the commode. You didn't see them?"

"All I saw was Tony."

"I thought you might have been the one who burned it."

"I just saw Tony, then I heard somebody moving in the other room. I feel so bad. It was Denny McCallum. He thought I was the killer, and I thought he was. If I'd stayed and called the police, they might have found him in time and saved his life."

"He had a lot of holes in him. That he lasted as long as he did was some sort of biological fluke. Some people just die harder than others."

"I was wrong to have run."

"Why *did* you?"

"Thought I was next. Thought if I sat down and used the phone, I wouldn't be alive by the time the police showed."

"Why didn't you phone the police after you checked into the Pacific Plaza?"

"I don't know. They were looking for me. I haven't slept in two nights, you know. I guess I'm just not thinking right. I was trying to figure it out, see? And then I phoned home and got your message. Obviously you figured it all out. Tell me who killed Tony."

I unfolded a photocopied twenty-year-old newspaper clipping from the back pocket of my jeans and handed it to her.

It took her half a minute to scan it. When she finished, she was weeping. "You were there, weren't you, Rhonda?"

"I put it out of my mind for so long, and then you showed up in Philadelphia and I realized I'd been thinking about it every day of my life and I didn't want to come out here, but I figured if I did, maybe the whole thing would be taken care of somehow."

"You were there? Were you driving?"

"Heck, no." She was slobbery now, wiping her nose and slick cheeks with the back of one wan hand. I fetched a freshly laundered handkerchief from my bureau and handed it to her. "Thanks."

"Who was driving? Jimmy?"

"I'm scared."

Five minutes later Rhonda and I emerged from the bedroom. I got her a glass of water and sat her down at the dining-room table in the dark. They were still dancing, slow-dancing now, all but Amber, who wandered into the dining room and said, "Are you sad, lady?"

Rhonda looked at Amber, sniffled, and said, "I'm all right."

"But why are you crying?"

I said, "She's crying because she's been worried for a long time and now she doesn't have to worry anymore."

"But you shouldn't be sad," said Amber.

Rhonda examined Amber's flushed face and said, "I'm sad because a long time ago a little girl just like you got hurt real bad. And I was there. And I should have done something about it, but I didn't have the guts."

I didn't recognize the music, something Philip had brought. I tapped his shoulder and cut in. Ever the gentleman, he walked across the candle-lit room and asked Jo to dance. Kathy and I moved together for half a minute. "Oooo, Ceeesco. We haven't done this for a long time. It feeels so good to be dancing in your beeeg, strong arms."

"Thanks, Pancho."

"De nada."

"I got the motive. I know who wanted to do it and why."

"Who's that over there?"

"Rhonda Yellowknife."

"I thought she was one of your girlfriends. So why on earth were those men murdered?"

"It's a long story."

"You're a good dancer, Thomas."

"Same to ya, sister." I could see Philip over Kathy's head, with Jo, watching us. He was steamed.

A minute later Philip tapped my shoulder. "My turn, eh, slick?"

I relinquished Kathy and examined the creases on the backs of Philip's slacks. The man obviously had never sat a minute in his life. Those were factory creases. Slick? Did he call me slick?

33 THURSDAY MORNING AFTER KATHY RE-turned from Denny's funeral service, she phoned the police and told them we would bring them Rhonda Yellowknife that afternoon.

I tried to reach Ronquist, Boyd, or Canfield, and finally tracked down a sweet-voiced woman at Boyd's campaign headquarters who advised me the Yellow Dog Party was already in full swing. Most of the participants had gone directly to the Olympic from the funeral. This year, the party would serve as the traditional wake for Jimmy Canfield's long-deceased dog who had been struck down by a Ritz Cracker truck, as well as for Denny McCallum.

Canfield phoned right after I spoke to campaign headquarters. "What about Rhonda? I thought you were a detective. You should have been able to find her."

"Where are you?"

"At the Yellow Dog. In the Olympic. Same suite Denny died in. Isn't that sort of obscene? We're having the goddamned party after all. It was the only time Floyd could fit it into his schedule."

"I'll be there in a while. I'll bring Rhonda."

"You got her? What the hell did she say about Saturday night?"

"Ask her yourself."

The Yellow Dog Party had begun with six constituents, but the membership had expanded and contracted over the years as more high school chums from Wilson learned of it, while other regulars moved to distant climes. This year, because of Denny, attendance had swelled.

Kathy came along more to bird-dog me than to monitor the proceedings. I squeezed Rhonda into the truck, too. And Jo Brown, who wanted to meet Floyd. She figured a guy willing to pay ten grand for a dinner date was worth a look-see.

On the tenth floor, Floyd Boyd opened the white door to the chambers and escorted the four of us into the plushly carpeted suite. There were about thirty men and six or seven women in the room. Almost everyone was the same age. Trays of hors d'oeuvres. A five-tiered cake sat on the dining table in the south conference room.

I noticed Gary Glenn among the celebrants at the far end of the room. Turning to Boyd, I said, "You know Gary?"

"Never heard of him. Oh. Glenn? I think he's been hired by the committee to do security work for me. Can you believe a guy running for state representative needs security? Crazy world, isn't it?"

"How well do you know him?"

"Not well."

"Did you know he was here? In this room?"

"Is he? I wouldn't be surprised. He seems a competent sort. Why?"

"Forget it."

Obscuring the antique china hutch in the right-hand corner of the room was a huge black-and-white poster of a dog. The infamous yellow dog. Inset into the lower corner of the poster was a photo of a Ritz Cracker truck. Below sat a bowl of crackers.

Most everyone wore dark clothing because of the funeral.

Jimmy Canfield, who had been lingering near the door, shuffled over and gave Rhonda a peck on the cheek, which she accepted graciously, before she gave me a funny little look. She knew there was a block of time Saturday night during which Jimmy had not been accounted for. And it bugged her.

Echo was gazing up at me from a white davenport. She wore shorts and a blouse, one bare knee still scabbed from a skating spill. She explained that her father was going to take her to the train in half an hour to meet her mother, who was coming in early. "Mom said I could get some roller skates when we get home."

"Next year we'll go skating again. You should be a regular zinger by then."

She didn't try to camouflage her elation. "We will? Skating? Really?"

Kathy gave me a smile and a wink. In the elevator she'd been teasing me about Echo's crush.

"So what's this all about, Black?" Boyd asked, glancing around the room. "Echo's got a train to catch, you know."

"Not for half an hour," mouthed Echo, soundlessly.

As if they were nothing, I pulled several sheets of paper out of my pocket and handed them to Boyd. Rex Ronquist was slumped in a chair near a window, legs dangling over the chair's arm. He had a drink in his fist and it didn't look like his first. Boyd kept stealing glances at Jo Brown. Kathy had introduced them while I spoke to Echo. Jo's face was still visibly bruised, and Boyd was giving her a rather squeamish going-over. That he resented any flaw in a woman had been evident from the beginning of this caper.

Boyd took the sheet of paper, a newspaper article from the *Tacoma News Tribune* dated June 29, 1969, and started reading silently.

There is no end to the sense of loss. It's been five months since Eugene and Agnes Driscoll lost their only child, Peggy, 4, to a hit-and-run driver in the alley behind their house.

At 6:37 P.M. on March 1 of this year, while playing ball with two other playmates, Peggy Driscoll left the safety of her fenced backyard on McKinley Street to retrieve a ball one of the tots had tossed over the fence. "We always told her never to leave the yard without one of us," said Agnes Driscoll. "Kids'll be kids, though," said Eugene. "That's just a fact."

Young Peggy took several steps into the paved alleyway behind the Driscoll residence and was struck by a speeding auto. The car ran over the child and continued to drag her for some two hundred feet before turning out of the alley. It was another five minutes before any adults realized what had happened. Neither of Peggy's playmates realized she had been struck. Peggy's mother thought the child was still in the yard until one of her neighbors ran to the back door screaming, "Your child has been killed. Peggy's been killed." At that point, Mrs. Driscoll phoned her mother in Topeka but collapsed during the call.

Witnesses said they had seen a blue-and-white Chevrolet speeding in the area earlier. "The car is thought to be a '56 or a '57 two-door Chevrolet sedan," said Tacoma police sergeant Albert Kincaid.

Boyd didn't bother finishing the article or reading the second one. "What's this, Black?"

I looked at Echo, who was sneaking flirtatious little glances my way, and suddenly modified my agenda. "You really want to talk about it here?"

He proceeded down the long corridor and through the dead-space hallway to the adjoining bedroom, the one Paris and Rhonda had never had a chance to use. I went over to Kathy before I followed him. "If I don't come out of the other suite with Boyd in five minutes, call an aid car."

"What are you talking about?"

"I'll explain later."

"Did you see Gary Glenn?"

"Boyd claims he's working on his security."

"There's something wrong."

"Yeah, I know."

In the other suite the window next to the bed was open, a slight humid breeze from the Sound unsettling the gauzy curtains. I could hear a truck's backing beeper somewhere below. And the diesel growl of an idling airport bus in the street. The stuffed yellow dog was sitting in the middle of the four-poster bed, bedecked in ribbons and medals, a scruffy black patch across his right eye.

Floyd Boyd closed the door, sat wearily on an aqua love seat by the door, and threw one foot up on the onyx coffee table. I stood with my back to the four-poster bed.

"So what do you mean by this, Black?"

I let my answer wait on a slim woman who had been using the bathroom in the suite. She apologized and scurried between us, snicking the door closed after herself.

"You know what it means," I said. "You were there."

Boyd rolled his head back in a studied maneuver, laid it on the back of the love seat, and smiled distantly. "I believe I do recollect some of this situation from reading the papers. They ever catch the driver?"

I smiled. He smiled back. "Floyd, you were the driver."

Boyd didn't react, just pushed his tongue around inside his cheeks and deadened his eyes into cold blue glass. "I knew it was going to be a waste of time," he said. "Talking to you. You're off on some bizarre wild-goose chase."

"I was doing you a favor by bringing you in here. I'd just as soon Echo didn't see you being led away in handcuffs."

"What? You're going to arrest me?"

"Right here," I said, pulling a pair of handcuffs partially out of my jacket pocket to show him.

"And take me to the cops?" He laughed. "For a twenty-year-old accident you only think I was involved in? Ho, ho. Cut it out, Black. It's not funny." Boyd looked at me, deadpan, tossed the papers I had given him at the coffee table, and steered his hands into his trousers pockets. One of the papers broke loose and pendulumed lazily to the floor.

"I did some research," I said. "Your father gave you a '56 Chevy when you turned sixteen. On March 1, 1969, you were on a date with Rhonda Lastusky in the Chevy. You were showboating. Speeding around town, places you thought might frighten Rhonda. Give the girl a thrill. Up alleys. The Driscolls lived only six blocks from where you had lived in grade school. You thought you knew every crack and bump in that alley. And you did. You knew everything about that alley except that a little girl was going to run into it. After you killed Peggy Driscoll, you spent the next few hours intimidating Rhonda.''

''Is that what Rhonda told you?''

''After all, you couldn't bring the little girl back, could you? Going to jail wasn't going to help her. And you were certainly not ever going to be speeding up any dark alleys in the future, now, were you? I mean, jail was there to teach a guy a lesson, and you had already learned your lesson. So why should Rhonda turn you in? You even cried for her.''

''You're guessing.''

''Rhonda thinks you faked the tears.''

''Think about this, Black. Maybe one of us around here did kill that kid. Accidentally. Maybe Rhonda lied to protect somebody else. Maybe the killer is in the other room with her right now.''

''Scares you, doesn't it? If I could figure it out, who else could? A nasty thing like this could leak to the press and sink a career.''

''Rhonda's confused. I'll speak to her.''

''The way you spoke to Denny McCallum? And Paris London?''

Floyd smiled, an innocent who-me look. He fixed me with his pale, charismatic eyes as a lock of his sandy Kennedy-clan hair dropped across his furrowed brow. ''What are you getting at, Black? You think Rhonda has anything to fear from me? Get serious. You must have gone to an awful lot of trouble to unearth those old articles. Even the police don't care anymore. Nobody cares.''

''The Driscolls care.''

''Who?''

''The parents of the little girl you killed.''

''What you've got is a harebrained theory and a mixed-up

woman. You realize as well as I do that nothing's going to bring that kid back."

"You've had twenty years to take out your excuses and polish them up, Floyd. I would have thought a smoothy like you would have cooked up something a little slicker than 'nothing's going to bring that kid back.' "

Boyd shook his head and rose. "If that's all you needed . . ."

I blocked the door. "Not yet, Floyd."

"Oh? You going to hold me?"

"I'm arresting you for a twenty-year-old manslaughter charge and for the murders of Denny McCallum and Paris London."

"You're kidding."

"You heard me."

34

FLOYD TRIED OUT A FEW STRANGE masks until he found just the right mixture of incredulity and scorn. "I didn't have anything to do with it."

If he hadn't been a politician, I might have believed him. "This dreamgirl gig was all a ruse so you could get me to look up a couple of potential stumbling blocks to your career." Floyd wanted to exit the room, but he needed desperately to hear my conjectures the way a Casanova needs one more woman. "I don't like being conned, Floyd. Your name popping up in the newspapers was apt to refresh some

faulty memories. You didn't want to be sitting fat in your
office in D.C. and have somebody call collect asking for a
suitcase full of cash, now, did you?''

Boyd's face was reddening. ''Black, you've got some
imagination.''

''You don't want to know how I can tie two murders at the
Olympic to a car accident twenty years ago?''

Boyd looked at me blankly.

''Rhonda knew about the accident, because she was in the
car with you. Paris London knew about it, because Rhonda
had confided in him. And why shouldn't she? Twenty years
had gone by and it was still bothering her, and what was
urgent about keeping something that old a secret? Denny
McCallum knew about it somehow, or suspected. After he
got his own dreamgirl out of his system, he came up here to
talk to Rhonda. It could hardly have escaped him, if he knew
about the accident and Rhonda's involvement, that her meeting up with you might have some dire consequences. Except
Rhonda wasn't here. Paris was. So they talked about it.

''I don't know how they ended up in the bathroom, but
they did, and Paris had the newspaper clipping Rhonda had
been hiding for twenty years. You walked in on them. They
leave the door open, or were you there all along, chatting up
Paris and waiting for Rhonda? Maybe Paris thought it was
kinky to fellate Denny while you were hiding in the other
room.''

''Black, you'd better think twice about what you're saying. You'll pay dearly.''

''You bamboozled me into running around the country
picking up witnesses that you could eliminate. Schwantz went
to your high school. You knew he was married to Jo because
you met them a few years back at a dinner party. Jo remembered it. Schwantz got juiced and mentioned some things you
might be hiding in your background. You let it pass, but it
needled you. See, Floyd, I figure there were half a dozen
people who knew or suspected that you killed the little girl.

''Don't look so surprised. That's how these things work.
Rhonda knew, and she told her girlfriend, Susie Capshaw,

who eventually told Randy Schwantz, whom she was dating at the time. Schwantz might not have known the whole story, but he knew enough. Who knows who else Capshaw told? Or who they told? Yet nobody ever turned you in. What business was it of theirs? Human nature says mind your own business. Floyd, the most popular boy in the school. Who was even going to believe it? Denny? He worshiped you. Schwantz? Capshaw, who learned the whole thing from Rhonda under an oath of secrecy? Most of these people, by the time they got the story, it was third-hand.''

"Capshaw," mused Boyd. "Susie Capshaw. I remember her.''

"You knew Jo from the PBS drives, and you also knew she'd been married to Schwantz, but you couldn't track her down on your own. You probably asked another private eye to trace her, and he wanted a legitimate reason. So you got some old tapes of her on the pledge drives from somewhere and conned your buddies into this dreamgirl baloney. This time you'd have a valid, if somewhat eccentric, reason to be hunting her. It wasn't hard for a man of your persuasive powers to convince your friends they were actually thinking up the shenanigans. Now you could track down Rhonda through Jimmy and Schwantz through Jo. You're an orchestrator, Floyd, I'll give you that.''

"This is all irrational conjecture, Black. I can come up with half a dozen scenarios equally as cockamamy. Rhonda was having an affair with Paris London and walked in on him with Denny. Her Irish temper? That makes more sense. If I ran over somebody, why didn't Rhonda step forward earlier?''

"Because Rhonda didn't understand that stepping forward and uttering a few sentences was the right thing to do.'' I grabbed his left wrist and started to put the bracelets on him. He offered no resistance, knew he couldn't fight me and thought it best not to try.

The door behind him opened.

Gary Glenn stepped through. Smirking. When he closed the door behind himself, I let go of Boyd and stepped back.

"What are you doing here?" Boyd asked.

"Don't fill your britches, Floyd. I'll take care of this. Don't I take care of everything?"

"Yeah, but this is different."

"He's just a PI. I can take care of him."

"Oh geez," I said, realizing I had outsmarted myself. Not all of the implications came clear at once, but I was beginning to see a whole new scenario.

I stepped back and put the handcuffs into my right-hand coat pocket in such a way that they were wrapped around my fist. They could serve as brass knuckles in a few moments. Not that brass knuckles were going to help much against someone as well-trained in unarmed combat as Glenn.

Glenn was cocky, his voice deep and reassuring. "Just take it easy, Floyd. You fell into a spot of trouble here."

"He's taking me to the police. I thought we had a deal. You and I, Glenn?"

"We do. And I'm not going to let him queer it. Mr. Black. Why don't you and I take a little hike downstairs to discuss matters?" It was plain that the two of us would be in mortal combat soon. Bloodbath was more like it. Here was a guy who could bust two-by-fours with his beak. "Come on. Move. That way." He nodded toward the door to 1138, which would bypass the Yellow Dog Party entirely.

I wedged my right fist in my sports coat pocket and moved it as menacingly as possible. Glenn laughed humorlessly. "Funny guy. Everybody in town knows you don't carry a gun, Black. That's why I don't need mine. Move." He smiled. "Or do it here."

I glanced around to see what sort of options I had. The room was spacious, had several coffee tables, a sofa, the love seat, a four-poster bed, and an open window with wind-flustered curtains. A cool breeze chilled the sweat on my face.

When I finally pushed out some words, my voice was froggy. "They're going to get you both."

"I don't understand," said Floyd, looking from Glenn to me.

"You just mosey back to your party and socialize," said Glenn.

Boyd grasped the doorknob. "Aren't you listening?" I said. "He's planning to kill me."

Boyd looked at Glenn quizzically and then at me. I could tell from his eyes that the truth of the situation had not escaped him. "I doubt that."

"Yeah? Think about it. I had it wrong. You didn't kill Denny and Paris London. He did. He must have."

"Shut up and move," said Glenn.

"Wait a minute," said Boyd, perplexed. "Why would he kill Denny?"

"Because you're going to help him out. That's the deal, isn't it? You're going to be a big shot and he's going to get your protection and influence? In return for not saying anything about what happened in that alley in Tacoma? Gary needs your protection. He's about to get kicked off the police force. Of course, if somebody else upsets your apple-cart first, then he wouldn't have any hold over you, would he? And you wouldn't win the election. Denny and Paris were talking about you in this suite. They both knew. He overheard them. He'd put a listening device in the suite. The cops found it when they picked up the bodies but didn't think it was related to the murders. Now I realize he put it there. He had been eavesdropping while they discussed you, Floyd. Paris and Denny both knew about the car accident. Glenn couldn't have any loose cannons on deck."

Floyd Boyd looked at the two of us for a minute, pondering all the repercussions, and then waved a dismissing hand over his head. "He wouldn't have killed them just for that."

"Ask him."

The room grew silent while Boyd tried to read Glenn's face. "I don't care," he said. "I don't even want to know if it's true. It's your business. You two. I'm leaving."

"This is attempted murder, Floyd."

Glenn faked a jump at me. "Get moving, bicycle man."

Boyd opened the door to leave, but instead of leaving put both hands over his head in a gesture of supplication, then backed into the room. Glenn turned his head toward the doorway.

Holding a .45 automatic in her tiny hands so that it looked like a chunk broken off a huge chocolate bar, Kathy Birchfield stepped into the room. It was my gun. There was no telling if it was loaded. I didn't keep it loaded, but she knew how to put it together and load it. I had taught her.

"Back off," she said to Glenn. Her arms were trembling, her voice breaking. "Turn around and walk out of here. Just walk out."

Glenn had been squared off with me, about two paces off, but now he turned sideways. His left shoulder was only a yard and a half away from the barrel of the gun. There were a hundred jitterbug/karate moves he could have done to get it away from her.

"She's used a gun before," I said.

"This foxy little gal?" Glenn grinned wickedly. "I find that hard to swallow."

"Get out," said Kathy.

I stepped forward, but Glenn made a move as if to kick me. He didn't, but the threat kept me from getting too much closer. Kathy's trembling grew more obvious. Glenn spoke, menacingly: "Put it down before somebody gets hurt real bad."

"You put it down, he'll break your neck," I said.

Glenn smiled. "Cute, Black. You're getting her in deeper because you're paranoid." Then, to Kathy: "You're threatening an off-duty police officer."

Floyd Boyd said, "Gary, let's think this through. There's two of them now."

"Put the gun down, lady." Glenn began squaring himself up with Kathy, took a step toward her. He might have been talking a kitten out of a tree for all the concern he showed. Yet, with her trembling, she could barely keep the pistol centered on him.

Glenn made a quick move, and the gun boomed. The impact kicked Glenn back a half-step. Then the gun boomed again. The second time he didn't move. Nor did he fall. Just stood facing Kathy while the rest of us tried to clear the ringing out of our ears.

Boyd said, "Oh God!"

I stepped around in front of Glenn. His eyes were wet and glazed. I held his shoulders and hiked my knee into his crotch. He collapsed over my leg and flopped facedown on the carpet. Kathy was stunned, still pointing the pistol until I reached across, took her hand, and directed it at the wall, then flicked the safety with my thumb.

The doorway behind Kathy began to clog up with curious partygoers. "There's been a shooting," I said. "Everything's under control, but someone should call the police." I closed the door on the random curiosity.

Boyd said, "Are you crazy? She shoots him, and you kick him in the nuts!"

I winked at Kathy. "These new bullets don't have much kick."

Glenn was on the carpet woofing like some sort of beached sea mammal. I frisked him, removed a .38 snub-nosed revolver from his waistband, then cuffed his hands behind his back. "He's not dead," I said. "Relax, Kathy."

"But I shot him," she said. "Dead center."

I rolled Glenn over and ripped open the front of his shirt. He was wearing a vest, which she'd hit twice. The bullets had only bruised and stunned him, perhaps broken a rib.

"Thank God. I thought I was going to be ill. He was the one who was shooting at your legs in Oregon, wasn't he?"

"I'm pretty sure he was."

"I thought I killed him. I felt so awful."

"Where'd you get my gun?"

"I've been carrying it since the murders. I figured if you wouldn't carry it, I would."

"What are you guys talking about?" Boyd asked.

Kathy slumped against the doorframe, let her gun hand drop to her side, and said, "I saw him sneak out of the Yellow Dog Party like he was looking for somebody. When I peeked down the hallway, he was eavesdropping, so I waited until he came in. I heard your voice through the door and could tell you were in big trouble."

"You!" I said, pointing a finger at Floyd Boyd's chest. Boyd had been edging toward the door again.

"I didn't do anything."

"You son of a bitch. He was going to kill me, and you knew it."

"I didn't see any weapons. You can't prove that allegation."

"I can break you in half if you move."

Floyd Boyd backed up against the open door and was quiet. With two fingers I examined the pistol I had taken off Glenn, a Charter Arms .38 with a two-inch barrel. Five shots. Ten to one the bullets in Paris and Denny could be traced to this.

"Listen, Black," Boyd gasped. "Listen to me. Don't turn me in. I didn't have anything to do with Denny, and nothing can be done about the other now. Everything's finished. Your fee for taking care of this could be stupendous. You wouldn't ever have to work again."

"I don't work much now."

Kathy looked drained. I took the .45 out of her hand, dropped the full clip heavily into my palm, and jacked the cartridge out of the chamber. Glenn was breathing in a coughing sputter that sounded like an outboard motor with a bad plug.

"I still don't get it," she said. "What's he doing here? What was he going to do?"

"Glenn found out about Floyd's history."

"Floyd?" Kathy looked at the politician.

"Floyd killed a kid with his car when he was in high school. Nobody ever found out about it, not officially. Schwantz knew. Schwantz went to their high school, too, dated a girl named Susie Capshaw who at one time had been Rhonda's best friend. Rhonda had been in the car with Floyd the night they killed the kid."

"Why didn't anybody else figure it out?"

"Partially because it was at the other end of town from where Floyd and his crowd hung out. Mostly because Rhonda got talked out of saying anything."

Kathy said, "Shrewd of you to figure all that out and come here for Floyd."

I could feel my face heating up. I hadn't figured anything out, had blundered into this like a puppy in a fish pond, and we both knew if she hadn't come through the door with the gun, I'd probably have spent the rest of the night kissing the bottom of an elevator shaft. "Thanks."

"But why didn't Rhonda tell the police? Her parents?" I shrugged. "You'll have to ask Rhonda. I doubt she has an answer that'll satisfy you. Schwantz probably told Gary here somewhere along the line. Schwantz wasn't going to use it, wasn't even sure if it was true, but Gary had been looking for something like this. He was in big trouble in the department, and a powerful ally couldn't hurt. So he did a little investigating and confronted Floyd with what he had. They struck a bargain. I don't know what it was, but it was enough that Glenn didn't want anybody else spilling the beans. That's why he was tailing me around town. He followed me here last Saturday night. I chased him outside but lost him.

"He must have come back. He found out who we were meeting and bribed someone on the staff for a passkey. Maybe he already had one. Cops have keys for all sorts of places. He put a bug in the suites here. Maybe he saw the newspaper article when he was here. We found the bug after we found Denny and Paris. He must have been listening from down the hall, or downstairs. Denny came up and talked to Paris about what happened twenty years ago. Denny was worried because he realized Rhonda was the one who'd been in the car, and he was beginning to get suspicious of this entire dreamgirl project. It's easier to evaluate something like this when your portion of it has already fallen through. I don't know what the two of them said, but it was enough to bring Glenn running.

"By the time he got here, they had other things on their minds."

"But why was he following you?" Kathy asked.

"He was afraid I'd figure out what this dreamgirl stuff was really about. He didn't want Floyd exposed. As long as he had the blackmail exclusive, Floyd was going to get elected and be in a position to help him. Maybe keep Glenn in his job. Get him another one if that didn't pan out.''

''I didn't know anything about any murders,'' said Boyd, flatly.

Echo walked through the doorway, staring wide-eyed at the huffing, handcuffed man on the floor. When Boyd saw his daughter, he began weeping silently. His life had just hit a crooked rail and jumped the tracks, but it wasn't until he was confronted with Echo's wide-eyed innocence that he realized how bad things were. It occurred to me that he had left his wife about the time Echo reached the age of the girl he'd killed. Whether or not that meant anything, I would never know. ''Your dad's going to take you down to King Street station, and then he and I have an important meeting downtown,'' I said. ''Right, Floyd?''

''You gonna let me go?''

''You'll be back.'' Echo's large brown eyes were moving from her father to me, her long lashes closing down on her cheeks like feathers. She knew something unpleasant was going on, but she didn't know what. ''It's been nice knowing you, Echo. Maybe next summer.''

''I thought we had a date to go skating. A for-sure date. You and me and Morgana and Amber.''

''A date it is, then.'' She gave me an uncertain smile, then slipped a small hand into her father's.

''Mom'll be here pretty soon, Dad.''

''I know, honey.''

After they left, we watched Glenn for a minute before Kathy said, ''Did you know Floyd gets his teeth cleaned secretly two weeks before he goes to his regular dentist? He likes hearing them tell him now nice he's kept his teeth. There's something a little strange about that, don't you think?''

''I'm beginning to believe everybody on earth is strange, but yeah, there is something strange about that.''

35

A WEEK LATER IN TACOMA I VISITED Agnes and Eugene Driscoll. They had moved from the house on McKinley Avenue to a trilevel on Bridgeview Drive overlooking the Narrows and Gig Harbor. The sun was setting over the Olympics, the clouds pink and purple.

The Driscoll household was more vibrant than I expected, their teenage son roaring off in a hot rod as I shambled up to their porch. The house was strewn with baseball and soccer trophies in front, the old man's bowling statuettes in battle formation in a rear window.

"Agnes Driscoll? I phoned."

"Mr. Black. Do come in." On the wall over the fireplace I spotted a battery of old photos of a small girl along with a canonized Teddy bear.

They sat me in the living room. Eugene was tall and ungainly, in work pants, a plaid shirt, and scuffed brogans. Homely was the kindest thing you could say about him. Agnes was almost as tall, with a long face and no makeup. Her drab brown hair hung limply.

"I found the driver of the car that killed Peggy. If you want to know. It occurred to me on the way down that you might not want to." The room fell into a deep hush. Suddenly the colors of the sky outside seemed noisy. A clock ticked. A child two houses away shrieked joyously. Eugene got up and shut a patio door, then sat down again. "An associate of his murdered two people a couple of weeks ago because they knew about your daughter's death. He's up on conspiracy charges for that murder. It's probably all they'll get him for.''

''You think he'll do time?'' Agnes asked.

''Not much.''

''We guessed somebody out there knew who done it,'' said Eugene solemnly, then got up and left the room. My guess was he didn't want to cry in front of a stranger.

Driving home in the truck, I pondered the little girl whose life had ended twenty years before. I had rectified some wrongs, committed a few of my own, but the dead were still too deep to retrieve.

All in all, it was turning into a strange week.

The coffin Bumpus had brought in for disposal exploded because of improper burial preparations on the cadaver. Fortunately for the peace of mind of the staff, it happened on a weekend. A janitor heard the ''whoompf'' and called me at home, thinking somebody had broken into our offices. The cleanup cost $6,500, which meant I was out fifteen hundred more than Bumpus paid me, plus a ten-buck bribe to the janitor not to tell Kathy.

That summer's Yellow Dog Party had been deemed a success by most of the attendees, even though one of the stars had been arrested at it. I had the feeling it was to be the last.

Kathy and Philip had spent the past weekend at the ocean together.

Gary Glenn had been suspended until the charges against him were settled. Early word was the gun I had confiscated from him at the Olympic was the murder weapon. He had been too cocksure to dispose of it.

Schwantz was suing me for what happened at the Copelands' Broadmoor house. If he was hoping my errors-and-omissions insurance carrier would rather settle out of court than dispute the case, he was going to be disappointed. The Driscolls instigated a lawsuit against Floyd Boyd, delivering the final blow to any chance he ever had for public office.

Charged with assault and battery on Jo and now with attempted murder and kidnapping in Myrtle Creek, Schwantz languished in the King County Jail. He would be extradited to Oregon after King County finished with him. As the state's leading witness, Earle Robb had escaped charges.

Rhonda had stuck around but was not dating Jimmy Canfield. I had a heart-to-heart talk with Denny McCallum's wife, Penny, and told her Denny had been planning to resume the marriage. She wept. She admitted Denny had been "reasonably sure" Floyd Boyd had killed some kid with his car when they were in high school. At the time she had deemed it an appalling confession, but then, Floyd was her brother. She speculated that contacting the authorities might have averted her husband's death, but I assured her rewriting the past was as futile as digging for pirate treasure in a city park.

Rex Ronquist was dating Tina Hosty. I had given her two grand for that first date, but she had returned the sum to Rex with the confession that she wasn't the woman in the picture. Rex said he didn't care and called me four times to thank me for introducing them.

Relieved that Randy was finally in the slammer, Jo Brown was back at work at the Leschi Café, and living on Twenty-fifth South with her daughters again. Nanette Corelli flew up from Yreka and was staying with them for a few weeks, baby-sitting the girls and getting to know Jo again.

After some calculating, I realized Randy Schwantz had to have been the one who took a shot at me in Jo Brown's house. Nobody ever charged him with it. Nobody ever would. Every dog in this circus had bigger fleas to chase.

36

THE NIGHT I DROVE HOME FROM THE Driscolls', I found Kathy alone at my kitchen table sipping coffee. Barefoot, she wore denim shorts and a Hard Rock Café, NY, T-shirt.

"Yo," she said, when I trudged through the back door. "How'd it go?"

"Grim."

"Sorry you went?"

"Not really. They've been waiting a lot of years for me to show up. Or someone like me."

"There's no one like you."

I doffed my jacket and sat next to her. Kathy stared at me for a long time. "What?"

"Nothing. It's just been a while since I looked at you close." She gave me a smile that was a bit less than carefree, but when I touched her hand across the table, she rolled her fist over and let me fondle her palm. "I want to talk to you about something, Thomas."

"You can talk to me about anything your fluttery little heart desires."

She laughed self-consciously. "My heart is not fluttery. It's very solid."

"Whatever. Sure. First . . ." I leaned across the table and kissed her on the lips. She wasn't expecting it, and at first didn't collaborate. After a while she collaborated just fine.

"What was that all about?" she asked.

"What do you think?"

"You making a move on me? Is that what you're doing?"

I grinned. "I suppose I am."

Kathy got up abruptly, went to the counter, sloshed tap water around in her coffee mug, upended it, watched the drips until they stopped, then faced me.

I followed and stood very close. Her hair was braided into a single thick ropy strand down her back. She touched my chest lightly with an index finger and put her other hand into the dark hair at her temple, corkscrewing a tendril self-consciously.

"I've been waiting for you to get back. I've got something to discuss. Well. It's not easy. Philip and I . . . We've been seeing an awful lot of each other over the past month or so." She began talking faster, running her sentences together. "Anyway, I've become quite fond of him. It sort of surprised me, because at first I didn't think of him in that way. He's very sweet, and he loves me very much. I know he tends to irritate you and I've been trying to figure it out, but I don't seem to be able to get a handle on it. I wanted you two to like each other. I was hoping you would become friends."

"Not bloody likely."

She swallowed. "Yes. I know. Anyway, the long and the short of it is, he's asked me to marry him again. Philip has." She was blushing. Kathy rarely blushed, but her face was bright pink now, as if confessing she'd run over my dog, or painted mustaches on all my photos of Jane Pauley. One would think a woman announcing a marriage proposal would glow, but the brightness in her face was definitely something else.

"Say again?"

"I know you don't like him, Thomas. But you're my friend, and I need you to approve. Please tell me I'm doing the right thing. Under all that joking and F-person business? Tell me you were just giving me a hard time."

"What did you tell him?"

"I said I would."

"That you'd marry him?" She nodded, and I thought she was going to burst into tears. She was still blushing. And perspiring. "So you're officially engaged to a man who wears black socks with Birkenstocks?" She nodded. "A man with one brown eye and one blue?" She nodded. "Your children are going to have big foreheads and tails. You know that?" She nodded again. "When did this shit happen?"

"Don't get mad. While we were at the ocean. Tell me you approve. I don't know why your opinion means so much to me, but it does. Be good about this. You could make it so difficult."

"Me?"

"If you didn't approve. Or . . ."

"You love him?"

She swallowed. "I think I do."

I smiled smugly. "You *sleep* with me."

"I do not. Well, not in the biblical sense. And only when I'm upset."

We regarded each other. In the murky kitchen her eyes were darker than usual. I moved her left hand to my shoulder, took her right and pulled it onto my other shoulder, then pulled her close. She looked up at me and shook her head. Her eyes started to puddle. I leaned down and she shook her head faster and I kissed her. She didn't speak or struggle. Nor did she encourage me. Not at first. Then she did. When we pulled apart, she didn't take her hands off my shoulders. I was holding her hips under her T-shirt, basking in the silky heat of her skin. She had been on tiptoes, sank down now. She sighed, and her breath smelled of vanilla.

"We can't horse around like this, Thomas. I'm engaged."

"I'd say you're engaged to the wrong fellow."

Kathy let go and pushed away. "Say that again?"

"It's not that difficult. You're with the wrong guy."

"Who should I be with?"

I looked at my shoes. "Me."

"You?"

"Yeah."

"But we don't . . . have . . . that sort of relationship. We might have. But it never evolved that way. You didn't want it and then I didn't want it and then neither of us wanted it. Best friends. Remember?''

"I'm not going to let you marry him, Kathy.''

"You sure you know what you're saying? You're not just depressed over what happened in Tacoma? People go off-center when they're depressed.''

"I love you, Kathy.''

"You've had a bad week, and I haven't been the sort of friend the past month that—''

I moved close and kissed her again. She was warm, almost hot. When I began to break away, she sucked my lower lip, holding me with the gentle vacuum of longing.

"You're freezing,'' she said. She pressed her ear against my chest so that I could smell her clean hair. "I shouldn't be here with you. This isn't right.''

"It feels right.''

"Unfortunately it does. Damn you, Thomas.''

"Yep.''

"In just a few minutes you've managed to get me more confused than I can ever remember being. About anything. You know that, don't you?''

"Uh-huh.''

"Thomas, you don't really mean this. You couldn't. Why hasn't something happened before?'' Kathy moved away, suddenly fidgety, padding barefoot across the linoleum, standing by the door to the basement, as if distance alone might ransom her from my onslaught. "We've been friends for a long time. You'd think if anything were going to happen, it would have happened a long time ago. We just don't have the chemistry.''

"Sure we do.''

"Then why hasn't it happened?''

"First you didn't want it. Then I didn't. Then we were buddies. Then we started working together, and you know that never works out. You don't have a relationship with somebody you're working with. It maybe never was going to be right. Except it is now.''

"That's the screwiest reasoning I've ever heard.''

"Maybe. But it's my screwy reasoning."

"Why are you doing this, Thomas?"

I had to think about that before I replied. "I guess I didn't know how bad it was going to feel to watch you walk off with another man."

"You're getting me all mixed-up."

"Uh-huh."

"Damn you!"

"Uh-huh."

"Tell me the truth. Why now?" In a situation like this it was hard to squeeze the truth through the eyelet of reality, but I thought she deserved my best effort.

"I didn't say anything earlier because I was terrified."

"You? Hah! Try something believable."

"Terrified that you'd laugh in my face. It would have killed me."

"That's how to get rid of you? Laugh in your face?"

"Yeah, it probably is."

Kathy began pacing back and forth between the sink and the basement door. "Now that I'm committed to somebody, all of a sudden I'm supposed to drop everything and jump into your arms. 'Sorry Philip, Thomas had first dibs.' Is that what you want me to tell him?"

"Yeah."

"Thomas, we're not lovers. I don't know why, but we're not. The enzymes just aren't there."

"I guess that last kiss was a total bust, huh?" She rolled her eyes and gave me a gut-stirring look that said it wasn't. "Tell me you never want to see me again. Or just laugh in my face. Otherwise there's no way to get rid of me."

She was incredulous. "But I've already told everyone I'm marrying Philip."

"I know, and I'm deeply offended. Usually I'm the first to know if last night's date has a pimple on his ass. You told everybody before your best buddy? Your old pal? I'm home, June. In here, Ward. Doesn't that seem curious? Maybe your subconscious is playing tricks on you. Ever think of that?"

She opened her mouth to say something, then reconsidered

it. "This is some monstrous joke you've been plotting for years, isn't it?"

"I'm not joking, Kathy."

"I told Philip I would marry him."

"Did you? I guess that settles it. I guess you have to live with him for the next seventy years. Bear his mutant children. Track down all his mismatched socks. Spit polish his glass eye. A promise is a promise."

"Don't be like this."

"Tell him you changed your mind. I'll tell him. We can send a singing telegram."

"So. Are you proposing? After all these years? Is that what this is? A proposal?"

I walked over and cupped her face in my hands. "I'm not asking you to marry me, Kathy. I guess what I'm asking is for you not to marry Philip."

"*Too, too* romantic."

"Old silver tongue." I grinned. She had often said she couldn't resist that grin.

"I can't handle this, Thomas. I don't know what to say. We'll still be friends."

"Friends isn't going to cut it."

"But we've been friends practically forever."

"Kathy. Come back to me." I kissed her again. "You don't have to make up your mind right away." I sat down. "I'll wait."

That brought a sad smile. "You want me to tell Mother I made a mistake, that I'm really not getting married? That I'm just going to hang out with old Thomas?"

I nodded.

She went to the sink behind me and showed me her back. She poured a glass of water and sipped. The refrigerator clicked on. Minutes passed.

"You come up with an answer?" I said.

"You really love me?" She was still facing away, but I could tell from the movement of her shoulders and the milky sound of her voice she was weeping.

"You know I do."

"You're pretty damn cocky, aren't you?"

"Uh-huh."

She spoke in a near-shout. "Was I supposed to wait forever while you made up your mind? Was that your goddamned plan?"

"I presumed you were living your own life. I didn't realize you were waiting on me."

"Neither did I," she said, quietly. She faced me, crisscrossing her bare arms over her breasts. Her hands were quivering. "This isn't easy."

"I don't imagine it is."

"You could have done this three months ago and made life simpler."

"So what's it going to be, sister? The alphabet guy or the man who lives upstairs?"

"I'm thinking. But you're going to have to give me some time on this. It might take a while."

"I can wait."